THE
ARIZONA
ALLIANCE.

by

Robert Paton

Grosvenor House
Publishing Limited

This book is published by
Grosvenor House Publishing Ltd
Link House
140 The Broadway, Tolworth, Surrey, KT6 7HT.
www.grosvenorhousepublishing.co.uk

A CIP record for this book
is available from the British Library

ISBN 978-1-78623-952-5

The

Arizona

Alliance.

INTRODUCTION

On the Arizona and Mexican border in 1867, battle was fought in the Sierra Madre.

An unholy alliance forged between Bounty Hunter, Bank Robber, Murderer, and U.S.-Marshall seek out the Apache encampment for gold.

The U.S.Cavalry want their stolen payroll gold back.

Gun-runners raid the Mexican Garrison for rifles to trade with the Apache for gold.

Locations move swiftly to exhibit hatred, greed and fear.

The Apache chief is driven by vengeance in a quest for the killing of his sons.

A Thriller From Start To Finish.

CHAPTER INDEX

The
Arizona
Alliance.

Chapter One

Wagon Train Massacre

'Thud'

He was cut off in mid sentence as the arrow pierced his back.

His hand moved instinctively for the gun but it was only a reaction and before he hit the ground he was dead.

Clementine was surrounded, they had appeared from nowhere. One moment she was talking with Larcy, the next he lay dead whilst she was dragged away.

Her eyes bulged with fear as a cloth was thrust into her mouth and secured. She remembered seeing her first Indian at the trading store in Tucson, but these were different, the other had been dressed in white man's clothes, seemingly harmless. These however were garbed differently with painted faces and a smell, which brought vomit to the back of her throat. They sat astride their painted ponies, radiating an arrogance of terror.

People began to move about amongst the wagons. The bustle of activity could be heard as the teams were hitched in preparation for the day's journey.

A wagon burst into flames, followed by a loud scream from a lone figure leading a pack of painted riders towards the circle of wagons. From all sides the Red men appeared.

"Apache"

cried one man as he snatched up his rifle and let off a shot, dropping a brave from horseback as the bullet found its mark.

Moving forward, the Apache charged the disorientated circle of wagons. The air filled with arrows leaving bowstrings, the whooshing of lances being thrust, and the shots being discharged by the teamsters.

Within the encampment pandemonium reigned, as people fled for cover, getting in the way of one another, completely unprepared for what was happening.

The early risers whom had hitched their teams and pulled out of the main body of wagons were the first to die. More than half the settlers were slaughtered in the long, sustained attack by the Apache. Then as quickly as they had come, the attackers were gone.

The wagon master organised defences during the respite. Burning shells of wagons were left to burn and livestock was herded into a much tighter circle.

Wagons were rolled closer together. The spaces between them being barricaded with whatever was at hand, table, chairs, water-barrels,

"Anything"

cried Burnett, the wagon master

"that will stop an arrow."

Ammunition was re-distributed amongst the settlers. Almost every wagon or family possessed a rifle of some sorts. With so many dead there were now ample firearms to go around. Those who could not shoot were to reload, others tended the wounded, whilst others still, cried over their dead.

There was a long wait after the attack.

"You reckon they're coming back, Burnett?"

"You can count on it, mister."

Spat back the old wagon master, "They're in no hurry and we ain't going' no place. Even if we was it would take us days to get there"

The reply troubled the man, who looked down at his fair haired son who in turn was ready to reload for him and wondered if he had any right to have brought the boy on such a perilous journey.

The Apache re-grouped, circled, and let off sniping shots at first. Gradually they closed in, screaming and letting off arrows to soar high into the air. They raced at full gallop as all behind the barricade of wagons watched. The frenzied horsemen drew nearer, forming a much tighter circle. They came within rifle range.

"Hold your fire"

screamed Burnett.

Arrows racked the wagons, some burst into flames, as a man the settlers let loose, Apache fell from their ponies into the flaying hooves of their own mounts. The teamsters fired from between wheels, from under wagons and from any place, which offered protection. The positions of bodies barely altered, the dead, merely went limp where they lay.

Others slumped over onto their knees, clutching as arrows tore into flesh. Men and women alike fired, many not realising the person beside them was dead.

The Apache sent an endless barrage of lances, arrows and tomahawks as they dipped from side to side on their painted ponies. A heavy toll was taken as the diminishing band of teamsters fought back with the full might of their limited resources in the desperation of the moment.

Again the Apache withdrew, reassembling out of range and sight of the wagons. The Apache who claimed a high death count on their first attack reeled under the resistance from those behind the wagons.

The area a hundred feet outside the ring of wagons lay littered with bodies. Teamsters blasted away with their rifles, which out-ranged anything the Apache could offer in firepower, dropping, fleeing or injured braves as they strove to rejoin the main pack. The bodies of over seventy dead lay strewn in the sand outside the circle of wagons, Burnett knew the tally amongst his own dead was as high, if not more.

Buzzards sat on the high rocks, viewing the scene below, for no matter who won the battle, it would be they who gained the prize of the carnage afterwards.

Burnett gathered his remaining force together. They were barely twenty in number.

"I don't believe we can survive another attack, the ammunition's low, so our chances are slim," said Burnett to his chief scout Abe Tucker.

"Can't we get help?" cried one of the women.

"No, we're on our own. When the bullets are gone, use your rifles as clubs, fight with stones, anything you can lift to defend yourself only don't get taken alive."

Hollinger came alongside Burnett.

"I haven't seen our Clementine since first light, she went off with your boy, Larcy."

"If Larcy's out there watching, don't you worry none. He'll take good care of her. There's little he can do for us so worry none about not seeing them."

Another circle of wagons was formed using only six wagons. Most of the stock they let loose, keeping only the horses. The oxen mules, cattle and the smaller ponies were released.

Whereas before there had been spaces under and between the wagons, now there were none. Every gap was barricaded so as to form a wall of solid timber with only the slightest niches to shoot through. The sick and wounded were propped up into a firing position, and the horses stomped around in the confines of the smaller camp. Men stationed themselves at the outer ring of wagons so as to give the earliest possible warning of attack.

The sun blazed high overhead as noon made its presence felt. Sweat trickled down backs and every eye was alert, with fingers locked around triggers ready to shoot.

Clementines gag was removed from her mouth and her hands unbound. She gaped with terror in her eyes as a Brave moved towards her. She ran, only to collide with another Brave. He ripped the dress from her back. Excited, he held the strip of material aloft, her long, fair hair fell around her oval shaped face onto the pale ivory coloured skin revealed as yet another brave completed the job of ripping the dress from her. She was half-naked, screaming as she was held down in the sand.

A warrior fell to his knees, she felt his body enter hers. Her screams cut through the air as she struggled against him, trying hard not to succumb to the overwhelming stench of horse as vomit rushed up the back of her throat.

The Brave arose, cursing. Another knelt between her legs, again she felt the penetration. He arose and another took his place, then another and another. She passed out, and still more Braves were to come.

"They're coming Burnett," cried one of the lookouts.

Everyone was positioned, so as to have a line of fire. The Apache again began their wild sweeping encircling of the wagons, riding faster and faster as they drew nearer.

Riflemen fired to offer cover for those who set alight the outer ring of wagons, when this was accomplished all the settlers returned to the inner ring of six wagons.

The flames licked high and black into the air as the Apache were held at bay by the heat thrown off, Here and there an eager young warrior would find an entrance through the ring of flames where a wagon had been removed to form part of the inner circle. Darting through these spaces they were met by a hail of bullets, as the teamsters were unable to control themselves any longer. The air filled with a stench of burning flesh as those who died on the earlier attack, were incinerated within the burning wagons.

Smoke spiralled high, as the Apache still came forward. Many now reached the settlers and ducked to avoid bullets from one side and the searing heat from the other. The air hung humid.

Indian ponies became possessed by terror as they reared with snorting nostrils, casting their riders afoot. Apache clambered over the wagons, scuffling between wheels, and leaping on horseback where a partition of the barricade gave way under the charge of a frenzied pony eager to rid itself of its rider.

The teamster's horses within the small encampment broke loose and ran for the narrow entrance, crashing underfoot all who barred their way white man and Apache alike.

Bodies were trampled to death as hooves flayed out in the ever decreasing confines of the wagons. Through the gap they poured, once they were through the gap the horses stopped for they could go no further. Ahead of them towered a wall of fire, behind lay the confines of small camp, which now also began to burn. They mulled around the fallen barricade blocking the gap. Some bolted to race around the wagons, careering into Apache on foot and trampling them under hoof amongst the already dead bodies strewn in the sand.

An Apache leapt from the back of a canvassed wagon already aflame, landing on Burnett he parted the wagon master with his scalp in one swift movement as his body jolted to the ground. The Brave buckled under the impact of Burnett's falling body and received a bullet in the skull from a fair haired young boy, glassy-eyed and bewildered as he was, still he managed to thumb shells into the rifle and fire. He received an arrow through the head moments later.

The air filled with loud shrieks as the Apache gained the upper hand, overpowering the last few settlers.

The fire died, and only a simmering of ashes remained. Wagon wheels and canvas supports were the only remains of the wagons, such was the all consuming thirst of the flames.

The Apache rode over the debris, collecting, where possible their dead. The battleground lay littered with corpses. Scalped heads seeping blood into the sands.

After little delay, the Apache readied to move. For this was a large party raiding on the Arizona border, hence they must return to their lodges in the Sierra Madre with their newly acquired booty.

Clementine Hollinger awoke to find herself strapped to a horse. Why her life had been spared she did not know or care as they rode through the remains of the wagons. She wanted to die, like all those she saw sprawled around her, her Ma, Pa,

Larcy, Mr Burnett and even little Johnny with his mop of fair hair, removed.

They rode away from the battle scene. The vultures swooped on the bodies of the dead, picking flesh from bones, starting first with the ponies, then the human offerings.

Chapter Two

Bounty Hunter

'A Ghost town,' thought Barrington Tyrane as he caught his first glimpse of Tubac. It was early light, the streets devoid of people, yet he could hear a dog yapping even from this distance. The wind howled, shutters flapped and doors creaked. He had seen many such border towns, merely one main street with a Bank, Saloon and a Hotel. The rest was made up of houses, hardware stores and lean-tos. He squinted his eyes as the wind lashed dust into his face, seemingly singling him out as the only thing that moved in the cold light of morning.

A yank on the rope reminded the packhorse not to dawdle. Tied across its back lay the body of a man, which to Tyrane meant nothing more than the $500 he would receive for the carcass. He raised a hand to scratch his chin, only to realise he hadn't shaved for a week as his fingers ran through what must be a beard.

He contemplated as he rode towards town, this one gave a lot of trouble. Yet he would spend the reward as easily and as quickly as all the others he had collected. $500 should last a month or two until he would have to go out in search of another bounty to sustain his needs.

For this was the path he rode, not one of his choosing but the one he had been dealt. For he was fast with a gun and when a man has a reputation, Ranchers will not hire him. Unless they want a neighbours land, or to have enemies kept at bay. However, once the deed was done, the fast gun was no longer needed. In those days Tyrane hired out to many such Ranchers with grievances against neighbours and although he could not recall having ever killed a man in cold blood, he had certainly baited them into a trap where they could do little else but reach for leather. After a few men died by his gun, his reputation had grown with each telling of the tale and exaggeration of the numbers.

Living such a life his name was added to the wanted posters. His recollection of reading the first reward poster on himself brought a wry smile to his lips. It had read –

WANTED
Barrington Tyrane
$1,000 REWARD
FOR THE
MURDER
OF
Zal Jones
DESCRIPTION
A brown Haired Man of stocky
build, with high Cheekbones and
a scar over his left eye.

Tyrane put his hand up to the scar, but it was on his right hand side. He had he admitted received the scar when he killed Zal Jones. The young man had come into town with a burr under his saddle, but he could not have known that when he singled out the tall stranger at the bar to vex his grievance on that he had little time left amongst the living.

For Zal had received a roasting from his old man and rode into town to take out his anger on anyone he had a mind to.

There were few men who would buck the son of one of the richest cattlemen in the state. Barrington Tyrane was one such man, but he had tried to ignore the young man's insults. For he had seen many such loud mouths during his years on the trail and furthermore did not want any trouble in a strange town.

Zal Jones, thinking wrongly that his victim's lack of response to his insults was afraid, did not let up on his tormenting. Tyrane turned to face him. Zal realised his mistake as he saw those hard eyes gaping out of no more than slits in the skin and the weathered face, which bore the marks of many a brawl. Even comprehending the error he made, Zal reached for leather. His gun never cleared the holster as Tyrane fired, boring a hole in Zal's chest. The body keeled over and as Zal hit the floorboards, blood gushed from his mouth.

Tyrane picked up enough information from those at the bar to realise he had better get out of town. Zal Jones had a tyrant for a father. So he rode hard, for he knew the wealth and power of Zal's old man would carry far. Across the Colorado River and into the staked plains he rode. Work was scarce and he fell in with a gang of rustlers, however, he did not like to rely overly on other people's ability so when the chance arose he moved on into the New Mexico territories and into Arizona.

There he again took up bounty hunting. The work offered a few hard weeks on the trail, followed by a month or so to spend the reward. Most of his prisoners he brought in dead. For it made good sense to kill his prey before they the hunted became the hunters, as could happen when a man was trapped and facing a long stretch in a six by eight cell or a dance on the end of a rope.

Steering his mount along main-street Tubac, Tyrane stopped in front of the jail-house. Sliding from the saddle he strode onto the boardwalk and into the Sheriff's Office.

"Got me a body outside, goes by the name of Red Thorburn. How soon can you make up the $500 reward on him?"

The fat, red-faced Sheriff came awake with a start.

"Look here mister, I don't know who you are, but just supposing that fellah out there's who you say it is, I'll need some proof of identity. Besides, the Bank doesn't open for hours yet so you'll have to set about for a spell,"

Tyrane, pulling a yellowed sheet of paper from inside his shirt thrust it into the Sheriff's hand.

"Jest match his puss with that picture, you'll have your proof of identity."

Arising, the Sheriff moved outside towards the horses. The wind howled down main-street A dog cocked his leg against a hitching rail. Pulling on hair, the Sheriff lifted the dead man's face, glancing from poster to face several times.

"Hm. Hm. I reckon that's him mister. About three hours before I can have your money ready. You want to, you can lie up in one of the cells till then."

"Yea, may as well. I ain't in a hurry no- how."

Tyrane walked his bay over to the stables. There being no one about he led him into an empty stall at the rear of the building. Giving the animal a good rub down he pitched some hay into a manger. The packhorse he led into another stall where he saw an old timer curled up in the corner. 'Obviously asleep on the job,' thought Tyrane as he kicked over a bucket of horseshoes, which brought the old coot to life in no uncertain manner.

"That bay back there, you see he gets his needs tended to. Feed this one as well." Tyrane dropped the lead rope into the old coot's lap.

The old timer was ready to curse Tyrane into damnation, but had second thoughts when he saw the formidable figure standing before him.

"Yessiree I sure will."

As he walked back towards the jail, Tyrane saw the Sheriff admiring a new acquisition amongst his wanted posters.

"Now" said the Sheriff, "Ifn' you was to bring in this fellow, you could earn yourself a sack of money real quick $5,000 dead or alive. You could bring him in the same way as that feller over the horse. They give you less trouble that ways I suppose?"

Tyrane stared at the poster. The man wanted was one

================

Salvador Gonsalves

For   Murder

Rape

Theft

Abduction

Rustling

$5.000 REWARD

================

Gonsalves the bandit rode with a pack, every one of which was as mean as their leader. They stayed in Mexico most of the time, only rarely would they venture into Arizona to rob a Bank or steal cattle.

"He's a mean one all right," said Tyrane. Noting in his mind the description on the poster and merging it with the facts he already knew about the bandit.

For the next week Tyrane relaxed, remaining in Tubac. Letting his body ease itself of the tensions of the trail. He took a woman a couple of times, even in Tubac he found that commodity. In fact he could not recall a town where he had been unable to find it.

After a week, Tyrane sold the packhorse, bought supplies and collected his horse, filling his canteens at the stables. He tossed the old coot a silver dollar for tending the bay and led the animal out into the street before mounting up.

The Sheriff strode over.

"You going after that Gonsalves fellah?"

"Maybe."

"Well if you do, keep your eyes open for Indians. The Apache's been raiding this side of the border lately. Couple of months back they wiped out a wagon train a few days ride from here."

"Obliged."

"That ain't all mister, that Red Thorburn you brought in, he has two brothers, they're bound to be laying for you once word gets out. One goes by the name of Kid Thorburn, the other's called Duke. The kids real fast so they say, mind you I'd be more concerned about Duke if I was you. He'd dry-gulch you as soon as say howdy"

"I know the type," said Tyrane, tilting his hat as an adiós He dug his spur into his mount, riding down main-street heading south-Easterly He was not especially going after Salvador Gonsalves, however should their paths cross then he would play the cards as he was dealt them and he would not forget the $5,000 reward tag. Three days out of Tubac, riding towards FT Huachuca the bay stopped, ears pricked and eyes alert. Tyrane rose in the stirrups for he, too, saw the vultures circling overhead and off-a ways

Easing spur into the bay, they moved on slowly. Keeping to the shaded side of the embankments as they weaved their way along the twisting sands As he passed from one shadow to another Tyrane caught glimpses of smoke rising from the place the vultures circled.

The bay sidestepped the bleached white bones of some long dead Longhorn. Sliding the rifle from its scabbard, Tyrane lay it across the saddle.

Tyrane was prepared for danger. If not then the difference between he and some others was that he still lived. How he still did so was a mystery in itself, for he had spent most of his thirty odd years in hell holes, either getting into, or trying to get out of trouble.

The bay stepped into the sunlight and there to the fore lay the still smouldering wagon. Two of the six-horse team with arrows in them, obviously killed to bring the convoy to a halt. Tyrane eased his finger around the trigger and nudged the bay forward.

The bodies of cavalrymen lay mutilated and scalped. Tyrane took in the entire scene, speculating that the convoy must have been pursued across the plain and been overpowered here, where the wagon would slow them down on the twists and turns. There were no dead Indians, though this was not unexpected as they would have carried off their dead. From the corner of his eye, Tyrane saw movement, in that same instant he swung the rifle around, exerting a more forceful hold on the trigger. An arm moved, Tyrane slid from the saddle approaching the wounded man. As he did so he looked all around for danger, for it was unlike the Apache to leave anyone alive. Standing over the trooper he winced, for the man was scalped and apparently left for dead. The trouper mumbled, spitting out words in between moans as his face contorted under extreme pain.

"GOLD"

The word brought a new sharpness to Tyrane's senses.

"Gold for the Garrison at Ft Thomas, must get through oooh."

Whether the soldier knew of his presence, Tyrane did not know, nor would he for the trooper broke into a bout of coughing and died.

"GOLD"

'He must have been raving," thought Tyrane, no one was stupid enough to bring gold through this country. Nevertheless, he poked through the burning debris for a look-see and came up with three gold coins.

"Now there's a strange thing," he mumbled. "Never known the Apache to bother with gold before."

This presented a problem. Tyrane was unsure of what to make of the findings. The soldier he reasoned was likely raving, yet at the same time he did find some coins. In fact it made sense for the soldier to be thinking of his mission. However, the Apache did not concern themselves with gold, gold was a white mans trait.

Moving towards the bay, Tyrane slid the rifle into its scabbard. The bay reared, casting him to the ground. Tyrane's gun was out as the animal bolted for the prairie. On landing, Tyrane let off three shots and two Apache fell from their ponies. The third bullet went into the skull of a pinto, it crashed to the ground taking its rider with it, trapping his legs underneath. Tyrane caught a glimpse of some twenty Apache with long, greasy black hair in that moment, before a blow to his skull sent everything black.

As Tyrane fell, holding his head, the young brave who fired the shot came running forward. He lifted Tyrane's hair and as he arched his blade a voice rang out. The young buck brought the blade to rest in the sand and turned to face his chief.

It was an older man than the rest, who barged his way through the semi circle of braves around Tyrane. His matt of greying hair was held down by a band different to the others, which signified he was a sub-chief. His nose had a remarkably evident dent in it, suggesting it was broken on more than one occasion.

"This White Eye will live, first he must suffer," shrieked the old man. "He has slain my two sons Matre and Samoa. For this he will cry out for death many times before being torn apart by ponies."

"The scalp, Geronobbi, I claim the scalp by right. It was my bullet which struck him first."

"The White Eyes will be taken to the lodges. There I shall avenge my sons, there you may have your scalp Hurritano"

The look in Geronobbi's eyes told young Hurritano not to pursue the matter. Tyrane's body was tied across a horse, and the party set off. First catching up with a larger party.

Tyrane could not fully focus his mind as his senses returned. His head thundered and he choked with every breath as his body bounced off the side of the horse. How long had he been unconscious, he did not know. Above his right eye was a gash where the bullet had struck. He tried to bring his thoughts into line, by rights he should be dead, he reasoned. However he was not, although this must be the nearest to hell he ever came. The drowsy feeling would not leave so he tried to focus his sights on those around. His lashes stuck together held there for a moment by the dried blood, which had run from his wound. His hands were secured to his feet by a length of rope, which ran under the horse's belly.

The desert plains drifted past and sand was continually kicked into his face. He picked out the Cereus Cactus, but other than that could get no bearings on where he was. A pony came alongside. Tyrane let out a curse as his hair was grasped by the roots and his head held upwards. Gaping all around in that instant, Tyrane saw the boxes tied to the horses in front of him. Tyrane also saw the grey-haired warrior's face, the sloping brow and the broken nose. The hatred in the old man's eyes was evident.

"You killed my sons White Eyes. You will die many times before the pain stops."

Tyrane tried hard to stare back in defiance at the greying warrior but his head was dropped and it fell against the side of the bay once again. 'Could those cases contain the gold of which the trooper was raving,' wondered Tyrane. He tried to raise his head for a better look and caught sight of an U.S. army stamp on one of the boxes.

This didn't make any sense. Apache would have no need for gold. They did not concern themselves with profit, he reasoned. No, they killed the whites for much higher reasons, yet here they were having attacked a convoy and now returning to their lodges.

None of this helped Tyrane from his present predicament,. His head still throbbed from the pain of his wound.

The sun grew more intense, up ahead Tyrane heard the splashing of water and suddenly he was submerged as the bay sidled down the bank and into the Yaqui River. Tyrane gasped air, by the time they emerged on the opposite bank, he was semi conscious and vomiting.

The whole of the next day they travelled deeper into the Sierra Madre. This Tyrane deduced by the crossing of the river, which had been his first real distinguishable landmark.

At noon the following day a huge encampment came into view. The river had cleansed his wounds and Tyrane was alert as they approached the wickiups As ever he took in all the visible terrain. The camp was well situated, and guarded on three sides. On one side was a range of cliffs, on another a lake. The only feasible entrance was by the route they travelled now. It was a rocky area, which gave way to an open stretch of ground leading up to the first wickiups

Young braves rode out to greet the war party. In the village, the old warriors and squaws came forth to see their sons and breadwinners. The wickiups grew more impressive as they rode deeper into the heart of the village. Tyrane's heart met with an empty feeling as he was led into an open area in the middle of camp. He saw the burnt patches where fires would be lit at night and where he supposed he would be one of the main entertainments.

The greatest chief of all, Victorio. A scar faced man, dressed in buckskin emerged. He surveyed first the gold, next the prisoner.

Tyrane listened to the exchange of words between Victorio and the broken-nosed sub chief, however, his understanding of the language was not good. The pack-horses were led forward and the cases unloaded. One box was smashed open, its contents of gold coins spilling out into a heap as it was emptied. There were three such cases.

Victorio pointed in his direction, Tyrane watched as the grey-haired warrior became angry on his relating of the tale. Victorio approached,

"You, White Eyes have killed the sons of Geronobbi. Your cries will haunt these lands long after you have gone, so much so shall you suffer."

Tyrane was thrust into a wickiup to the ground, where he was staked out.

Lying in his spread-eagled position, Tyrane's mind raced. Remembering some of the tortures he had heard of the Apache use. He had witnessed a few, once coming cross the remains of a man who had a stake thrust up his bowels. The stake had been lit and when its end burned away, the remaining eighteen inches of stake was left inside the body. Another time he saw a man set out naked in the sun to fry as the sun burned him. There were many other tortures he knew of. First however, he expected to be warmed up to the occasion before being allowed to die.

"Must escape."

He cursed, yet a lot of blood had been lost and he was a captive under close guard.

Craning his neck backwards, Tyrane saw the legs of the brave stationed outside the wickiup. He was not even sure of his whereabouts. Somewhere in the Sierra Madre he knew, however had it been The Yaqui, The Bavispe or The Rio Aros he crossed two days ago. Due to the time spent in unconsciousness, he was unable to judge in time or distance.

Darkness settled, from his prostrate position, Tyrane watched the smoke filter out through a hole in the top of the wickiup. The fires were ablaze outside. The flames rose to light up the night, casting great shadows across the walls of the wickiup, as the bustle of movement reached his ears.

Drums beat out their slow monotonous sound, yet Tyrane hoped they would not stop playing. For he knew they were a prelude to the forthcoming activities. Faster and faster the drums sang, until suddenly they stopped.

Two braves pushed Tyrane out into the arena. A huge fire blazed, at which Tyrane shielded his eyes as he was hauled past it, to be presented before a ring of chiefs. Sitting around the immediate area were braves. Tyrane scanned those before him before his eyes came to rest on the broken-nosed warrior sat amid the sub chiefs.

He was led before the old warrior who eyed him with distaste. Geronobbi arose to address the council.

"This White Eyes killed my sons. They must be avenged before they can rest in the land of their forefathers. My sons fought bravely against the Blue-coats only to be slain by this one."

He incited pointing to Tyrane.

"Who shall suffer for his deeds."

Tyrane was taken between two stakes and a rope tied to each wrist before being hoisted above ground level and his feet being bound to the stakes also.

Brush was brought and lit beneath him. As it took hold the flames licked his legs as they cut into the air, causing Tyrane to twist and attempt to stand higher in his bonds, which made little or no difference as the heat intensified.

The watching braves jeered, tormenting him as his face contorted under the pain of the burns on his legs. The young buck broken nose stopped from parting Tyrane with his scalp came forward, brandishing a torch he passed it under Tyrane's chin, forcing him to stretch backwards. It singed his growth of beard. He was having difficulty breathing as the hot air rose all around. Each breath became like inhaling toxic gases, causing him to cough and choke and sag his body nearer to the flames, which ever searched out his flesh.

Sweat dried quicker that it was being produced, whilst every thread in his jeans appeared to be alight and burning into his shins and thighs. The boots grew too hot for his feet to bear and became like a detached part of his body without feeling the heat grew so great. He suffered this, sometimes conscious sometimes not before being cut down and staked out on the ground once more.

Tyrane gritted his teeth as each movement brought his clothing into contact with his body. His lungs gasped in the cool night air as his body grew cold very quickly. The sweat dried on his torso, to remain a cold feeling. He shivered, barely conscious of those around him.

Hurritano brought kindling, to start a small fire not far from his head. Tyrane heard the crackling of the twigs as the flames took hold. Arching his body looking overhead, he saw the fire and felt its heat as more twigs were added. The flames licked higher, Tyrane tried to pull his head away from them.

When Tyrane pulled his body a few inches away from the flames, Hurritano added more brush to bring the fire closer. Beads of perspiration appeared on Tyrane's forehead as he attempted to sink his neck further into his body to escape the searing heat. His ears blistered first. His head became so painful, that even with his eyes closed he still saw the red heat of the fire.

Tyrane smelt the sweat rising from his body, heard his hair singe and the rancid smell of burning hair rushed to his nostrils. A feeling of hopelessness came over him as the slipped into unconsciousness.

As his body became limp, the fire was doused. The instant relief he felt, no man could explain, for although his skin was peeling and the pain was intense, it was as if a knife had been removed from his brain.

Tyrane's mind filtered back into focus. His bonds were tightened, the hot ropes bit into flesh offering little movement to right or left.

Hurritano approached him again, carrying a lance, which was white hot on leaving the fire. As the hot end neared him, now turning a dull, reddish colour, Tyrane saw upon the flattened blade, small pebbles. Hurritano permitted Tyrane to see the pebbles drop into a bowl of water. The loud simmer and the hissing rise of vapour left no doubt as to their heat. The hot end picked up more pebbles. The lance was passed over Tyrane's body it came within an inch of his flesh. There was no way to retreat from the heat as he tried to sink deeper into the sands underneath. Any sudden movement might cause his tormentor to let the stones fall and cut through his body. As the lance was passed over his face for the second time, causing his nose to blister, Tyrane dreaded the stones being used to blind him.

The frenzied chant of the warriors ceased as the rifle boomed. The startled Hurritano let the pebbles fall into the sand beside Tyrane's head. They only missed connecting with him because he arced his head to one side, but he could smell the singed hair burning on the side of his head.

The Apache turned as one to look in the direction of the shot, for it was a warning signal indicating riders approaching the camp.

Tyrane did not know the reason for his reprieve, however he used the opportunity to heave in great lungs of air and get his body flowing to an even rhythm once more.

Into the encampment rode the intruders, weaving a course through the wickiup s and braves who lined their path. The first rider to appear into Tyrane's view wore a large sombrero, over his shoulder were draped carbines of ammunition in a cross-cross fashion. He was a lean man, clean-shaven with a bronzed face. His face was obscured by long black hair though he had rather pointed features.

Tyrane recognised him immediately as Salvador Gonsalves. Behind him rode a great bull of a man, again with the carbines draped across his shoulders. His head was a mass of shaggy black hair. Tyrane could not distinguish where the hair stopped and the beard began. Just two bright black eyes pierced the black mass. He, Tyrane assumed was Amine, Gonsalves second in command. He too, wore a sombrero, as did the rest of the men who followed. They were all draped with carbines and loaded with weaponry.

Victorio stood up.

"You come quickly Salvador Gonsalves, this is good, do you bring the guns?"

"Not so fast Great Chief, I was told you wanted to buy guns with gold. First I must take the gold with me to purchase the rifles you want."

"No," said Victorio.

"You will take with you only enough gold to buy rifles, the rest will remain here until you return."

"Now you see here," interrupted Amine

"I see the Great Victorio does not trust me any more than I trust him," said Gonsalves.

"Enough!" cried Victorio

"We will talk, take the White Eyes to the wickiup, he shall live to see another sunrise."

Amine looked on dispassionately as Tyrane was thrust into a wickiup and staked to the ground. He lay there favouring his right side, for his left shoulder was the more painful.

Outside he heard the raised voices as Gonsalves tried to get more gold to take with him.

It was a strange quirk of fate, thought Tyrane for although he had not set out deliberately to find Gonsalves, the Mexican had certainly found him. Outside they argued on how much gold for how many rifles, how long it would take to return with the guns and where the exchange should take place.

Victorio and his braves would obtain guns in battle, but they could never amount the kind of arms the Mexicans could bring them for the payment of the gold. The gunrunners would be free to move through their native land unobserved striking at some unsuspecting garrison where an arsenal of arms was known to be kept.

What good this information did Tyrane he did not know as he listened to the broken Spanish and little Apache, not understanding all of it. He became at first alert, then apprehensive as he saw the blade appear in the wall of the wickiup. He saw the silhouette of a small figure cast by the light from the great fire.

When the blade reached the ground a hand appeared. Pulling the slit open, the small figure stepped inside. In the half-light Tyrane saw the figure approach and lean over him. He now realised it was a white woman, as he moved his lips to speak she put her hand over his mouth. Indicating the guard outside she bade him quiet, as she worked her way around cutting his bonds. Tyrane studied her face. Her fair hair was much in need of a wash and she was agile in her movements.

With his bonds cut, Tyrane loped over to the tear in the canvas. He picked up a blanket and water container before stepping into the cold night air.

She led the way, stopping often, continuing only when the way was clear, keeping to the shadows cast by the fire. After a little way she stopped and turned to him, speaking for the first time.

"The horses are this way, quickly before we are missed."

"What's your name, what are you doing here?"

"Hollinger, Clementine Hollinger's my name."

Tyrane followed, content to let his liberator lead the way.

"If we can get to the horses, you can take me out of here, I've been afraid to try it on my own. I wouldn't know which way to go,"

Tyrane knew his chances of escape were slim, alone he stood some kind of a chance but with a girl along he stood none. He looked at the frail figure who stood before him so expectantly and hoped she would understand, though he doubted it. He swung his fist and smashed it into her face, dragging the body into cover he continued heading towards the water.

Tyrane reckoned himself as being somewhere between the heart of camp and the lake. There was no way he realised of him escaping without a horse. Logic dictated that the animals would be corralled somewhere between the cliffs and the waters edge.

Stealthily Tyrane slid his body into the refreshing water. He followed the line of the lake around until it led him to the whispering sound of horses, where he stopped to seek out the guards.

In this country a man would die without a horse, little wonder the Apache valued their animals above all else. It would be suicidal to think no one was watching over such prized possessions. He saw two braves, they were on the blind side of the water from the livestock.

Tyrane did not like the way in which he treated his rescuer, however, should he get safely away from here he intended to inform the authorities of her predicament. The animals whinnied, standing back from him as he moved amongst them.

Confident of being well concealed from the lookouts, he cut strips from the blanket with the knife he had taken from the woman. He fashioned each strip into a crude rope, his movements being nullified by the stomping of hooves. Making a noose he slipped it over a back's head. Singling out another black he put the makings of a bridle over its neck, it offered some kind of a hold and controlling the animal would be that much easier.

With the remaining piece of blanket he cut a slit in the middle and popped it over his head. It only reached as far as his stomach, however, it did offer some protection from the wind to his shoulders. Leading both the blacks he mounted one, leading the other by the bits of knotted blanket. As the moon shone from above Tyrane listened for any commotion from the village, there was none. Hence his absence was not yet discovered.

Tyrane cleared the first skyline before digging spur into the big black. The animal lunged forward pulling the spare horse into close contention. Tyrane rode hard and fast, putting as much distance between himself and the Apache village as was possible. For the best part of the night the big black galloped until, as the darkness fell away and the murky light of dawn appeared his forelegs buckled underneath pitching Tyrane sky-forward. The spare animal stomped his hooves as Tyrane returned to the wounded black. It was sheer exhaustion, which caused him to falter, but he was finished. His foreleg shattered.

Taking the blade, Tyrane tried not to watch the bulging eyes as he ran the blade across the throat. The crimson omitting from the open throat wet his jeans as he transferred the bridle to the other black.

The Apache would be coming after him, of that he was sure. However, with the lead gained in running the big black to his death, he stood a chance of not being missed until daybreak.

Chapter Three

Bank Robbery

Ojo Caliente said Freeze, and the Bank teller was no hero. Ojo shoved a flour sack across the counter, indicating for it to be filled and quick. The young cashier gaped at the man who stood before him.

Ojo Caliente had a long, thin face with a pointed nose, his moustache was barely a thin line of hair above his lip. When he entered the Bank, the cashier had noticed the low slung holster and alert look of the man. Now here he was with the barrel of that low slung gun being pointed at his head with no one else in the Bank even remotely aware of what was going on. The individual cubicles set up at each teller shielded the clients from one another.

The cashier stuffed the notes into the sack, he could cry for help he knew, but would be killed for his trouble. He trembled as Ojo snatched the sack from his fingers, Ojo knew if he took just one pace backwards all in the Bank would know a robbery was in progress. He beckoned for the cashier to lean forward, indicating silence by putting the gun to his lips, Ojo grabbed him by the collar and brought the barrel crashing down on the teller's head. The body relaxed on its stool, slumped across the counter. Ojo, bracing himself for trouble wheeled around heading for the door. Just as he reached it there was a crash,

28

the cashier had fallen from his stool. A guard leapt, his rifle swinging, across the room. Ojo's first shot took him through the head, he was dead before he hit the ground.

Ojo fired two more quick shots into the Bank before rushing along the boardwalk to the rear street buildings. One shot landed harmlessly in an oak cabinet. The other ricocheted off the ceiling, coming to rest in the prostrate body of the cashier.

Ojo's horse was on main-street, however, was of no use to him now, for the whole town was brought to life by the shots. He ran gasping for breath as he darted his way around the outbuildings to the rear of main-street He heard a cry,

"Someone's robbed the Bank."

The adrenaline pulsated through his veins as both body and mind raced, searching for a solution. He must find a horse, or somewhere to hide although the latter was unlikely. Reaching a blind alley he scrambled up onto the fence barring his way. He hesitated before jumping back down as an open window caught his eye. It was a floor off the ground, though from his elevated position he could just reach it. If someone were inside he may have to worry no more about a horse, or anything else as he may be shot.

He pulled himself up and came through the window rolling to land flour sack in one hand, gun in the other. Fanning the room with his gun he took it in at a glance, it was empty, but in use. The smell of cheap perfume hung in the air and a woman's clothes were scattered on the bed.

Ojo concluded he must be in a saloon. The door handle turned and the door fell open. She stood there the water dripping from her body, the tin bath lay steaming in the background. Ojo cast his eyes over her.

The flour sack fell to the ground, its contents spilling out.

"So you've made a mess of robbing the Bank eh! Where do you think you can hide up here, certainly not under the bed," she taunted, in no way trying to hide her body.

"Shut your stupid mouth,"

retorted Ojo, pressing his ear against the door, listening for anyone approaching.

No one was coming yet, but soon this whole town would be looking for him and when they came they would bring a rope.

She picked up the money sack stuffing it below the mattress.

"Get your pants off and git into bed quickly mister. They'll have this town sealed off in no time looking for you."

Ojo made to protest before realising his only chance was to hide out until dark. He surmised the situation. The only one who knew what he looked like was the cashier and he was dead.

Ojo slipped between the sheets, she looked at him alarmingly for he still carried his gun.

"I keep that with me wherever I go."

Suddenly he heard the kicking open of doors along the corridor and the bustle of activity as voices were raised.

Ojo thrust the barrel of his gun into her body as the door was thrown open. A thickset man stood in the doorway, gun in hand. Ojo saw the star pinned on his shirt pocket.

"How long has this fellah been here Marie?"

"Well now Deputy, you don't expect me to time the man do you? I don't charge by the hour you know. Just what do you mean by bursting in here any ways?".

Ojo shifted the barrel of his gun to bear on the Law-man's chest.

"The Bank's been robbed. Someone slugged the teller and killed him. He won't get away though, the town's been sealed off."

"Well, he's not here,"

Ojo reckoned it being only ten minutes since he shot the guard. This town sure had come to life in the meantime. The

Deputy took a long look at him, Ojo curled tighter on the trigger. Marie felt the tension in his body.

"If' you don't mind Deputy I have a client here who sure as hell ain't going to come across with you standing there."

Another figure appeared in the doorway.

"What the hell is this, a peek show?" shrieked Marie, hurling a tray at the two men.

"Nobody here Slim," said the Deputy.

"Just a client who wants to get on with his business," he added, closing the door.

Marie turned to the man lying beside her. He was thin and wiry, in any event she learned to take them in all shapes and sizes.

Ojo threw back the covers, side-stepping towards the window. There was not much visible, however, he could hear a lot of shouting and the galloping of horses.

"Must get to my horse," he said aloud.

"You'll have to stay here until after dark mister."

Ojo considered this for a moment. It was true, he could not go downstairs as yet.

"Where do you come in on this? You could have given me away. Of course you would have been killed for your trouble, but you didn't even try."

He did not have to wonder for long.

"I want out of this here one horse town. Some of that there Bank money will do it for me. I'll hole you up here for a cut until after dark. I can get you something to eat and to whet your whistle and I can sure as hell keep you occupied in the meantime," she added, glancing down at her body.

Ojo eyed her suspiciously. He saw no harm in whiling away the remaining daylight hours with her. However, in no way was he going to allow her out of his sight.

"Have you any whiskey?"

"Sure, some in that cabinet, left over from a little party I threw last night. About the same number of people here, as was last night, too."

Ojo pulled the cork out and took a swig.

"Alright, so you can hole me up in more ways than one until dark. If you behave yourself and do as your told I'll leave you enough to take you to wherever it is you want to go."

"It's a deal mister, I'll do just as you say. Although whether I would call that behaving myself, I don't think."

Ojo sneered, telling her to call for some food and for it to be left outside the door.

"Just tell whoever brings it, you have a shy customer."

Whilst he ate, Ojo watched her well-manicured fingers flicking through the banknotes.

"$2,880."

She gasped, her eyes widening as she did so. It was roughly what he expected. To hope for more would have required a full scale Bank Robbery, the risk of such a robbery did not appeal to Ojo. Marie was already in bed when Ojo slid between the sheets beside her. His hand thrust between her unresisting thighs and his body wrapped around hers.

An hour before midnight, Ojo awoke. Pulling his body away from hers, he quickly dressed, Marie watched him suspiciously. Pulling the covers together, Ojo bound her to the iron bedstead before counting out money onto the cabinet.

"If you make a noise and someone has to untie you, you will have to explain about this money I'm leaving. On the other hand you should free yourself within a couple of hours, by which time I shall be long gone."

Ojo stepped through the window clasping the money sack. Landing on the move he peered to both right and left before venturing towards main-street, his gun leading the way.

The roan still stood at the hitching rail long away from the Bank. Ojo, stashing the flour sack into his shirt strode towards his horse. There were few people about, though he heard the music and clinking of glasses coming from the saloon, also a low murmur of voices.

"Don't move mister,"

The voice came from behind and to the left.

"I've been watching that horse, it's the only one that's been here all day, ever since the little fracas we had at the Bank. All the others have been and gone, looking for the fellah who killed the cashier. I'm the one who's found him though, ain't I?"

"What is it you want Mister?"

"Well now the Bank's offered a ten per cent reward on that there money, which adds up to nigh on $4000."

"Not four thousand dollars mister. Someone at the Bank's taken some dollars for themselves and pinned it to my tail, but tell you what, I'll give you $500 off'ns you will just -"

All the time he spoke, Ojo turned slowly his adversary. His voice trailed off as his eyes fixed on the tin star and the face of the man who earlier had come to Marie's room. He realised there was little chance of talking his way out of this one.

"The money's in my shirt, you want I should take it out?"

"Ah Ha!" The Law-man nodded.

"No funny moves, first toss your gun over here."

Ojo inched his hand towards the low slung pistol grip.

"By the fingertips mister, that's right."

The gun on the ground, Ojo started taking the money from within his shirt. The Law-man temporarily relaxed his guard.

As Ojo withdrew the bundle of bills, he tossed it skyward. In the instant the Deputy looked up, Ojo kicked him in the groin. The gun went off harmlessly into the night.

The low din from the saloon stopped as heads appeared over the swinging doors. Ojo snatched up his gun and fired.

The Law-man arced his back as the bullet ripped through flesh. Ojo fired two shots towards the saloon, sending a hat from its owner's head. Others ducked out of sight as shots rang out from along the street and men came running along the board-walk.

Ojo leapt onto the roan, digging spur into the animal's side. It reared, lunged forward and pulled on the bridle, taking its unwelcome weight galloping down main-street Ojo pulled on the reigns, veering the roan away from the main-trail, steering it southward he rode hard and fast, clutching the little money still remaining in his shirt. He rode the animal into the ground for the first hour, before slowing the pace to a canter. He wouldn't be going back to Lordsburg for a while he reckoned. .

He was also wanted in Deming, Silver City and Santa Fe. As the roan cantered he counted the money, $2000 or thereabouts. He cursed his luck.

Riding all night and half the next day, it was noon when he sighted the relay station. Switching the reigns he turned the roan into the coral. He had come a fair ways and reckoned on taking the stage on the next leg of the journey. His pursuers, if any, would probably keep off the well-beaten tracks, never thinking a man on the run would exchange his horse in favour of a stagecoach. It was a ploy he had used successfully in the past.

"Hello inside, anybody there?"

The clanging on an anvil stopped and a man covered in sweat emerged from the barn carrying a red-hot horseshoe.

"I'm looking to trade my horse and saddle, then catch the next stage going South."

"I can take your horse mister, though I've no need for a saddle. The stage comes through in about an hour or so. Set yourself inside, we can trade whilst you eat."

'Sly bastard,' thought Ojo, a hungry man with food being shoved under his nose isn't going to put up much argument about price. He would be too busy filling his face.

The meal was good, the man's wife sure could cook. He didn't get too bad a price for the horse either.

The stage rolled in. The horses needed changing and the passengers tended to. The driver was first to enter the shack, a man in his mid forties. Followed by a sour faced old shotgun guard who looked all of a hundred years old.

"Hear you want to buy fare. How far you fixing to go mister?"

"What's the end of the run?"

"Sonora," replied the driver.

"That'll do me fine, you got a spare seat?"

"Sure have, only one passenger so far, you make two."

"Sounds as if you expect some more."

"We pick them up all along the line mister. You wouldn't believe some of the places they show up. Miles from nowhere some of them, no horse, nothing and flag me down."

The passenger entered, a large, burly man who looked rather well to do. His white moustache matched the colour of his hair. He had bulbous cheeks, with a swagger of authority he set himself down at the table, his cup was soon filled with thick, black coffee.

"This here gent's going to be joining us on the coach Mr Cameron. You two gents can get along. If not it's going to seem a mighty long trip for you both."

The big man nodded towards Ojo.

"Howdy"

"Mr Cameron here's just had some excitement. The Lordsburg Bank's been robbed."

Ojo's hand moved towards his gun.

"We was just pulling out as it happened, so we delayed some, then Mr Cameron here caught the stage and we've been trying to make up lost time since," quipped the driver.

"He been giving you a bumpy ride Mr Cameron?" Put in the relay master

"Was anyone injured?" enquired his wife.

"One man killed," replied Cameron.

"The thief got away with over $40.000.

Ojo nearly choked on his food, thinking that someone at the Bank had used his robbery to their advantage and helped themselves.

"You were lucky not to be injured."

"I was fortunate to be out back when it occurred," explained Cameron.

Once Cameron's legs were stretched and his belly filled, the Teamsters were readied to roll.

Ojo tossed his saddle up tops and climbed in ahead of Cameron, wanting to face the front. On entering the stage he snatched up a wallet lying on the seat and stuffed it into his pocket.

He observed that since his arrival at the relay station, Cameron had not once let go of a small black bag. He now sat with it on his knee, his fat fingers clutching the handle. The stage rumbled out onto the trail, soon it was well on its way.

Cameron chatted incessantly and how he was going to visit his brother's ranch near Fronteras, in Mexico. Ojo allowed him to talk away, not really listening, certainly not contributing anything to the one sided conversation.

It took several days to reach Fronteras, where Cameron left the coach. Ojo thought it strange that the big man had not mentioned the loss of his wallet, though it bothered him little.

Disregarding the personal papers, Ojo removed what money was inside and tossed the wallet out onto the trail. The stagecoach was gaining its full momentum as it pulled away from Fronteras.

No sooner had the stagecoach departed than Cameron enquired when the next stagecoach was leaving for Mexico.

Ojo Caliente was the only passenger as the Sonora Stage travelled south westerly. The driver seemed to be in a hurry as the whip cracked and insults were hurled at the six-horse team. Ojo was bounced around the interior of the stage and was now regretting having traded his horse as he rigidly held his body in the seat, stopping himself from being hurled to the floor.

Barrington Tyrane put the water pouch to his lips. The last few drops fell onto his parched skin. Having crossed the Yaqui River a day hence, he was looking for somewhere to hide up until nightfall as the first rays of sunlight spread across the sky.

Tyrane had ridden the second black sparingly. Riding for a while, then walking. In doing this, the Apache village lay some days behind him. The water although scarce, he gave to the horse. However, late the previous night the black and stumbled. As with the first animal he had no choice but to put it out of its misery. He cursed the way bad luck had ridden his trail. All night he had walked and unused to travelling on foot he was exhausted.

On finding a small overhang, he snuggled up tightly and slept, awakened only when too much pressure was exerted on his burns. They were healing and the only time they bothered him was during sleep.

The day passed, when he awoke it was evening. He had slept heavily and did not like the fact he had done so. His thirst returned soon after awakening, water was needed, but he had none.

When he set off, the darkness had covered the land once again. The only bearings to be had were by the stars. The going was slow, repeatedly he stumbled over rocks. Even bones on one occasion, though he could not be sure. Each time he picked himself up and continued putting one foot in front of another doggedly.

On crossing a stretch of open ground, Tyrane stopped, for the land seemed hard and well trodden. Dropping to his knees he felt around in the dark, fingering the cut in the earth's crust made by a wagon wheel. He reckoned on daylight not being far away, so looked for a place to hide.

The morning passed and noon arrived, bringing with it the intense heat prevalent to the terrain. Tyrane watched the trail, but no one came. Still he watched, not daring to allow himself to fall into sleep, for it was a well-worn track and had been used recently.

He had not seen nor heard an Apache since his escape and was convinced he had shaken off all pursuit. The sun travelled across the sky.

It was mid-afternoon when he saw it in the distance.

A small disturbance of dust, growing larger as it neared. Feeling for the knife, Tyrane lost all thought of his impending thirst as he strained his eyes onto the advancing dust cloud. Slowly but surely, the nearer it came the more tense and taut became his muscles with the expectation of what was approaching. Sweat trickled down his spine, the hair on his neck stood on end. Still the dust cloud approached. Beneath it he began to determine the shape of a wagon.

Letting out a great sigh of relief, he relaxed.

The thought of fire burning into his brain became a distant memory, as fear of recapture by the Apache drifted into nothingness.

The stagecoach rolled nearer.

"A stage route," he cried in elation.

Coming from behind his rock, Tyrane climbed on top of it. He wanted whoever was riding shotgun to see he represented no danger.

The sour-faced shotgun guard saw the figure on the rock.

"Hey mister, you inside. If you can use that gun of yours then have it ready."

Ojo shoved his head from the side of the stage, sighting the figure waving what looked to be a piece of blanket.

Old sourpuss up top had the carbine bearing down on Tyrane's chest.

"Whoa, Whoa, steady now," cried the driver.

"What the hell are you doing out here mister?"

Ojo interrupted.

"What happened?"

"Apache."

"Ah Ha, I didn't think you got those burns out of choice."

"Obliged if you'd drop me off at the nearest town," cried Tyrane to the driver, shifting his attention from the man in the stage.

"Git aboard, then we can git away from here."

Put in sourpuss, "I've had my scalp too many years to be parted with it by some Apache."

"Go on git, you mangy critters move!"

The whip lashed and the team pulled in the harness. Inside the coach, Ojo passed Tyrane a canteen, wetting his lips he began to swallow. Ojo watched as the Adams apple bobbed back and forth.

"Ah, I needed that."

Wetting the piece of blanket, Tyrane dabbed it onto his burns.

"How'd you happen to get taken alive mister? The Apache don't usually take no prisoners."

"When they came up on me I let off some shots. I killed the sons of one of the chiefs. He didn't want me to die so quickly. So I was taken to their camp."

Tyrane paused.

"I escaped,"

"Not before they had some sport with you I see," said Ojo, indicating the burns.

"Aha it weren't no picnic mister, but I intend to return for that gold."

As he spoke, Tyrane realised the slip he had made. Ordinarily he would never have been so revealing, but he put it down to the state of his body and mind.

Ojo was suddenly taking more than a passing interest in the conversation.

"My name's Caliente, Ojo Caliente."

"Tyrane."

"Just Tyrane, no other name."

"Just Tyrane."

The stagecoach bumped along the road. Ojo studied the tall stranger who sat opposite him. He was the second person on this trip, on this stage who had aroused his curiosity.

Chapter Four

Marshall And The Bandit

Zeb Pluckard drew reign on the piebald.

'About an hours ride behind them,' he surveyed, studying the tracks. Tilting back his hat he wiped the sweat from his forehead.

"Sure as hell ain't getting any younger."

Trailing these three hombres was taking its toll. Zeb was a big, brawny man with black hair greased back and a thickset moustache, with a broad forehead and a strong chin. He was at an age one did not usually attain as a U.S. Marshall.

He had been following these three for a week and was gaining on them rapidly.

At the last camp the ashes had been warm, he reckoned on sighting them around noon.

Zeb was in no hurry now his quarry was within striking distance. He always seemed to be rushing through this country, never stopping to take in the breathtaking beauty of the high mesa's and wide open plains. The tranquillity of such places was unique. Though the vegetation was sparse, there were water holes to be found a plenty, with outcroppings of gorse, mesquite and sage growing around their edge.

Even out here, days from the nearest town with shifting sands all around, Zeb felt in his element.

He knew that the three men he trailed would be no easy task for they were involved in a fracas back in Nacozari, killing the bartender and Faro Dealer. They reckoned they had been cheated, Zeb knew the Faro Dealer to be honest. He was also told that the three were the worst for drink when the trouble started. First they killed the Faro Dealer, then when the bartender reached under the bar for his shotgun they killed him, emptying some dozen or so slugs into his skull and proceeded to wreck the joint.

This was not one of his official assignments. However the Sheriff at Nacozari was not up to tracking down the three perpetrators.

Zeb was in town purely to look up his old friend the Faro Dealer. When the townsfolk learned he was both a U.S. Marshall, and a friend of the deceased they turned to him for assistance. He had been returning to Tombstone, from Casas Grandes, where he had tracked two renegades and once again, as he had done many times before was acting on his own initiative in trailing these three.

U.S. Marshall Zeb Pluckard paid heed when his piebald let out a whinny.

Ahead he saw the smoke drifting upwards from a thicket. Dismounting, he walked the piebald, cocked his rifle and spun the chamber of his pistol before re-holstering.

Satisfied all was well with his weapons the Marshall advanced on the thin line of smoke.

The terrain was rocky with sparse gorse leading to the grove where the three killers camped.

As he drew near, Zeb could smell the aroma of hot coffee. He didn't believe he was expected, nor that the killers even knew of his existence. Their guard was down, Zeb scanned the camp, picking out the exact location of the three men.

One was standing over the fire helping himself to a coffee, another was sitting to his right inserting shells into the chamber of his gun. The third member of the trio was lying some distance away from the others. Zeb recognised this man from the descriptions given by the townsfolk, also from the wanted posters bearing his name.

Emanuel Santes, a murderer, thief, abductor and many other things besides. He was a short, bull of a man, some five foot six in height. What he lacked in height he more than compensated for in physique. There was two hundred and ten pounds of power packed muscle to the man. Atop a stubby neck sat a tiny head, which in comparison to the rest of his body was out of place with deep-set eyes and a well-groomed moustache, which fell to the edge of his chin. His mass of black hair was obscured by the sombrero he flapped, shielding his eyes from the sun.

Santes was a loner as a rule. His tantrums were not tolerated by some of the bands of Mescalero' he rode with. Always he would ride out when the notion took him, Zeb was in no doubt that he rode with these two only because it suited his purpose at present.

Zeb, aware he could bear down on his quarry, did not do so. For if any of them should manage to get to cover, his present position did not offer much protection.

Crawling steadily, Zeb found himself behind a rock, which offered both concealment and an escape route, should he need it. Propping the barrel of the rifle against the rock, Zeb let the butt rest in his shoulder and looked along the sight. He was unconcerned about all the movement he made, for he believed it better to take all necessary risks early in an encounter, rather than later.

The sitting Mexican spun the chamber of his gun. Zeb sighted him, intending to take him first as he represented the most danger, his gun already being out. Next he would take the leader, Santes. The man with the coffee pot represented the least danger, for his hands were occupied and it would be several moments before he became involved in the shooting.

This was the way Zeb thought out the situation. His finger curled on the trigger, taking the pressure.

"You out there, stay perfectly still, your!"

No sooner were the first words uttered when the man with the coffee-pot dived for cover, sailing past his sitting accomplice as he did so.

Zeb eased on the trigger. The Mexican in flight, stopped in mid air, his body crashing to the ground, blood trickling from behind his ear.

Zeb had a line on the sitting target, however the wrong man stopped the bullet. He fired again, not having to shift his aim. As he did so, so too did the sitting Mexican.

The two shots exploded in unison, there was only one sound. Zeb's shoulder was ripped by a bullet as his victim groped backwards. A red circle appearing on his shirt, growing bigger as the blood came forward.

Swinging the rifle, Zeb's stomach churned in the realisation he was alone. The two bodies lay by the campfire, however, the third member of the trio was missing.

There was no time to surmise where Santes was. A bullet ricocheted into the rock besides him, spraying splinters into his face. Zeb leapt behind the rock, thumbing fresh cartridges into the rifle before wiping the dust from his eyes.

As his vision came into focus, only then did he see the redness and feel the dampness of his shirt. Zeb fingered the wound, concluding the bullet had passed right through.

The Marshall worked out from the lone shot fired, the general area Santes was in, though he could not get an exact fix on the trajectory of the shot. This of course was always assuming Santes had not moved his position in the meantime.

From where he was, Zeb reckoned he could not be seen. Also Santes would not know if his accomplices bullet had done any serious damage, nor even if his own ricocheted shot had scored a hit.

Thinking these factors out, Zeb concluded if he remained quiet, Santes would have to investigate, hence making the first move and revealing his position.

Placing the rifle before him, Zeb lay on his stomach. Moving slowly, he pulled his body along, stopping only to lay the rifle ahead of himself. Then pulling himself along again. Doing this was time consuming. Fifteen minutes passed before he crawled forty feet.

He froze as he heard Santes call out.

"Gringo, you would like me to believe you are dead? No. My name is Emanuel Santes and I am not stupid. What do you want?

Why do you trouble us?

Who are you?

Why do you follow us to this place?"

There was silence, Zeb lay still, not daring to betray his position, uncomfortable as it was. The time passed, another ten minutes before he again began to crawl. He was able to crouch once he was at a safe distance, Zeb swung around to the opposite side of the encampment and began to inch his way towards the clearing once again. Using the same principle as before, first he crawled, next lay the rifle to the fore and dragged his body after it. Zeb saw the rock, he hoped Santes would believe he still hid behind.

It was over an hour since Santes fired his sole shot. The sun was shifting across the sky, Zeb's shadow lay behind him. His eyes scanned the entire camp area. He saw no sign of movement. There was no knowing from which direction the Mexican would come, for during his absence Zeb was sure Santes would have shifted his position several times.

The campfire was low, the last flames clung to the embers. A vulture soared overhead, casting its shadow as it circled. Another hour passed. The sun moved further across the sky, the shadows grew longer.

A bush moved. Santes emerged from the bracken, his gun in hand leading the way, moving with an agility, which belied his body. Zeb placed the rifle against his shoulder, snuggling the butt into his cheek. His finger curled around the trigger and he waited as Santes moved more into the open.

Santes was only a few yards from where he believed his attacker to be. As he approached each rock he flattened his body against them.

Zeb, with the rifle bearing down on the Mexicans chest, only needed move his finger a fraction to release a bullet.

"Hold it right there Santes, freeze."

Santes stopped dead in his tracks, startled by the voice, which rang in his ears.

"Real slowly, let the gun drop."

Santes hesitated. A bullet smacked into the rock mere inches from his face.

Zeb back on the trigger again.

"I said, drop it Santes."

Santes' mind raced. Who was this Gringo who knows my name. Have we met before perhaps?

"The next bullet won't miss."

As his pistol landed in the sand, Santes gazed all around. He too, could tell from where a shot was fired, however he could see no sign of his attacker.

Kick the gun away, I can drop you before you move an inch, so be real careful."

Touching his toe to the pistol, Santes sent the weapon some six feet from him. Zeb emerged. Santes studied the face of his captor, but could not recall ever having met before.

Advancing towards Santes with his rifle aimed at the Mexicans belt buckle, Zeb's finger itched for some movement, which would give him just cause for releasing another round. He stopped to examine the two bodies, collecting the dead men's guns, doing likewise with Santes weapon when he reached it.

"You Gringo bastard. Why do you do this? Who are you?"

Pulling back his vest, Zeb revealed the U.S. Marshall badge pinned to his shirt.

"That is no good here Gringo. You have no power in Mexico. If you will let me ride out, I will forget what you have done and permit you to live."

"Shut up. Get that fire going."

As Santes added kindling to the fire, Zeb positioned himself at a respectable distance from the Mexican and peeled back his shirt. The pain, not noticed before came ever more prevalent. He kept one eye on Santes at all times.

"Boil water, then put some coffee on."

Zeb cleansed the wound, wrapping it as best he could. Santes fixed the knot, securing the dressing.

"One wrong move and you're a dead Mex."

Their eyes met, Santes was in no doubt the Marshall would pull the trigger, at this range the blast would blow him away.

Zeb concluded his injury was not serious, however, he did not want to risk the several day journey back to Nacozari. The nearest place he knew of was Sonora, so he reckoned on making for there.

Pointing to the two bodies, he called to Santes,

"Bury them."

"What! I have no shovel."

"Use your hands, do it Santes and do it now."

Raising the barrel of his pistol ended any protestations.

"Then put rocks over the bodies."

Dragging the bodies, Santes lay them in the shallowest spot he could find. Not having too much digging to do he was soon laying stones in place.

With the fire doused Zeb let loose the two dead men's animals. Santes arose from completing the graves.

"Saddle up and keep your mouth shut."

It would be a two-day journey to Señora

Too much riding could re-open the wound, resulting in a loss of blood, which would be fatal where Santes was concerned. He tied Santes into the saddle, his hands fastened, his feet linked together underneath the horse's belly by a length of cord. Zeb fixed another length of rope from his piebald to the Mexican killer's animal.

"On you go Santes, I'll be right behind you."

The two men loped off. Whenever Santes veered off a true course Zeb halted the piebald, bringing Santes mount to an abrupt standstill causing him to lunge forward in the saddle.

"Hey you Gringo bastard, you think you will live long enough to get me to jail. I do not think so. You bastard, you will never live to see another day if you put me in jail. I will break out and kill you one day. This I swear."

"I warned you."

Belated Zeb. Removing the bandanna from around the Mexicans neck, he thrust it into his mouth, fastening it there with the sweatband from around his own neck. They made good ground for the rest of the day. As the light grew dim, a place was found for the night. Dismounting in a small arroyo, Santes was set to building a fire.

The last flicker of daylight was present when they rode into the arroyo, now as the coffee boiled it was darkness all around for night came quickly in this desolate country.

Zeb, tying Santes hand and foot, bound him to a rock within the firelight. Satisfied the Mexican could not break his bonds, Zeb retreated into the darkness. He could still see Santes, however, doubted whether the Mexican could see him. He sat watching, concerned, for his prisoner had made no attempt at escape. A man like Santes, killer though he maybe valued his freedom, Zeb decided to take precautions.

Sliding out from under his blanket Zeb put dead brush in his place. Donning his hat at the head of the blanket, to all intent and purposes it would appear as if he still slept there. For good measure he emptied the rifle and lay it alongside the hat before disappearing further into the darkness, settling in an uncomfortable knoll.

Santes strained his eyes, trying to keep them focused on the Marshall, at times he believed he saw him, however it was only shadows he saw and when they remained in one place for too long he realised he had lost all trace of the whereabouts of his captor. His hands were bound behind his back, with a separate length of rope tying his feet and yet another length securing him to the boulder. The hours passed, still Santes remained awake. He was trying to adjust his body so as to be able to reach the top of his boot.

After much struggling he attained the position he wanted, however, his shoulders were hard pressed against the boulder as a result, allowing little movement of the arms. Leaning his body over to one side he could just touch the top of his boot with his fingertips. He strained every muscle in his body to gain another inch of reach.

The tips of his outstretched fingers made contact with what they sought, the knife within the boot. Straining his body to its utmost, Santes eased the blade out but it dropped to the ground. Cursing inwardly he allowed his body to go limp again.

Re-adjusting himself to his former position after much struggling, he was at last once more sitting with his back to the boulder. On top of the knife, pressing his shoulders against the rock and arching his back to what little degree was possible, Santes threw his body away from the rock and let it drop. He shoved himself back, using his feet, dragging the knife nearer to his back and his hands. Repeating this exercise several times he was at last able to grasp hold of the blade.

Cutting his bonds was a difficult business due to the awkwardness of his hold on the knife. After many cuts from the blade he was at last able to succeed in freeing his hands.

Santes sat for a while taking in great gasps of air, getting his wind back.

Cutting the rope from his feet and releasing his anchorage from the boulder he breathed easily. Moving off into the darkness, Santes went in the direction he had seen the Marshall go.

Treading very deliberately Santes tested the ground before putting his full weight behind each step.

With the knife still in his hand, he came upon the seemingly sleeping figure of the Marshall. Moving with infinite skill and experience he crept nearer. It was very dark away from the fire.

Santes snatched up the rifle, allowing his knife to drop, as his hands clasped around the weapon, his finger curled onto the trigger when the rifle cocked there was a loud, empty sound.

Marshall Zeb Pluckard was to the left of Santes as the sound brought him out of his light sleep. Three loud clicks then filled the air as Santes tried to put as many bullets into the prostrate figure before him. Santes pulled back the blanket, at the same time kicking away the hat and cold chill overcame him as he heard the voice calling from the darkness.

"Freeze Santes, or I'll put a hole clean through your head."

Santes let the rifle drop alongside the knife, which he had let go in his haste to possess the seemingly more deadly weapon.

"You bastard, you knew I was coming. You planned this."

Zeb indicated with a wave of his gun, for Santes to move towards the dying fire. He did not further reply to Santes remarks, he was only grateful he had come awake when he did or the outcome may have been very different.

Picking up the rifle, he also lifted the knife. Putting it in his belt he followed Santes to the dying embers.

"Don't bother to sit down Mex. It's nearly daylight so we may as well set out."

"Hey Gringo bastard, what about some coffee and something to eat."

"I said mount up and you call me a bastard once more, and you may not get to Sonora."

Santes didn't delay in saddling up the horses. It was an hour before the first light of dawn crept into being, promising another scorcher. Zeb hoped his early start would enable him to reach Sonora sometime during the day. He did not relish another night on the trail with Santes.

Zeb's shoulder began to bleed, with each jar of the horse he winced, feeling the wound opening.

Santes remained quiet, he did not welcome having his bandanna shoved back into his mouth.

By noon Zeb was slumped in the saddle. Trying to sit erect and look alert whenever Santes looked around, which the Mexican did frequently.

"The next time you turn around Mex., I'm going to put a bullet in your shoulder to give you something to worry about."

Santes cursed, many times he longed to cast a glance backwards but was afraid to do so. He could feel the hatred his captor had for him and was in no doubt that a gun was always pointed at his back.

It was late evening when they rode into Sonora, by this time Zeb was doubled over in the saddle.

Heads appeared at windows and people arose from tables, coming out onto the boardwalk to see the two figures riding down main-street

Santes reached the jail-house first, the Marshall came alongside waiting at the hitching rail. A portly figure appeared from within the Sheriff's office.

A great, lumbering man with ginger hair. His face was friendly.

"What is going on here Senores. Who are you?"

Zeb revealed his U.S. Marshall's badge.

"This is Emanuel Santes, he is wanted for murder. I'm taking him in, but need somewhere to stop over until my wound heals up."

For the first time the Sheriff saw that Zeb was injured, leaning in the saddle and favouring his right side. The stains of blood were now plainly visible from under his vest.

"This gringo bastard had no right to arrest me. His authority does not mean anything in Mexico. Besides, I do not know what he is talking about. I ask you, do I look like a man who would kill anyone?"

"Pedro,"

Screamed the Sheriff at the top of his voice,

"Take this one inside and lock him up."

The crowd gathered around began to bustle with activity, everyone offering an opinion.

"I know of you Emanuel Santes," continued the Sheriff,

"And if the Marshall here cannot hold you, then I can. You are wanted for rape, rustling, abduction and murder here in Mexico. So you can forget about living to an old age."

"Bastards, there is no jail can hold Santes, I -"

His cries waned off as he was bustled inside.

"You people go about your business, there is nothing for you to see."

Zeb fell into a chair in the Sheriff's office,

"Pedro, go and fetch Mrs Brady from the Boarding House, tell her to bring bandages."

He switched his focus to the Marshall.

"This wound it is days old, you have lost a lot of blood Senores."

"Happened yesterday, about noon, been riding most ever since,"

"Was he alone, this one, Santes?"

"There was three of them, the other two are dead. They killed two people in Nacozari, one of them was a friend of mine."

Zeb gave the Sheriff Santes' knife.

"This was his, it almost made the difference."

Mrs Brady appeared on the scene. An elderly woman with grey hair, she had stayed on in Sonora after her husband was killed driving the Wells Fargo Stage. She moved efficiently, soon a fresh dressing was in place.

"Much obliged Ma-am, is there a room going at your place for a few days?"

"I'll go and get it ready."

"Can you send a telegram for me Sheriff?"

"Si Senores."

"To Tombstone. Let them know my whereabouts and how long I should be held up here."

"Si senor, and I will have it brought to your room should there be a reply."

The next day Zeb was feeling much better. A good night's rest and a lazy day sitting around town closed the wound. The bandages would be off in a day or two at most.

As he relaxed in the Cantina a young boy came running in.

"Senores, you must come quickly, there is a message coming in over the wire for you."

The boy waited expectantly. Zeb dug into his pocket, coming up with a coin he flicked it towards the lad.

"Si señor,"

"Say I will be along in a few minutes."

Whilst the boy hurried back down the street, Zeb moved across to the Sheriff's office.

"Just looking in on my prisoner, Sheriff."

"Si Senores, in the back."

Opening the door leading to the cells, Zeb merely glanced inside to reassure himself all was well. Santes spat as he left, just missing his target.

"Bastard."

The Marshall quickened his stride as he went towards the telegraph office, as he approached, he heard the key tick tacking out its message.

"The boy said you have a message for me."

"It is coming through now Marshall."

The operator glanced a quizzical look towards him, Zeb caught the glance and moved closer to read the message as it came through.

To U.S. Marshall Zeb Pluckard.

Stop.

You have no jurisdiction in Mexico.

Stop.

Should not have tracked two fugitives to Casas Grandes.

Stop.

Having done so, you should have returned immediately and not have embarked upon present undertaking.

Stop.

You have been reprimanded on previous instances for similar misconduct.

Stop.

Return to tombstone at once.

Stop.

Prisoner in Sonora must be released.

Stop.

Captain R.C. Floydd.

Stop.

Zeb stood incredulously gaping at the message for several moments. Snatching up the piece of paper, he crumpled it into a ball hurling it across the room before bursting out of the office heading directly towards the jail-house

He was seething, his face contorted with rage at the order to release Santes. The fact he may not remain a Ranger for much longer was not a total surprise. For it was not the first time he had bent the rules in his pursuit of perpetrators. Only because his services were of value to the Rangers had they tolerated his behaviour, however now the Army was so much in force, it was inevitable the role of the Rangers would be curtailed.

Zeb knew they were lenient with him in the past only because of his good record of bringing in his man. However, now he was beginning to show signs of slowing down he realised they were using this as a good reason as any to take his badge away for his own good.

Zeb had come to terms with his situation by the time he reached the jail-house, but not with the order to release Santes.

As the door flew open, the great lumbering Sheriff had no time to move before Zeb stood towering over his desk. He removed his U.S. Marshall badge.

"I'm giving you this, send it back to Tombstone for me."

"What do you mean, Senores?"

"I mean. I have just now received a telegram stating I was not authorised to arrest Santes. Resulting in my dismissal and further-more demanding I release the prisoner."

"This is bad Senores. I cannot understand the workings of your government. The man is a killer, no?"

"Nevertheless he must be released. If you will give me the keys I'll do the job."

The Sheriff rummaged around in a drawer, before Zeb disappeared into the back of the building clutching a large ring, which held an assortment of keys. In his absence the Sheriff took down Santes' gun, removing the bullets.

As the Marshall entered, Santes leapt from his bunk to the bars of the cell.

"You gringo bastard. What do you want?"

Zeb looked hard at the Mexican, hatred in his eyes. He turned the lock, opening the cell door beckoning Santes to come out.

"Where are you taking me you gringo bastard?"

"You may go Santes, just get out of here whilst you still can,"

Santes moved from the cells, into the Sheriff's office.

The Sheriff handed him his knife and gun.

"Then it is true, I am able to leave."

"That is correct Santes, you may go."

Ex U.S. Marshall Zeb Pluckard came into the office from the cells, Santes face widened in a broad grin showing his yellowing teeth.

"What did I tell you, you stupid gringo bastard. You cannot keep Emanuel Santes in your stupid little jail."

The Sheriff stayed between the two men as Santes moved towards the door. Outside, Santes turned to laugh at the Marshall once again.

He turned to face the barrel of the Sheriff's gun.

"Emanuel Santes, you are under arrest for murder and many other crimes of which I shall inform you later."

Zeb smiled wryly at the realisation of what was happening.

"Pedro,"

Yelled the Sheriff, and his deputy came running along the boardwalk.

"Take this prisoner inside and lock him up, take away his gun and knife before doing so. Do not bother to use your gun Santes, it has no bullets."

Santes snatched out his pistol, and fired. There was only a click clicking motion as the hammer fell against empty chambers.

"You bastards," cursed Santes as he was hustled inside.

"Do not lose him Pedro, he is my prisoner now,"

The Sheriff, turned to address the Marshall.

"What will you do Senores? You no longer have a job with the Rangers? To me, this Senores, seems a harsh punishment for what you have done."

"Not really Sheriff, this has been on the cards for some time. I've had a long line of run-ins with my Boss, but he wouldn't fire me, no, it's probably because I'm not getting any younger. He has only used this as an excuse to tell an old man he's past it. I was fifty on my last birthday you know."

"But you do not look old Senores, what will you do?"

"I suppose I could always go back to cleaning up Border towns, we Rangers don't save any money because none of us lives long enough to enjoy it."

"That would be very dangerous Senores, why do you not stay here in Sonora, and here. Please take back your badge. You might want it."

Zeb accepted the badge, putting it into his shirt pocket.

"I'll stop around for a while Sheriff. At least until I'm completely healed up. I could always ride back to Tombstone and hand it in officially.

========================

The wagon rumbled on, it was midnight when it rolled into Sonora.

Both Tyrane and Ojo alighted from the Stage.

"I'll drop you off here. This is as good a Boarding House as any and Mrs Brady cooks good eats If you'd just tell her the Stage is in and that the shotgun and myself will be along in an hour or so after we whet our whistles."

"Will-do driver," nodded Tyrane.

The Stagecoach churned off along the street, leaving the two men on the Board-walk Both took in the surroundings. Looking up and down the street, surveying everything, making mental notes of where specific buildings were situated before entering the hotel, each man had acted independently in his assessment of the town. Each had seen the other making the same checks as himself. Each man knew that the other was no greenhorn.

Ojo rang the bell in reception. Mrs Brady came through from the back room, for all the notice she took of Ojo, he might well not have been there. Her eyes rested on the tall figure standing before her in a piece of blanket.

"I don't usually dress like this lady."

"We'd like a couple of rooms and some hot water for a bath."

"I only have three singles, two of which I keep for the Stagehands. The other one's occupied, I can let you have a twin."

Tyrane looked towards Ojo apprehensively.

"We'll take it."

"It's a dollar a day gents. That includes two meals."

Ojo peeled some banknotes from his pocket.

"That should cover us for the week."

"Top floor, second right."

Tyrane fell in behind Ojo on the stairs.

"Much obliged, you know I don't have any money."

"Forget it, I've been in similar positions myself before now."

As he said the words, Ojo was thinking about the gold Tyrane had mentioned. There had been no mention of it during the past two days. However Ojo concluded that this stranger, far from being demoralised by his present predicament, did not have a look of desperation about him. Instead, there was a confidence radiated by the man with him on the stairs. He figured the best way to learn what Tyrane knew was to keep him close at hand and this situation suited his purpose admirably.

They turned right at the top of the landing. Someone was moving about in the room opposite.

"We have neighbours," voiced Ojo, inserting the key in the lock.

Ojo slung his gun belt over his bedstead. Tyrane allowed his exhausted body to drop and was asleep within minutes.

Next morning at breakfast Ojo had given Tyrane a shirt to wear. The garment was evidently too small, the buttons stretched to capacity across the chest. They were the last to arrive to eat. The Stage driver and shotgun Guard were already getting stuck in.

With them sat another man who greeted them both.

"Morning gents. My name's Pluckard, Zeb Pluckard."

"howdy," asserted Tyrane. Ojo gave a nod.

"Zeb here's a U.S. Marshall,"

put in the Stagecoach driver. Ojo's neck hairs crinkled, his hand edging towards his gun.

Chapter Five

Gun-Runners

Seeking rifles in return for gold, Salvador Gonsalves and his men headed for the Garrison town of Janos.

"There will be much gold for us when we return with the rifles Salgo," as Gonsalves was called by his men.

"Si Amine but first we must obtain the rifles."

"We have two boxes of gold still to collect from the Apache It would be unwise to risk such a prize by a foolish action eh Salgo."

"Fool, Salvador Gonsalves does not buy which he can steal."

Salgo and Amine were riding at the head of the band. The rest of their group was strung out in two's and three's behind. The remainder of the gold the Apache had kept until the guns were delivered into their hands.

Salgo was leading his men to Janos.

He knew the Garrison there had enough guns for his purpose. Also that the Militia were away dealing with troubles in the territories, with only the barest contingent of men remaining.

Salgo believed his men would have little trouble looting the town. No one would dare stand up to their number.

The Garrison at Janos was sighted late in the evening. Sending out scouts to assess the situation, Salvador Gonsalves directed his men to rest for the night, however to build no fires. The men protested, but were grateful for the rest alone, after the exertions of the past few days.

Salgo had driven them hard in his eagerness to reach this present position. The scouts reported back, confirming the Garrison was under- manned. Salgo grinned, he was well pleased for although he believed his men could overpower the Fort when at full strength, he did not wish to lose any of his band needlessly. Not with the impending exchange with the Apache yet to come.

That night whilst most of the men slept, Amine, under instructions from Gonsalves stole out of camp with six followers. Emphasising silence, Amine led them through town with stealthiness men of their profession possessed. Bypassing the outbuildings, keeping to the backstreet they moved through the town, which was only one long street with the Garrison at one end.

Amine led them towards the stockade. The white stone wall stood out in the moonlight. With two men stood with their hands linked together, a third ran at them. As the runners foot made contact, the two men thrust upwards. The runner was ejected skyward, his hands clasping for a hold on the wall. He scrambled his body over, flashing looks in either direction for fear of sentries.

He beckoned below for the rope to be tossed up. Each of the invaders scrambled up and over the summit of the wall, remaining motionless on the ledge, for fear of being silhouetted in the moonlight. Amine gave his orders, four men moved off in pairs. The remaining two dropped from the ledge to hit the ground within the stockade, following Amine in search of the ammunition store.

The other two pairs went about their business with ruthless exactitude. Creeping up on the few sentries on duty, one sank a blade into the victim's body whilst the other stifled his cries and lowered his body down. One by one the sentries were dealt with, the fact they stood guard singularly made the task of the assassins easier.

Amine stepped stealthily along the side of the building, his body hugging the wall. Shoving back his sombrero he poked his head around the corner to survey the front of the building. He sighted the guards, both of whom were puffing on a cigarillo. Amine saw the red end glowing as the two men took it in turn for puffs. He turned, signalling his two followers to go around the other side this took several moments, in the meantime the guards finished their smoke and were lounging against the wall.

Amine watched for the signal telling him the other two were in position. They were. He saw the blade of a knife appear protruding for an instant from the other side of the building before being pulled back from sight. He knew what he must do, however he never relished his part in the proceedings.

Stepping out from his concealed position, Amine approached the two guards.

"Un momento Amigo,."

The guards stuttered in disbelief, reaching for their rifles, in their preoccupation they did not hear the other two come up behind them. The blades sank deep into the flesh near the base of the spine, paralysing the victims for an instant before a twist brought the blade out and relief for the guards in death. A rifle clattered to the side walk

"Quiet, you fools,"

cursed Amine breathing heavier and faster after playing decoy. The guards were quickly propped up against the wall, rifle butts shoved between their legs to keep the bodies upright.

"It is locked, Amine,"

exclaimed a voice from behind.

Amines hand moved for his pistol.

"It is us, Amine"

They were joined by the other four.

"Of course it is locked, did you expect it to be otherwise."

"The guards they are all taken care of?"

"Si Amine, they are all dead,"

Amine flashed an evil smile, he was well pleased with the night's proceedings so far. The seven of them set off towards the Barracks.

Singling out the sleeping soldiers, the mouth was held whilst the throat was cut. Each pair moving methodically amongst the sleeping bodies, hands groping, in the instant between suffocating the cries as the blade sliced into victim's throat.

There were few soldiers at the Garrison, in all some dozen were accounted for plus those on sentry duty. This left only the Officers Quarters to be overpowered, then the Fort would be theirs.

This presented a problem, not because of the numbers involved, they were few, but because each family would have its own Quarters. Furniture would be scattered haphazardly about, unlike in the men's Barracks where everything had a place and a purpose. Amine decided against tackling this last obstacle until daylight, the danger of knocking something over in the dark was too great, in any event he knew the Fort to be his.

There was much grumbling as he told the men to return to the sentries and prop them up so as to outwardly appearances all was well within the Garrison, however he soon had his way.

"Remember Amigos, there will be much gold for us all when we leave this place."

This quietened the protestations, ceasing all complaint. Once their task was achieved they took up positions offering a good view of the courtyard and settled down for what was left of the night.

Salvador's body shook,

"Salgo, Salgo wake up. Amine he is gone, and others also. Gonsalves stirred from the depths of sleep to scowl at the man who awoke him. The whole camp was stirring, setting about making ready with weapons and horses. Salgo gathered his men around him.

"Amigos. Today we ride into Janos. We go to take the guns from the soldiers. We will trade them to the Apache for much gold."

There were those who believed many lives may be lost in taking the town. Salgo put their minds at ease.

"Amine, he has taken the garrison. It will be easy."

"We have only to take the town Salgo?"

"Si that is correct, mount up for we must act quickly."

The early risers in town saw them first. Some ran to awaken others, a few fled for guns, whilst more hastened towards the Garrison.

Salgo led the men in a charge. Along main-street they galloped, shooting anything and everything that moved. There was little resistance from the sleepy townsfolk. Dismounting, the bandits ran through buildings driving occupants out into the street, they killed at will.

The town was like the total confusion of a battlefield. Men still fired from horseback, peons fell from windows their bodies crashing onto rafters and boardwalks below. Some were still clad in nightshirts, others half dressed fleeing for safety.

Inside the Garrison, officers ran from their quarters to be met by a hail of bullets, those who escaped death threw up their arms in surrender.

"Move to the middle of the parade ground, tell your women to come out also," cursed Amine

Terrified townsfolk hurled themselves, pounding against the outer stockade walls.

"Let them in," signalled Amine.

With the bar removed the gates fell open and the townsfolk swarmed into the courtyard to be confronted by the Militia, their wives and their families already overpowered. Turning to flee they were herded inside by those on horseback and those firing from the stockade walls.

Gonsalves and those with him, ferreted out the last resistors. Showing no emotion, they shot to kill anyone found hiding.

The town was littered with bodies. Some draped across beds, others suspended from windows. Still more lay in the street, in water troughs, across hitching rails, tables and boardwalks.

The lock was smashed on the munition store.

"The guns, they are here, just as Salgo said they would be, look!"

screamed Gomez, a weasel-faced little man in a frenzy. He waved a rifle for Amine to see he was already inside the arsenal and awaiting further instructions.

"Amine" Barked Gonsalves upon arrival.

"Have the officers of the militia brought forward."

Amine fired into the air, the screaming and wailing ceased and silence fell over the crowd. Not one of them uttered a word as Amine spoke. The only sound was of a child crying.

"I wish for the officers to come forward."

A moment of stillness passed before two men pushed through the crowd, under protests and pleas from their wives not to do so.

"Quiet."

Under instructions from Amine, both men were dragged bodily across the parade ground. The crowd began to scream as they realised what was happening.

"Bring your rifles."

Those on horseback passed the four men weapons. Each man simultaneously checked the rifle was fully loaded.

"This is to emphasise to you that when I tell you to do something, it had better be done at once,"

A hush fell over the townspeople.

"Fire."

A volley of shots exploded, the two officers slumped to the ground, their bodies riddled as each rifle was emptied.

A woman screamed. Another fainted at the loss of her husband.

Salvador Gonsalves raised himself aloof in the saddle.

"We shall remain here for only a few hours. If you do as you are told, then you will be allowed to live. If not -"

He gestured towards the two bodies crumpled on the ground.

Fear filled the faces.

"There is much to do, all the guns must be loaded onto wagons. You will be given tasks to perform, do not delay in carrying them out."

The men set about their tasks, carrying boxes and preparing the wagons for their journey. The older women were set to work cooking, whilst the younger ones were herded towards the barracks.

Amine made trips into town to bring tools to strengthen the wagon for a long journey. He supervised as the repairs and replacement of old wheels took place.

Salgo had feared that with so many soldiers away, there may not be many horses. However, his fears were ill founded as he rounded up all he needed from around town.

Pushing the younger women into the barracks, the killers unbuckled their gun-belts

"No please, you have killed my husband, do not do this to us,"

A surly man stepped forward, striking her across the face.

"Any resistance and you will join your husband."

The women drew back, resisting the mauling advances.

"You know what is happening in the barracks Salgo?"

"Si Amine, the men they are entitled to their pleasures. They have been on the trail for a long time. It will pass, and it may take their minds off the gold, eh Amine! It is much gold to share between two, however, between thirty it is not so much."

"Si, I understand Amigo but when?"

"First we must make the trade with the Apache, then we shall make our move,"

As the morning drew on, the raiders were flopped against walls or just laying on the floor, unable to stand under the influence of much liquor consumed.

The lookouts however remained on watch, whilst even fewer still kept the prisoners up to their tasks.

The town lay devoid of life, all that remained were the buildings. A gust of wind blew down main-street causing the Cantina shutters to flap this was the only sound to be heard. Buzzards circled overhead, hesitantly awaiting to swoop amongst the carnage.

Salgo had decided he had delayed long enough. The men were aroused from their drunken stupor. Two wagons loaded high with rifles and ammunition creaked under the burden as the axles turned and each one moved into place, ready to move out. A team of six pulled each, with a spare team tied at the rear.

Salgo did a mental count of his men, three had been lost in the taking of the town, leaving some twenty eight including himself and Amine

Water was secured to each wagon. Sacks of flour, coffee, beans, sugar, salt and soda, along with salted meat and bacon were loaded onto a third wagon, which was the only one canvassed.

A thorough search was made of the garrison, any found hiding were shot. The entire surviving population of Janos was huddled into a corner of the stockade.

Salvador and Amine mounted their horses, the men stood beside theirs. Teamsters awaited the signal to crack their whips and move out. Amine raised himself in the saddle, the leather creaked as he shifted his great weight.

"Mount up, we ride."

Snapped Salvador, his voice piercing the air.

The wagons moved out of the garrison, those on lookout came down. Salvador dug spur into his animal, racing to the front of the column.

Down main-street they rode.

Janos was a dead town as it faded into the distance. Those to the rear looked back amid the rising dust to see Buzzards swooping.

Salvador kept the wagons rolling at a steady pace, covering ample ground during the remainder of the day.

The scouts reported, telling their leader of a good place to camp for the night.

Darkness was upon them when the cavalcade drew rein. Very shortly, apart from the sentries, everyone was sleeping off the day's exertions.

Salvador roused Amine, beckoning him to the covered wagon. There they removed the gold given as part payment for the guns. Discovery now would mean death at the hands of their own men.

The transfer complete. Replacing the gold with sand they moved out of camp, avoiding the sentries. A half-mile along the back trail they stopped.

"This is where we shall bury it Amine It would be very foolish to take it back to the Apache, we shall return when we have made our trade for the other two boxes of gold coin."

"Si Salgo."

"Are we not leaders. We shall drive them hard. The journey back to Sierra Madre will consume their every thought. They will have no time to think. Only if by some accident, someone should discover the gold is missing, will I tell them it is buried for safe keeping and will be awaiting us on our return."

The hole was dug, and the gold safely interred, the place would be easily remembered without a marker. Quickly the two men made their way back to camp unnoticed.

Amine dreamt of how he would spend his share of the gold.

Salvador spent the remainder of the night thinking of how he could seize all the gold, for he had no intention of sharing with anyone, let alone a stupid fool such as Amine

The stars twinkled overhead, far off a coyote gave a lonely howl. Slowly the night passed, still Salvador lay awake, thinking.

At first light the men set about making ready to move. Neither Salvador nor Amine gave any respite in their relentless driving. Passing the outermost tips of the Guadalupe Mountains, before turning south into Sierra Madre.

Chapter Six

Unholy Alliance

Tyrane sidled alongside, snatching Ojo's gun from its holster.

"Nice weapon."

"Looks like it's seen some use."

Ojo was indignant at being disarmed. Before he could unleash a flurry of insults at Tyrane, the Teamsters arose.

"Well folks, reckon we'd best be moving. Still have a schedule to keep you know. Good luck stranger, hope things work out all right."

Tyrane nodded and the men departed. Old sourpuss did not utter a word as he closed the door behind him.

"Sociable cuss ain't he," inferred the Marshall.

"Uh, uh,"

Agreed Tyrane, re-holstering Ojo's gun. As he tucked into breakfast, Tyrane eyed the Law-man He was not sure whether the Marshall had seen Ojo's hand moving towards the weapon, but he pegged him as no fool and assumed he had. Introducing himself, Tyrane waited for his room-mate to do likewise.

Ojo's mind raced, 'what was this Marshall doing here,' he wondered.

"Cameron's my name," voiced Ojo, as he recalled the name in the wallet he had picked up on the stagecoach.

"So you've been in Sonora for a week eh, Marshall?" asked Tyrane.

"That's right, ever since I brought in the prisoner."

Ojo relaxed his vigilance. For if the Marshall had been in Mexico as long as he said then he would know nothing about the fracas in Lordsburg.

"I've heard of you Tyrane. Heard you got a raw deal in Texas. Some young punk gave you a hard time didn't he?"

Tyrane's curiosity was now aroused. Here he was confronted by a U.S. Marshall about a killing, yet the law-man showed no animosity towards him. Nor any inclination the tin star was going to be flashed.

"When do you reckon on leaving Marshall?"

"Not for a week yet, I want to see Santes safely on board the jail wagon before I leave. He's the feller inside awaiting a noose, but first he must be taken to trial."

Zeb rose to leave, to make his daily check at the jail-house

"See you around Marshall."

"Oh, I'm not a Marshall any more. I lost my badge over this Santes affair."

Tyrane seen off another plate of beans in the Marshall's absence.

"What do you make of him Tyrane, strong looking cuss ain't he?"

"He doesn't interest me, I've problems of my own. If you don't mind my asking, what are you doing down this way. It ain't exactly the most popular part of the country?"

It was a prying question, not the sort Tyrane usually asked. Yet he could think of no good reason why anyone would come to this place.

"Health reasons."

"Thought as much."

"No matter to me, in any event the Marshall says he's handed in his badge. So you wasted effort giving a name."

"Yea I know that now, so what's the difference.

Ojo was becoming annoyed, here he was trying to learn more about Tyrane and instead was feeding the stranger information about himself.

"What do you plan on doing?"

"Seeing as how you have already paid for my room, I may as well rest up then I can see about getting me a stake together."

"This should last you a whiles."

Ojo placed two five-dollar bills on the table.

"Why are you helping me mister, you don't know me?"

"Told you before, I've been in similar spots myself, I know the score."

Tyrane did not believe a word of it. He had not known this man for long, however, during their short association he concluded he was not the sort to do anyone any favours.

"You appear well heeled mister, that something to do with your being down here for health reasons?"

Ojo became more perplexed, however managed to contain his annoyance, explaining he had left Lordsburg in a hurry, but had not brought as much money with him as he intended.

"I lost some on the way. What about yourself. You say you were captured outsides of Tubac. What were you doing there?"

"I was chasing a reward poster."

"You intend on going after your prey?"

It was an ironical question. For Tyrane knew he did intend to track down Salvador Gonsalves, though not for the reward money but for the gold he may have received from the Apache.

Tyrane realised he must get a bundle together fast if he was going to beat the Mexican to the gold. The ten dollars would go mainly towards a good piece and some cartridges. He got up to leave Ojo alone at the table.

"If your still around and available, I may have a proposition to put to you in a few days. I'll let you know more then."

The Marshall strode into the jail-house, it was his second home during the last few days. He and the Sheriff got along fine and with nothing better to do he called in regularly to pass the time of day.

Zeb was always sure to take a look out back to ensure Santes was still under lock. It had become a ritual with him, he would enter the cell-block and Santes would rise from his bunk to hurl abuse.

"You gringo bastard. I will kill you when I am free of this place."

Zeb left Santes with his face pressed against the bars, still casting insults at him after he returned to the front office.

"That one, he does not like you very much Amigo, however he should bother us for only a short while longer."

The Marshall stuck his head around the door leading to the cell-block

"You hear that Santes, soon you're going to be no trouble to anyone with your feet swinging in the wind."

Santes clutched the bars of his cell, shaking them with all his might in his rage to get at the Marshall.

The following days passed without incident. Tyrane practised his draw with his new weapon whilst still in his room, then made sure of his accuracy by using up a couple of boxes of shells in practice.

Ojo spent the time in the Cantina, waiting for Tyrane to make the next move in providing him with more information about the gold he had mentioned on the stagecoach.

Five days went by, Tyrane felt fully recovered, or at least he told himself he was in his eagerness to be on the move.

He was fluent with the new side-arm, though he realised it pulled slightly to the right. In not shaving since his arrival in Sonora, Tyrane's growth resembled a beard. He took advantage of Ojo's curiosity to obtain more money with which to pass the time of day and purchase some clothes. However being where he was, all the garments had a touch of the Mexicans about them. Still, he managed to buy some jeans, a frilled red shirt, and a topcoat. The coat was the least liked of the garments in that it was made of cowhide, although a thick lining was the deciding factor in its favour. However Tyrane was not happy with the embroidery someone had so painstakingly taken the trouble to sew into the hide, nor the red blotches on the leather.

That night he borrowed Ojo's razor and was in the process of shaving when his room-mate entered. Ojo was vexed at the way he was being played for a sucker, forever giving yet never receiving anything in return.

"Just help yourself to my things when it pleases you," he said.

Tyrane continued to shave.

"You said something about a proposition when we arrived, you haven't let out much about it since. Sure, you've dropped a hint here and there but I don't know what's all about. So what's the full story, I'd like to know what kind of money we're talking about?"

Tyrane continued to shave, relating between strokes the tale of the gold boxes.

"Those Apache who captured me had a lot of gold, I intend to get some of it."

"Against the Apache, you must be crazy."

Ojo didn't like the sound of this.

"Maybe, but I'm talking about $50,000 to $100,000 and for that kind of money I could go a little crazy."

Ojo's point of view changed immediately on hearing the sum in question. For that kind of money he would go up against the entire Apache nation, or at least that's what he told himself as Tyrane continued to give out snippets of information.

Ojo had found himself in similar situations to the one he found himself in now, where the chance of big money was equalled by the chances of being killed. He had always decided in favour of living.

Tyrane explained about the gold, though he stopped short of its whereabouts.

"The two of us won't be able to do it alone."

"Now you wait here," protested Ojo.

"I don't intend to share that gold with anyone."

"Don't be greedy. There's enough for four of us to have at least $20,000 plus apiece. Furthermore I reckon I know where we can get the other two members of the team."

Tyrane went on to explain how the Marshall was indisposed at the moment.

"So he might be interested."

"And the other one?" inquired Ojo.

"The man in jail, he has nothing to lose, he's only going to keep an appointment with a rope."

"Your insane, the Marshall would never stand for it."

"The Marshall won't know until it's too late, that's always assuming he's interested in the first place."

"Oh, he'll be interested all right, but to release Santes. I don't know about that."

Tyrane wanted no arguments.

"The Mex. is a killer and it's the Apache we're going up against so he's in. If you don't like it you don't have to come."

Ojo gave Tyrane a black look. There was no way he was going to be left out of things.

"All right I agree, but I'll be keeping this Santes feller ahead of me. I like to know from which way the bullets are coming."

Tyrane saw why Ojo had little choice but to accept the situation, as he knew he would.

"Anyone would think you were a preacher, we're all tarred with the same brush us four. We all kill for one reason or another, the only difference is why? I kill out of necessity for the bounty, Santes kills because he like to, the Marshall kills out of a sense of duty. I don't know about you Ojo, why would you kill, for a share of $100,000 maybe?"

Tyrane knew he had exaggerated the value of the gold, but it fixed Ojo's mind. Tyrane laid it all out, first they must get the Marshall with them. Then keep him preoccupied while Santes was broken out of jail.

"What about supplies and horses?"

"You're the one who keeps coming up with the money. So just come up with some more and remember, after this you won't have to worry about money again. Either that or you won't have any need of it."

The significance of the last remark sank home.

"Have you enough left for our needs?"

"I expect so."

After eats the following morning, Tyrane knocked on the Marshall's door.

"I have some work you may be interested in. Ojo's at the Livery. We can discuss it there together."

"You go on ahead, I'll join you shortly,"

The Marshall continued administering the slightest touch of oil to his pistol before reassembling the parts.

Tyrane picked up his coat on the way out as he heard the wind beating the shutters against the wall.

Tyrane strode into the wind, towards the stables. As he drew level with the swinging doors of the saloon he froze, on hearing his name being called by an unfamiliar, arrogant voice.

"Your name Tyrane, Barrington Tyrane?"

Turning to face his inquisitor Tyrane at a glance took in the ever so casual, yet prepared stance of a gunfighter. He was a young man of barely twenty years, with a mop of red hair sticking out from under his cocked hat. His gun hand hung close to the ornate holster he wore.

"Yea my name's Tyrane, what's it to you?"

"Mine is Thorburn. Folks call my Kid Thorburn."

Tyrane felt a tingling sensation creeping up from the base of his spine. Such loudmouths as this kid he had met before, but his mind was preoccupied with another matter as his memory flashed back to Tubac. 'He'd two brothers who would dry-gulch you as soon as look at you' had been the warning. "Or dry-gulch me whilst his brother looks at me," mumbled Tyrane.

His eyes swept the rooftops before him. However he was unable to scan the opposite side of the street for fear of the kid making his own play.

The arrogant stance of the kid became more erect. Tyrane felt eyes boring little holes into his back, the kid flexed his fingers.

Whether it was a signal for his brother Duke to make his move, or merely a distracting ploy, Tyrane did not know. His gun flashed out of its holster into his hand, as it drew level it spent a shell from the chamber. The gun pulled to the right, as during practice. The bullet tore into the flesh of the kid's upper arm, crashing his body backwards through the swinging doors.

Almost in unison another weapon barked from along the boardwalk. On letting off the first shot Tyrane half turned half fell in an attempt to do a quick reconnaissance on the opposite buildings. As he turned he saw the Marshall's gun leap in his hand. The figure of Duke Thorburn staggered forward to the parapet, capitulating to snap on impact on hitting the ground.

Tyrane immediately swung his pistol to cover the flapping doors, heads began to appear from the windows of the Cantina. From somewhere behind the saloon Tyrane heard a horse whinny before breaking into a gallop during the short silence after the shooting.

"Then there was one."

Mused Tyrane remembering the warning he received in Tubac.

The bemused Sheriff acknowledged Zeb's greeting with a wave as emerging from the office he was in time to see the Marshall cross the street with Tyrane.

"What was all the shooting about?" asked Ojo on their arrival at the corral.

"What's this all about Tyrane? Voiced Zeb ignoring the. question.

"I'll fill you both in."

The livestock mulled around in the corral. Ojo had already selected his own mount. A bay gelding, not for its speed but for its endurance qualities. The three leaned against the corral watching the animals go around.

Tyrane narrated his tale, giving only the sparsest details of his capture and escape. He did not mention Clementine Hollinger, preferring to put the matter aside for the moment, for the Marshall he believed, would almost certainly want to help the girl, whereas Ojo would not. If and when the opportunity arose, he would put the matter right himself.

Tyrane reckoned that of his three would be travelling companions the Marshall was the one in which he could put the most trust.

"The boxes were bursting with gold coins, the one chance we have is that we can attack at night, take them by surprise and put as much distance between them and us as is possible before daylight."

"What were the Apache doing with the gold in the first place?" asked the Marshall.

Tyrane gave no reply. The fact that the gold was there was sufficient enough knowledge he reckoned and they would have to make do with that.

"Will there be only the three of us?"

"No Marshall, there's another man coming. Incidentally, just how much have you severed yourself from the law? This fourth man isn't exactly one of the good guys and this gold once belonged to the U.S. Army.

"I'm with you and you can forget about my past. At least as much as I can forget about yours. That includes you mister. I dug out a wanted poster, it doesn't bear your name but the description fits you for a murder in Deming. The name on the poster was Caliente, or something like that."

Ojo was perturbed that a wanted poster could give such a good description as for the Marshall to link it with him.

"One thing Tyrane," added the Marshall.

"Who's calling the shots around here?"

Ojo looked towards Tyrane expectantly, hoping for a share in the say for the money he was putting in.

"I am," stated Tyrane,

which left no doubt in the minds of either of his associates.

The three of them prepared for a long journey. There were supplies to be bought, food, ammunition, rifles, and water bottles. Tyrane purchased twelve sticks of dynamite without the knowledge of the others. He could not foresee a use for it as of yet, but intended to have it along. In all, they bought five horses, three saddles and two pack animals. The Marshall had his own horse, the piebald. All was in readiness.

It was a full week since the stage had pulled into Sonora. Zeb said his goodbyes to the Sheriff, lingering at Mrs Brandy's to thank her for nursing him. The horses were saddled and the loads secured when he arrived at the stables.

"Where's the fourth man."

"We meet him out on the trail," replied Tyrane.

"In case you're wondering Marshall, we're leaving at night so as no one sees which direction we take. We'll ride out, then circle round."

"Into the Sierra Madre?"

"That's right."

The horses were led out under the stars. The moon shone down as the six animals moved along main-street.

"This friend of yours, he sure is a cautious feller. Wanted in Mexico huh?"

The Marshall's remarks were lost in the wind whilst they swung to the south. They were a mile out of town when Tyrane turned to the Marshall.

"We part company here for a while Zeb. You take the pack animals on ahead, wait for us near the fork in the road. Ojo and I will meet you there with the fourth member of our team."

"He must have come a long way to need a fresh horse,"

"Not such a long ways Marshall."

Tyrane scowled at Ojo for his trite remark.

"See you at the fork where the road turns east,"

Zeb, edged his mount forward, taking up the slack on the rope leading the two pack animals.

"That was a stupid thing to say. He would never agree to breaking Santes out of jail, but once he is out there's not much he can do about it."

They rode along the back-trail, approaching the town tentatively keeping to the rear buildings back of main-street. There was little activity this night, what there was came from the saloon. Hitching the three horses they continued on foot to the jail-house

The Sheriff was half-asleep at his desk when Tyrane strode into the office. He had not expected this, he believed a deputy would be on guard at this hour.

"I thought you both left with the Marshall, did you forget something?"

"You could say that,"

Tyrane produced his gun from its holster so fast it was like one motion before its barrel was pressed under the Sheriff's nose. The fast draw did not go unnoticed by Ojo.

"The keys to the cell, where are they?"

Lines appeared on the worried law-man's brow, he began to look older than he was.

Tyrane snatched the keys and disappeared into the rear of the building. In Tyrane's absence Ojo began to tie the Sheriff to his chair. He stuffed a gag into his mouth, securing it there.

The Sheriff looked around the room. His eyes coming to rest on his gun-belt hanging on the far wall, of no use to him there.

Santes was on his feet by the time Tyrane reached the cell.

"Who are you, Why are you here?"

The key clunked in the lock and the door fell open. With his questions unanswered Santes donned his hat following his liberator into the front office.

Ojo was securing the Sheriff's bonds, Tyrane quickly assured Santes of his intentions.

"$20,000 in gold coin Santes, that would make you a big man here in Mexico."

"I will come Senores. For this much gold I would risk my life."

"You might do just that," replied Ojo.

Santes found his gun-belt and pistol in a wall cupboard. His hand clasped around his knife, before deciding to leave it behind. The three men moved casually out of the building so as to attract no attention from the drunks tottering their way out of the saloon. The Sheriff gaped after them, struggling with his bonds. They reached the horses before Santes stopped suddenly.

"I must go back for my knife."

"Damn your knife, you can get another one," cursed Ojo.

"Oh sure, I can just ask someone if I may borrow their knife so I can cut their throat with it."

Santes turned, hurrying back towards the jail-house

"You two wait here, I will not be long."

The Sheriff's bulbous eyes widened in their sockets when Santes entered the office. The Mexican crossed the floor, picked up his knife and moved behind the law-man's chair. The tied man attempted to keep his eyes on Santes, however was unable to do so due to his enforced position.

Santes waved the blade before the Sheriff's eyes, moving it slowly backwards over his head. The law-man arched his back, trying to keep sight of the blade. Flicking the knife to his other hand, Santes thrust the blade between the rungs of the chair. The great bloated body shot forward, groaned, then slumped, his eyes rolling, fixing on his gun-belt still hanging on the opposite wall. Withdrawing the knife, Santes wiped the blade on his chaps before placing it in his boot. Running out of the office he rejoined the others.

They dug spur into their mounts and galloped.

"Did you find the knife Santes?"

"Si Senores I have it. Amigo, where is this gold you speak of?"

"There are four of us altogether, the other one's up ahead, waiting with the supplies and ammunition. We ride for the Sierra Madre."

"Against the Apache?"

It did not take long to reach the fork in the road.

"howdy," called Zeb from his vantage point.

Santes turned in the saddle, instantly recognising the voice of his captor even though it was too dark to see him.

'Click'

Santes felt the muzzle of Tyrane's gun in his ribcage.

"Easy now, don't get excited," he whispered.

"And no moves."

The Marshall led out the supply animals, he saw the sombrero, cast in the moonlight.

"Keep your hands away from your gun Marshall."

"What the hell's going on, I'm with you remember."

Tyrane spoke in a cool commanding voice.

"Move in closer Marshall. I want you to get a good look see at the fourth member of our team."

Zeb's eyes went wild at the realisation of who was under the sombrero.

"Santes." He spat the name.

"Are you mad Tyrane. What's he doing here and how did he get out of jail?"

Ojo forced the issue. Giving the Marshall every opportunity to drop out of the venture.

"We broke him out Marshall. He's got a gun, and he knows how to use it. Furthermore he will use it, which is more than we know about you."

Ojo's animosity towards the law-man came to the fore.

"You're supposed to have disregarded your badge, so why not throw it away."

"Cut it out," broke in Tyrane.

"Now get this and get it good. There are only four of us, against God knows how many Apache. So if and when we get out of this, you two can settle your differences."

The logic of Tyrane's remark was not lost on Santes. He relaxed in the saddle and felt Tyrane's gun being moved from his ribcage.

"Well Marshall, it looks like its up to you."

"Are you with us or against us?"

"I'm with you. At least until this is over."

"It is I who shall be dealing with you, you gringo bastard. Your days of living are numbered."

"The sooner we're on our way, the better I'll like it," said Tyrane.

The four riders set off into the darkness, leaving Sonora behind, to its problems.

Tyrane thought of the troubles ahead, for he had collected unenviable types around him.

Ojo was a Bank robber. Perhaps even a murderer if what the Marshall said was true. Of Santes he had no doubts, the Mexican was a homicidal killer. The Marshall he found it difficult to weigh up, however his vendetta against Santes made him a dangerous member of the party. At the same time, Tyrane knew Zeb was the only one he could safely turn his back on once the whereabouts of the gold was known. His own limitations he knew, he had been bringing in bounties these past years and had done his share of killing.

There he had it. Four men, riding into the Sierra Madre against who knew what odds. One Bank robber, one murderer, one ex U.S. Marshall, and one bounty hunter.

Suddenly for no apparent reason, Tyrane remembered Clementine. The fair-haired girl who had given him his new lease on life.

The four silent figures jogged along in the dark. Each with his own thoughts, yet each with one all consuming thought. The gold, and how they would spend it.

The following days were full of tension, Tyrane trying as best he could to keep Santes and the Marshall apart. The hatred the two men felt for one another was evident for no words to be necessary.

The deeper they rode into Sierra Madre the more intense became the humidity.

The crossing of the Yaqoi River was the first real landmark Tyrane recalled. The vegetation was not so sparse here and each tended his horse, seeing that each animal had plenty to drink. The water bottles were replenished and the journey continued.

It was the fourth day out of Sonora, camp was made. At dawn the first awake kindled the fire. It was Zeb this morning and he went about his chore.

Ojo tended to the horses needs.

Tyrane relieved Santes on watch, each man took a two hour watch each night. This meant Santes took the last watch, for no one wanted the Mexican to have to waken him in the dead of night. This rota worked, however it was difficult to change it in any way for to put Santes and the Marshall on consecutive watches would be inviting trouble.

The foursome set out, Tyrane's horse leading the way.

"How much gold did you say we would get Amigo?"

Tyrane was growing tired of the same questions being asked day after day from the Mexican, however he said nothing. Ojo was not so tactful.

"I'm growing weary of listening to your mouth, Mex."

Tyrane dug spur into his mount, drawing clear of the others. The sudden quickening of pace brought an end to all grievances as each man craned his neck to see where Tyrane was riding for. The sight before him confirmed he was on a true course.

"What is it Amigo?"

"My horse, I had two, one I rode to here where he buckled under me. The other took me to within reach of the stage route where you picked me up. I missed finding the other animal, but when we crossed the Rio Yaqui I knew we were on the right trail. This confirms it. We should reach the Apache village by tomorrow night."

The informative reply sank into the minds of the threesome as they gazed down at the bleached white bones of the dismembered framework.

"We'll make camp here. We can ride for the remainder of the day afterwards."

Ojo scanned the surrounding terrain for some indication of their route.

"Do you see something you recognise, Tyrane?"

"So, it appears I am not the only one with an anxious mind amigo, and a greedy one perhaps."

Ignoring Santes, Ojo continued his surveillance. Focusing his gaze across the sun-baked sands. Zeb had a fire going, it was kept low. This was the first time Tyrane had shown caution against smoke.

"What shall you do with your share of the gold Amigo, buy yourself a Ranchero perhaps?"

"It's possible," replied Tyrane. Realising he had given little thought to what he should do should he survive this undertaking.

"For me it will be easy Senores, I shall have much respect."

Continued Santes,

"With my gold I shall be the most famous bandit in Mexico. Everyone will wish to join the band of Emanuel Santes."

"Santes and his gang of murderers, that's what will be said about you,"

"Who ask you, you stupid gringo bastard. Shut your mouth or I will kill you as easily as I killed the other bastard in Sonora. -"

Santes realised his error as the words left his lips. The full impact of the remark penetrated the already hostile minds of his companions.

"What the hell does he mean? What happened back there in Sonora when you two broke him out of jail?"

Tyrane's patience with the Mexican snapped.

"Not what you think Marshall," added Tyrane, turning his attention to Santes.

"What did you do when you went back for your knife Santes?"

"You mean to say you let this maniac out of your sight back there."

"Sure – I killed the Sheriff bastard."

Santes told the tale as much with his arms as with his mouth.

"When I returned for my knife, his eyes they followed me round the room. For he knew I was going to kill him as I will kill you for putting me in jail you gringo bastard."

Zeb watched as Santes remonstrated how he committed the murder, then wiped the blood stained knife on his chaps. For the first time, Zeb saw the dried bloodstains.

Zeb exploded in anger. He leapt towards Santes crashing him down, landing blows to his head. Over they rolled, the coffee-pot was knocked from the fire, it sizzled as a cloud of vapour arose on contact with the heat.

Santes was no novice to fighting. As the Marshall rose, he brought up his knee to smash into the law-man's groin. Zeb fell backwards, Santes got to his feet. Racing forward he swung his foot, catching Zeb on the side of the head, then dived on top of him. Over they both rolled, pounding punches into one another's bodies and faces. The horses shied away as they rolled amongst them.

Zeb's lip was split open, Santes ear began to bleed. The two men struggled to their feet, circling one another. Crashing blows to one another's body. Zeb was much taller than Santes, yet the Mexicans amazing physique enabled him to overcome any disadvantage in height.

"Hadn't we better stop them, they'll be no good to anyone if they kill each other," said Ojo.

Santes arm arched through the air, to come crashing down into the Marshall's face. Heaving with all his might, Zeb threw the Mexican from him and scrambled to his feet. Santes charged again, connecting with a blow to the ribs, which knocked the wind from his opponent. Somehow Zeb withstood the force of the blow, turning Santes from him. The Mexican staggered forward and fell, Zeb leapt upon him, bringing his knee down on Santes ribcage. Pounding blow after blow into the Mexicans body whilst he had him pinned down. Zeb did not see Santes hand fumbling with the boot. Santes allowed his hand to grasp around the handle of his knife, the blade flashed through the air as it arced its way towards Zeb's body, piercing the flesh - .

Chapter Seven

U.S. Cavalry

At the same time as Barrington Tyrane and Ojo Caliente arrived in Sonora by Stagecoach, Major Beresford the Commanding Officer at Fort Thomas paced the floor of his office.

The Major grew more concerned with each passing day as still no word was heard of the gold shipment.

The delivery was not scheduled to take place at any specified time, however even allowing for the most wild of delays it was long overdue.

The Major sat behind his desk scrutinising a map. As rough as it was and lacking in so much detail, he was still able to determine the route the gold shipment should be travelling.

"Corporal Conrad,"

He barked at the young man standing outside his office. Conrad shuddered, came to attention, then marched briskly into the office.

Stopping before the Major's desk he stood rigidly to attention.

"Yes-sir, Corporal Conrad reporting Sir." His heels clicked and his arm brought his hand up level with his forehead. Beresford acknowledged the salute by a nod of his head.

"Go and find Captain Houston and Sergeant O'Mallahan. Tell them to report here, on the double. That's all Corporal."

Conrad stiffened, clicking his heels, bringing his arm up to salute. At a nod from the Major he marched out.

Conrad was new to Fort Thomas. A young man, twenty five years of age, with cropped blonde hair. He had arrived at Fort Thomas under the command of the Captain some three months previously and had done little but click his heels ever since.

Supposing the sergeant would be the easiest to find, he went after him first. In the back room of the supplies store the sergeant was playing poker. He was a grey seasoned, battered old campaigner.

Conrad approached the seated men quite formerly before speaking.

His heels clicked.

That was the first time he had been noticed by any of the players.

"I wonder who that can be?"

Drawled O'Mallahan from behind his cards.

"If you please sergeant, Major Beresford would like you to report to his office."

O'Mallahan helped himself to two cards.

"Well now, if it isn't the little tin soldier."

"The Major said to come at once sergeant."

"Well I'd better make this the last hand boys. You tell the Major I'm on my way corporal."

Conrad left the supplies store amid stifled laughter, going in search of the Captain. After several fruitless inquiries he found him.

Captain Houston was a full six feet six in height with a bronze chiselled face. Now in his late Twenties this was his first posting since passing out of the Military Academy.

He was a world apart from the other officers at the Fort, thought Conrad. His uniform was always pressed, his buttons polished and the bars on his shoulders always clean, not the stained colour worn by other officers. Having always trained under the likes of Captain Houston, Conrad could not comprehend apparent lack of formality within the Fort. Things would go on from day to day, yet certain disciplinary matters to which he was accustomed were not always observed, although no one ever failed to salute the Captain, or return his greeting.

"Captain Houston, Sir."

Houston turned as Conrad's heels clicked together. He returned the salute.

"Yes Corporal what is it?"

The Major would like to see you in his office Sir."

"Very good Corporal, inform him I shall be there directly."

As Conrad reported back to the Major, there was a rap on the door, Houston walked in.

"You wanted to see me Sir?"

"Yes I do, that will be all Corporal."

"Sir!"

Conrad was brushed aside as O'Mallahan arrived.

"Sir, Captain."

His salute served them both.

"What took you so long Sergeant, playing cards again if past experience is anything to go by. A good hand was it?"

Houston eyed both men critically. He could not understand the Major's condonation of card playing. Nor his apparent genial, almost friendly attitude towards the non-commissioned rank. What Houston did not know was that both Beresford and O'Mallahan had a great respect for one another, having fought many campaigns together through more years than either would care to recall. Each having saved the others life on more than one occasion.

"Sit down please gentlemen."

Beresford related to them, all he knew about the gold shipment.

"This gold is imperative. I've noticed there's been a restlessness amongst the enlisted men lately. They've had nothing to do, and even less to spend whilst sitting about waiting for action."

He ran his finger along the map, tracing the supposed route the shipment should be taking.

"This shipment is larger than most. Mainly because the men are due back pay, however it's also needed to purchase horses both for this Fort and others besides. I'm speaking gentlemen about gold coin, so you will appreciate my anxiety."

O'Mallahan was flabbergasted by the sum given. Houston played around with it in his mind, deciding it was too much for the reasons given by the Major. However, he kept his opinions to himself and bade the Major to continue.

"I want you to take a platoon of men Captain and investigate the reason for the delay of the delivery."

He added,

"I'm sure I don't have to stress to you the importance of this mission."

"No Sir, if the shipment is late then I shall find out why."

"It is already delayed Captain."

"Then I shall pursue the reason for the delay Sir."

"Yes I am sure you will Captain. You had better go and organise your departure."

Houston briskly marched out of the office. Beresford turned to O'Mallahan.

"As you know sergeant this will be Captain Houston's first assignment. Possibly even his first time in action, he will be green, so help him all you can. He has the making of a good officer under all that starch. I appreciate he will be in command, however try to guide him as best you can. He's no fool, he knows your experience and will turn to you for advice."

"Yes Major, I'll do my best sir."

"I'm sure you will sergeant."

"Do you think it's the Apache sir?"

"The Red man has no need of gold."

"No, but they like to take uniforms sir, especially from dead bodies. It could be Magnus, or even Victorio."

"I doubt it sergeant, Magnus was last heard of in Chihuahua deep in Mexico, more than likely it's Renegades. Though I hope to God it's not."

"If you will excuse then sir."

"Certainly, and don't forget to come back O'Mallahan."

"As if I would sir."

Supplies and ammunition required for the forthcoming campaign were readied. By midday the platoon was ready to pull out.

Major Beresford emerged from his office with Captain Houston, last minute instructions were given.

"Prepare to mount, mount. Foorrrwwaard Ho,"

yelled O'Mallahan, echoing the captain's command throughout the platoon of fresh faced eager recruits, none more so than the corporal riding at his side.

Visible contact between the outgoing platoon and the Fort was soon left behind, Houston rode to the fore. Preceded only by the two scouts. Sergeant O'Mallahan and Corporal Conrad rode directly behind with the men in uniform two's, the pack animals bringing up the rear.

Houston signalled, and O'Mallahan moved forward to join him, leaving Conrad gaping from side to side wide-eyed with anticipation at the thrill of the forthcoming adventure.

"I expect the major asked you to keep me under your wing sergeant, is that correct?"

"Well, not exactly sir though he did mention this was your first time in action, so to speak."

"That is correct sergeant,"

said Houston.

"Though I shall not tolerate any interference from you on how I conduct this mission, is that understood sergeant?"

"Yes-sir, all too clear sir."

Said O'Mallahan, easing his mount back to rejoin Conrad. He could not help but notice the ever so slight smirk on the corporal's face.

'Could he have overheard,' he wondered. He reckoned not, although if only the odd word had reached his ears, the rest would not be hard to piece together.

The day passed and camp was made for the night. At first light the platoon was on the move.

Skirting around the outermost of the Dragoon Mountains they linked up with the San Pedro River. Continuing south-west they followed the river for three days. Vegetation was plentiful, thickets of Aspen and Junipers dotted the embankments.

Crossing the San Pedro River, two more days passed.

The scouts came riding hell for leather towards the column. Between gasps for air they related to Houston the exact whereabouts of their find.

It was the first all important news of the gold shipment. Houston listened carefully, impatient for details as he was told of the remains of a burnt out wagon being found.

"They've been dead for a while captain. The bones was picked clean, though that could happen in a few hours. It's the state of the remains which gives us the time factor."

"I see," contemplated Houston.

"We shall investigate. In the meantime you two men look for signs, anything which may give us a clue as to whom is responsible."

"Oh I can tell you that now sir, it was Apaches."

"Apache,"

breathed Houston deeply. He had never met an Apache, the prospect of encountering them on his first campaign did not appeal, as he tried to recall the tales told around the Fort.

Only wagon prongs and wheel rims stood out amongst the debris. The sands had shifted slowly, half-burying bodies though here and there a bluish uniform was visible.

Human skeletons were not intact where carrion had dragged off a limb to devour elsewhere.

"It wasn't only animals that mutilated these bodies,"

said O'Mallahan, disturbing the silence.

"What do you mean sergeant, are you saying human beings could have done this sort of thing?"

"I said it wasn't animals, but I wouldn't call Apaches human beings either."

"That's enough sergeant, things are bad enough without you elaborating on the details."

Houston felt a sinking empty feeling in his gut as he considered the vulnerability of their position. There had been ten men riding with the gold shipment, now here he was in the same location where the massacre had taken place and with only a few more in number, at his command.

"Have the men make camp sergeant. We shall bury the dead before continuing."

The captain was hesitant in his voice, a fact which did not escape the wily sergeant. He considered opposing the burial, yet thought better of it, now was not the time to contradict the captain's orders. A mass grave was started upon.

The strong aroma of coffee soon warmed hearts. O'Mallahan could not see the captain's face, however if it was as frightened as that of the young corporal by his side, then the captain was a mighty worried man.

Those detailed to search for signs, returned with little news. The scouts found the barest trace as to the direction taken by the perpetrators. How old the tracks were, it was hard to assess, though O'Mallahan reckoned about a week before they themselves left Fort Thomas.

Houston knew it was not logical to bury the dead, for it could possibly alert any hostile in the vicinity of their presence. However he needed time to think, to collect his thoughts, and in any event he believed it his duty to perform a last act of humanity for those whom had been slain.

The interment complete, Houston spoke a few words over the unmarked spot. Each man stood alongside his horse in silence.

"Have the men mount up sergeant."

With assistance of the scouts, Houston put his party as being a days ride east of Tubac and two days south west of Fort Huachuca.

It took only a half day's hard riding to find the first campsite of the Apache, how old it was, was as hard to gauge as before

"We shouldn't go no farther cap'n."

Houston ignored O'Mallahan's protestations, focusing his attention more on the scouts who rode far to the fore in search of signs. They rode back and forth, losing the trail on many occasions due to the passing of time and the velocity of wind, before picking it up again.

The party they trailed was a large one not concerned with covering its back-trail This factor, plus the assumption by the scouts that the route led into Sierra Madre enabled them to keep a true course.

Little over a week had passed since the outset from Fort Thomas, Houston realised now the enormity of his task. This country was much bigger than he ever realised and more desolate than he could have imagined. The instructions given in the Major's office seemed far removed from the reality of the situation. The thoughts of what he should do next lay heavily on his mind.

It had seemed so simple at the outset, merely meet up with the shipment and escort it to safety. Even the possibility of having to apprehend attackers appeared quite simple. What he had not considered was that first he would nave to find the looters. That, plus the fact that they were following the Apache back to his home ground, preyed on his brain.

The heat was intense as the sun rose to its summit. The fresh-faced youngsters who sat astride their animals so proudly at the outset, now slumped in the saddle, riding out of formation, and bickering amongst themselves as to the credibility of their task.

O'Mallahan again approached the captain on the subject of returning to the Fort.

"You've done what you set out to do cap'n, track down the gold shipment and pursue any attackers, those were the major's orders.

"Come with me sergeant,"

O'Mallahan soon joined the captain some-way ahead of the main body of men.

"What you do not know sergeant, is that my orders were to return with the gold."

Houston waited several moments for the full implication of his remark to be realised.

"Taking all steps necessary to achieve that objective, this gold is vital, do you understand that sergeant. Without it there could be rebellion amongst the men at our own and at other

Forts. They haven't been paid for months, some of them will start to desert, before we know where we are the Forts will be undermanned. They are the only strongholds for hundreds of miles, without them law and order would be obsolete. The Apache and outlaws would turn Arizona into another badlands. Is that understood sergeant. I am in command of this platoon, you will do just as I say."

"Yes-sir"

The outburst of the Captain took O'Mallahan aback. Houston had been letting his command of the men slip, now as he rejoined the head of the column there was a hard, determined look on his chiselled face. A look, which did not go unnoticed by the slumped figures on horseback who quickly moved back into formation.

Having reasserted his position as commander, Houston reflected on what would be thought of him should he return his first campaign a failure. He had wanted to tell O'Mallahan what other purpose the gold was to be used for. In building a new Fort, however knowing the sergeant's doggedness he deliberately held back this information to reveal should the sergeant raise the issue again.

All signs vanished, as if the Apache had now begun to cover their tracks. Two days ride into the desert of Sierra Madre, no stone was to be found unturned, nor any sign of horse droppings or marks on the ground. The platoon was spread out in two's and three's to search and to cover an area half a mile in width whilst still advancing southward.

Corporal Conrad remained close to the Sergeant, listening as the older man gave instructions on what to look for. The half-breed scout rode amongst the men checking for himself that no sign was overlooked.

O'Mallahan had no illusions. He knew all trace of the hostile was lost, to stumble upon their trail now would be luck in its extreme.

"You see the way the sand hugs around one side of stones, that's because the wind has blown it there. Ifn you see any stone without sand around it, you tell me."

"Whys that sergeant?"

Asked the young recruit.

"Because, as there's no sand around it, then it must have been moved, seeing as how there's been little or no wind this last day or so."

"You mean an Apache may have moved it?"

"That's right, though not necessarily the ones we're trailing."

The recruit listened eagerly as the sergeant related to him what different formations of the land could mean, where water could be found and what should be growing where. It was all too much to take in at once.

Conrad grew more closely attached to the sergeant as the days melted into one another. O'Mallahan was aware the task he had set the men was nigh on impossible, for even when no wind was apparent, the sands still shifted. Furthermore no Apache was apt to leave any sign which was visible to the naked eye, not unless he wanted to.

On riding out of a sandstone gully the water was heard. The waters of the Rio Yaqui surged before them.

There were disgruntled remarks amongst the men as the Captain showed no indications of stopping other than to take on fresh water.

The scouts rode for a mile down either bank of the river searching for signs, none was found.

It was the twelfth day since leaving the Fort.

"There has been talk of desertion cap'n, not to me in person, but I know who is involved. They are at the end of their tether, saying we should go back."

Captain Houston turned to face O'Mallahan, his face glistening, bronzed under the hot sun, sweat ran down his face into the stubble on his chin.

"If any man attempts to desert his post he will be shot. I will not have any such talk amongst my men, if you know them as well as you say you do then make sure the ringleaders get my warning."

"You fire a shot and every Apache for miles will hear it cap'n."

"Apaches,"

protested Houston, cracking up, a shrill pitch entering his voice.

"That's all I've heard since we entered this desert. I haven't seen a sign of an Apache or any other Indian for days. We...."

The argument was brought to an abrupt halt as the scout came riding in. He was strung across his horse with an arrow in his leg. The body crashed to the ground and there was a high pitched yell, followed by arrows soaring high into the sky.

Houston was speechless. O'Mallahan pulled him down to the ground as the arrows plummeted earthward. Houston's mouth moved but no words came forth No enemy could be seen. O'Mallahan watched, unable to move, as the arrows sank into the bodies of the young, raw recruits. There was no time to issue orders, let alone carry them out. The more experienced men, using their horses as shields moved towards a dip in the sand rifts, where at first there appeared to be no cover, it did offer some slight sanctuary.

Indicating the way to the others, O'Mallahan moved amongst the dead, relieving them of their weapons. He was amongst the last to reach the shelter of the dunes. Even as his body fell alongside that of the captain's, he realised the situation offered little cover should the Apache alter their direction of attack.

They were trapped some fifty to seventy feet from the waters of the Rio Yaqui River in a small crack in the sands, sheltered only by the sparsest growth of mesquite.

With each man readied for the impending onslaught O'Mallahan took stock of the casualties. Ten men were missing. Their horses were still amid the others, rifles as yet to be removed from scabbards.

The position was vulnerable from the rear. However, the Yaqui would stop the Apache from getting close from that direction until after dark.

"How do we fight if we can't see them sergeant?"

"Jest keep your heads down, shoot only if you see where an arrow comes from."

O'Mallahan scurried across to where Houston lay shaking.

"There can't be many of them sir, or they would have attacked afore now. It must be a scouting party, but if we move they can pick us off as they like with no fear of loss to themselves. I suggest we stay here until after nightfall cap'n, before making our break. Like as not though they sent someone for help."

Houston breathed heavily, his gun was still in its holster, as yet unused. He grasped at any suggestion, which took the burden of command from his shoulders.

"Yes, yes sergeant, that's what to do. We'll wait until dark and try to slip away."

What was to be done after that, he did not even consider. Looking around at the hostile faces about him, Houston sank deeper into his gloom. The older men ignored him, whilst those who had come west with him now eyed him in a new light.

"Of course cap'n, us being able to sneak away from here doesn't help us find the gold none. After all, we've spent the last few weeks on the trail. Well we've found them, there's your Apaches cap'n, what do you aim to do about it."

Added O'Mallahan, unable to resist the barbed remark.

As the sun rose, so too did the temperature. The horses whinnied, unable to move from their tethered position yet sensing the waters nearby. Only sporadic fire continued, no Apache had yet been sighted. However, another life was claimed as an arrow found its mark.

An hour passed with neither sight nor sound of movement. Nerves began to take over.

"Do you think they've gone sergeant?" Queried Conrad.

"No, they're still out there all right boy, just waiting for someone to poke his head up. An Apache can wait boy, you remember that. He's the most patient animal alive, besides which we ain't going no place."

"AY II EEEE."

All heads turned as the ginger-haired, one stripe rose with an arrow in his back. His hands moved compulsively trying to remove it, then he lay still. More arrows came across and in their present position they were vulnerable. Each man leapt for the cover of the opposite bank, yet no sooner were they there than more arrows came from the direction of the first onslaught, each soaring high before dropping in their midst.

A Trooper snapped, he leapt to his feet.

"They can pick us off as they like, what chance do we have here?"

In full view, his body was struck first in the shoulder, then in the chest choking off his words. He fell forward forcing the arrow through his body.

"Let that be a lesson, stay where you are. Watch for arrows, but in no way betray nor abandon your position." Screamed O'Mallahan.

"That's right men," broke in Houston.

"We can get out of this, just hold on until dark."

This was the first semblance of an order Houston had uttered since the initial attack. He was looked on with disgust, as the once impeccable officer, was now trying to re-establish his authority.

The vigilance continued as the daylight hours passed and numbers dwindled, punctuated only by the breeze rustling through the dry growth.

Nothing could be done for those mortally wounded. Darkness came suddenly and with it a brief silence followed by night noises.

The whispering of the horses was the loudest sound. No one wanted to be the first to peer out into the darkness.

Chapter Eight

Apache Encampment

Tyrane's gun leapt as he fired, the loud crack carrying far across the desert. Santes froze as the shot echoed in his ears then he snatched out the knife from the Marshall's shoulder. A look of glee came across his face as he saw the law-man grimace.

The two exhausted men lay panting.

Tyrane holstered his gun, making sure it was firmly in place.

"Don't worry none about the Apache, we've got other troubles.

Look -"

He gestured towards their back-trail, it was a couple of miles away, but gaining on them. The sky was black with thunder, it boomed, the lightening cracked.

Ojo stood agog as it descended upon them.

"It is a storm we must be quick."

Even as he spoke, Santes ran towards his horse, he ignored the red liquid, which ran from his ear, as he wrested the blanket from off his horse. Then pulled the animal to the ground.

Tyrane secured the pack animals to his own mount.

Ojo protested.

"What's all the fuss, it's only a storm!"

As he spoke, the wind began to howl around him, drowning Santes reply,

"You have never seen a storm in this desert Amigo. It could blow you away."

Tyrane pulled his bandanna over his mouth.

"If you want to go on breathing, I suggest you get something over your mouth, keep it shut and keep a tight hold of your horse. He's heavier than you are, so hold onto him."

The storm devoured them, swallowing them up in a hail of sand and sticks.

The Marshall was slow to act and was coughing as sand entered his lungs.

Even as he secured his sweatband Ojo tasted the sand stinging his face and entering his eyes.

The horses were terrified, their eyes protruding and wild.

Tyrane called out.

"Try to keep in contact with one another, don't wander, stay in a group."

The words were swept from his lips, carried on the wind to some far off place. Perhaps someone would hear them, however, those they were intended for did not.

"What the -"

Tyrane cursed as he nearly fell over the body in front of him. He snatched up the reins quickly and squinting his eyes saw Santes huddled against his horse's belly underneath his blanket.

Pulling on the reins, Tyrane sent his own mount to the ground.

""Whoa there, steady now fellah"

Crouching against the horse Tyrane pulled his hat tighter over his eyes, holding it there. With his other hand he kept a tight hold on the pack animals.

The Marshall choked to the point where he believed he was going to bring up blood. His whole body lunged forward with each cough, causing his head to spin. In a delirious state he stumbled, letting go his hold on the piebald. Fumbling, trying to retrieve the reins he moved away from the others, before, collapsing, on all fours and blacking out.

Ojo still struggled to remove the sand from his eyes. He could not see and as his eyes watered they attracted more dust. He rubbed his eyes red raw.

The storm raged. Then as quickly as it came, it was gone.

With the passing, sand settled and the roaring of thunder and flashes of lightening died away.

Tyrane moved first. He ventured to his feet. The sand fell from his clothing, he beat the garments and still more fell. The roan stood and Tyrane secured the line from the pack animals to its saddle horn.

He took in the surrounding landscape as he flayed his hat against his jeans. It was completely altered, what with rocks being overturned, vegetation being uprooted, and sand dunes being created in new locations. In no way did the terrain resemble that which they had recently ridden over. All tracks now obliterated.

Santes moved in front of him. First there was only the slightest motion from beneath the blanket. Then the Mexican thrust out his blood stained face amid a mound of sand.

"I see you decided to remain with Santes Amigo, that was wise."

As he arose, Santes left a deep imprint in the sand.

"That was a good idea of yours Santes. You've obviously been through such a storm before."

"Si Amigo, many times."

Ojo lay not far from them, his face still buried in his hat.

"You can come up, it's over."

Sitting himself upright Ojo asked for water. It was only when he handed him the canteen did Tyrane realise Ojo could not see. He slipped off his bandanna, wet it and handed it to him.

The particles of dust removed from his eyes, Ojo came to his feet, also surveying the altered terrain.

"Things sure look different huh, where's the Marshall?"

The threesome looked around but could see no sign of the law-man

"Perhaps the bastard was carried away by the storm, I hope."

"Maybe, but we need him," said Tyrane.

Santes tended to the pack animals needs whilst Tyrane and Ojo looked for Zeb.

Ojo sighted the piebald standing motionless, nudging its head against something on the ground. Riding forward, he sighted the prostrate figure of the Marshall.

Tyrane, sighting the sudden movement by Ojo turned his roan in the same direction.

The piebald backed away as Ojo leapt from the saddle to examine the body. The side of Zeb's face was red raw where the wind had bounced sand and hail. As he turned the body, Ojo saw Zeb's other cheek, which resembled a pincushion due to it being pressed against the sands.

Ojo felt a heartbeat, however, knew the law-man to be in a bad way.

Tyrane arrived bringing his canteen, Zeb's lips pleaded for more as the wetness fell onto his parched skin.

"Easy, just a little at a time. How do you feel?"

The water reviving his senses, Zeb saw Tyrane kneeling beside him. Ojo was off a way to the left.

"Where's Santes?"

"He's all right Marshall," Answered Tyrane.

"If all he can worry about is where the Mexican is!"

At that moment, Santes arrived leading the pack animals to interrupt Ojo.

"I am here you bastard. Do not worry, I will not leave you whilst you still live."

"How bad is it, Marshall?"

"I'm all right, let me get to my feet."

Tyrane aided him up and into the saddle.

"That shot you fired, could it have been heard?"

"More than likely. In any event we ride."

"It may have been put down to the storm,"

"Bastard, if an Apache heard the shot he would not confuse it with a storm. This I know."

They rode. Although the landscape was totally disarranged Tyrane was sure of his direction.

Ojo rode alongside the Marshall, inquiring about the piebald.

"You must have had him for a long time for him to stand over you like he did, but for him I wouldn't have seen you."

"Sure, me and the old fellah have ridden the trail a long times together."

The storm as it transpired was a blessing in disguise. For there were no tracks to betray them, and for the moment the fight was forgotten. The tension between Santes and the Marshall was eased somewhat, though with the Marshall injured Tyrane reckoned the best thing was to rest up for the night, rather than press on.

As they rode into the late afternoon, Tyrane ever vigilant marked time, looking for a place to stop. He sighted a rock formation and veered the roan towards it.

It suited the purpose admirably, offering shelter from the wind.

Santes took the first watch this night.

Around the low-lit fire the others huddled, each with his own thoughts none looking directly into the flickering flames. Wheezing badly the Marshall brought up the subject of Santes killing the Sheriff of Sonora.

"I knew nothing about that Marshall, neither did Ojo here. He was right beside me all the time."

Ojo nodded in agreement.

"I believe you Tyrane, but when this is over I mean to settle with the Mex. For now though he's certainly proved he can hold his own, we're going to need all his help when we reach the gold."

"None of us may come out of this alive. That was an almighty number of Apaches I escaped from, it wasn't easy."

Ojo sat listening, hoping for some snippet of information that may be forthcoming. When none came, he baited his question.

"You never did tell us how you came to escape. Just how did you manage it?"

For the first time in weeks Tyrane thought of the fair-haired girl who had cut his bonds. A young thing he reckoned not much more than nineteen or so.

"Well, I had a bit of help, a woman, she freed me."

"A woman?"

"Don't tell me you have notions of rescuing her whilst we try to steal the gold."

"That's my business, Ojo."

Santes, on hearing the raised voices left his post to investigate.

"It's our business if you intend to jeopardise this under-taking just because you feel you owe this woman something. That's not why we're here."

Ojo stopped speaking, his gun flashed into his hand as he heard footsteps approaching.

"What is this about a woman?"

"You should be on guard,"

"Shut your mouth you bastard or I will put my foot in it. My watch it is over. Someone else can go out there."

"There's only two watches tonight Santes. The Marshall here won't be able to take one."

"That's right, so get back out there and complete your quota."

Ojo re-holstered his gun.

"Go to hell, that bastard can take his own watch. If he cannot do it then we will have to leave him, we have no need of passengers."

"I, Emanuel Santes carry no one, least of all bastards."

Having said his piece Santes sat down. His hand never leaving the hub of his pistol grip.

"I'll take my own watch, Tyrane."

"All right, you take the next one Ojo. Then waken me, the Marshall here can take the last one up until dawn."

Ojo still wanted to know more about the woman.

"Her name is Clementine, that's all I know about her. She was captured by the Apaches when the train she travelled with was attacked. She cut me loose and I escaped. If we can bring her out with the gold then we do so, if not -"

"Where did this gold come from?"

"I believe it to be Army Payroll of some kind. When I was captured, I had just come across a burnt out wagon. There were blue-coats around it, a scalped, one of them lived long enough to mention the gold, before I was taken."

"Then you didn't actually see the gold for yourself?"

"Yes, at the Apache Lodges, where we're headed now."

"Then it is government money, which we are after. Does that not bother you Marshall bastard?"

Ojo left the light of the fire to take up his place on lookout. When no answer was forthcoming from the Marshall, Santes chuckled.

"Shut it Santes," warned Tyrane.

There was silence.

Ojo settled with his back against a rock, his rifle across his legs. Looking outward there was no sound from behind him.

Santes and Zeb slept at opposite ends of the makeshift camp. On wakening Tyrane to take up watch, Ojo hit the sack.

It was daylight when Zeb stirred. His eyes took in Tyrane fixing himself a coffee.

"I took your watch – you needed rest."

Zeb rode alongside Tyrane.

"How long before we reach this village you talked about?"

"We should sight it around noon. We may have been there last night but for the storm. It has confused the landscape, also it was dark when I made my escape."

"Thanks for taking my watch. Those extra hours made all the difference."

"Forget it, it's going to take the four of us to pull off this job."

The small party rode from side to side of hillocks and sand dunes, crossing the last lap of the desert leading to their destination.

Due to the movement of his horse, the pains returned to Zeb's chest causing him to cough once more. Although he tried to contain his discomfort, it was evident to Tyrane that the Marshall was not well.

His fever rose, in holding himself back, Zeb found it necessary to burst into bouts of coughing.

"That's it you bastard, cough yourself to death and bring the Apache down on the rest of us."

Although Zeb did not pursue his vendetta against the Mexican, Santes took advantage of every opportunity to criticise the Marshall's inability to sit upright in the saddle and to comment on the noise his coughing was making.

"Now we permit cripples to ride with us."

They heard the noise simultaneously, each man halted his mount, remained still and listened for any other sound in the vicinity. There came to them a low hum, far off, yet not too far not to warrant dismounting and continuing on foot.

Zeb's discomforts faded into nothingness, once out of the saddle. He moved as stealthily as the others, making no sound.

The village appeared larger than he remembered and Tyrane realised and admitted to himself that for a while back there on the trail he had been unsure that the route he had taken was the right one.

Their present position confirmed his fears as the approach led somewhere between the cliffs on one side and the open terrain on the other. The water in the background glistened amid the tops of the wickiups

Tyrane, knowing he had tried to return the same way as he had left did not mind his error for their present position offered concealment.

Tethering the horses amid the rocks on their back trail, the four men looked out over the encampment from their vantage point, which was slightly more elevated than the wickiups

"Take it all in fellah s, try to make mental notes of where everything is. It may make all the difference between us getting out of here with the gold or remaining as permanent residents."

The waters on the far side took up all the terrain in that direction, to leave that way with the gold would not be possible. This left the huge cliffs towering above the wickiup s on one side and the open ground leading to the lodges and the waters edge on the other.

"A natural fortress if ever I saw one,"

"I didn't say it would be no picnic, but the gold's down there Ojo."

"Just waiting for us to go and get it, eh Senores, what do you have in mind?"

"Well, as you can see, we're somewhere between the cliffs and the open stretch leading up to the lodges. As long as we don't move out from these rocks our position is safe."

"That does not get us the gold Amigo."

"I'm coming to that. The Apache have their ponies other there between the cliffs and the wickiup s, giving them access to the water. I want you Santes to get up amongst these cliffs, somewhere where you can look down on the ponies. Assuming there is a way up there, I want you to collect any dry tinder. There's probably plenty about after the storm, then at a signal from me set fire to each bundle of tinder and let it fall amongst the ponies. This should stampede them through the village, can you do that?"

"Si Amigo, if there is a way up amongst the cliffs I will find it. However I have one not so small point."

Each man turned to Santes as the Mexican awaited their attention.

"It would be very foolish to leave Santes trapped on the cliffs, for if he should then escape, he would kill you."

"No one's about to run out on you Santes."

"What about me and the Marshall, Tyrane?"

Explaining that if he and Ojo set out now, they would be on the other side of the water by nightfall.

"We'll have to swing wide to avoid being seen," said Ojo.

"That's right and we can ride the pack horses bare back. That will give us fresh saddled horses when we come out of the village."

"With the Gold?"

"Yes."

"We can forget the pack animals once we're amongst the Indian ponies, for we can have our pick. We'll rope enough of them to bring both ourselves and the gold out. When I fire three successive shots, I want you to let the burning tinder fall Santes. That will be the signal."

"Si Amigo."

"Ojo and I can help to stampede the ponies in the direction we want them to run."

"What about me?"

"Marshall you stay here and look after the horses. When the stampede gets under way, let the Apache go after their mounts. Don't reveal your position until we come out, then give us all the covering fire you can lay down."

The plan seemed as plausible as any other that was suggested, so it was agreed upon. Moving back, they returned to the horses.

"Take these with you Santes."

Santes put out his hands and onto them Tyrane thrust dynamite.

"It may help if you throw a few of these during the proceedings, but not before you get the signal."

"Si Senores, I understand."

Taking rope and sufficient ammunition, Tyrane set off with Ojo on horseback.

"Make sure my horse is here when I return bastard."

With this last remark, Santes set to finding a way up amongst the cliffs. He needed to also circle around away from the camp.

Zeb tethered the horses, watering them before taking up a position where he could watch the comings and goings from the encampment.

As he watched, a young boy attempted to seal up a hole in the canvas of a wickiup.

"What about this woman you mentioned. How do you intend finding her?"

"She has to find me Ojo. I'm going in there after the gold. When the Apache didn't bring me back she must have realised I got away. She's probably been living in hope of rescue ever since. If she has any sense then when the action starts she will head for the wickiup where I was held captive. It's near the centre of camp, that's where the gold will be."

"Perhaps she can tell us which one it's in."

"It would sure save us some time, maybe our lives."

At the back of his mind Tyrane worried about leaving Santes and the Marshall together for even a spell. At the same time, he told himself that both men were professionals in their own right. So would bury the hatchet, at least until the next part of the plan was completed.

Ojo knew the chances of them all coming of this alive were slim. He decided on being one of the survivors, irrespective of the cost of life to his companions.

Each man braced himself for the job he must do.

Santes was in no hurry. When one trail led to a dead end he returned and started again. Taking his time he explored the passages amid the cliffs, each he realised would be known to the Apache. This he took into consideration. Yet they would not know of his existence until he wanted them to.

After an hour of going over the same tracks, he came across a narrow path. A horse could not walk along such a path, however Santes could. The path tapered to a ledge, always twisting upwards so Santes proceeded. It led him onto a cliff edge, which towered above the Apache village. The cliff on which he stood was not the tallest, for behind him stood another, which dwarfed the one on which he stood.

From his place of concealment Zeb watched the small boy put the finishing touches to the repair job on the wickiup.

'Damage must have been caused by the flash storm,' he reckoned.

Halting some distance from the waters edge, Tyrane and Ojo dismounted.

The last moments of daylight were spent knotting together ropes in such a fashion so as to hold the gold bullion cases securely to the ponies' backs.

"I reckon on a box to each horse Ojo. There was three cases of gold, and we need a mount apiece plus one for the woman. That makes six mounts, best make plenty of bridles."

"We'd best have the ponies well picketed before Santes lets loose with the dynamite."

Darkness fell, with it came the night noises.

Tyrane lay looking up at the star spangled sky. This was all he knew, the wild life and the open prairie. With its small towns and saloons. Somewhere in the back of his mind he had a vision of a ranch. He put himself into the picture forming in his imagination.

The vision shattered as Ojo indicated it was time to move.

"Yes, let's go!"

Ojo led the horses to the waters edge, allowing them to drink. Both men mounted, silently slipping into the water. The crossing proved slow and difficult on the bare-backed animals.

The moon shone down silhouetting them for an instant before each man swung his horse out of the silver gleam, which stretched itself across the water. As soon as the water was left, Tyrane began selecting the sturdiest looking ponies. Ojo tied them together to form a chain.

'Would Santes be in position?' wondered Tyrane.

"Would the Mexican have succeeded in finding a path to the cliff tops? Well no matter."

Ojo, not as trusting of Santes as Tyrane, appeared to be worried.

"He's unreliable, I don't like it."

Tyrane saw the beads of perspiration on Ojo's brow.

"Don't worry Ojo, Santes is just as hungry for the gold as you are, he'll be ready,"

The ponies secured, they moved along the waters edge away from the cliffs. Halting on hearing voices above the whispering sound of the horses. Smoke filtered through the wickiup tops to be whisked away by the darkness. Braves strutted about in the cool night air. Fires were aglow in the camp throwing off light, which revealed the innermost wickiups patterned detail.

Tyrane drew his gun and turned to Ojo who nodded he was in readiness. Tyrane aimed for the chest of one of the two braves on sentry duty, his finger moved as one motion. Three shots cut through the comparative silence of the night. Ojo put his full weight behind the lead rope holding the ponies.

Tyrane dropped the second sentry, sending him sprawling.

The night echoed the shots, bouncing them off the cliff walls to be cast back into the darkness.

Overhead, Santes lit his torch. Walking along the cliff edge he put it to each bundle of brush, kicking them over the edge as they caught alight, bursting into flames.

Down they plunged, sparks erupting as they landed. Some fell amongst the ponies, others against wickiups causing them to smoulder and flicker into flame. One landed atop a wickiup, blocking the air hold, causing the inhabitants to rush out into the night.

Fear frenzied ponies reared in panic, Tyrane emptied the remaining shells from his pistol into there midst, driving them towards the wickiups

The inadequate enclosure holding the ponies crumpled under hoof The near-most wickiups collapsed beneath the thunder of hooves as the sleepy eyed dodged being trampled under the stampeding horde.

Following immediately behind the main charge, Tyrane and Ojo moved deeper into the village. Tyrane thumbed fresh shells into his empty chambers.

Clementine Hollinger was amongst those to waken. Rising from her stinking corner of a wickiup she gaped outside at the pandemonium.

For weeks, or was it an eternity, she had lived in hope of rescue, ever since the Braves had returned without the body of the tall stranger she befriended. As she watched, the flashes of light from the cliff top burst into flame on their descent. Hoping, for she could do no more than hope and pray, and praying had been a lost cause. She pulled a blanket around her shoulders and moved into the chaos, which reigned. She hurried towards the centre of camp.

Tyrane quickly spent the replenished load his gun took. Following in the wake of the stampeding herd with Ojo to his left and in close contention he quickly replenished the pistol, methodically thumbing shells into the empty chambers. The two men rode closely together.

Tyrane, believing Ojo was too preoccupied with the goings on around him, relieved him of the chain of spare animals. Away somewhat from the confusion surrounding the corral, the two men rode cautiously, fanning bullets into the area immediately before them.

A half-naked Apache raced towards them. Waiting until the last possible moment Tyrane unleashed two bullets, which smacked into the chest of the runner, sending him crashing amongst Ojo's horse's hooves. The warrior turned, spitting blood. The horror on his face was only momentary before being flayed by a mighty hoof.

Painstakingly they neared the glowing fire at the centre of the encampment.

Tyrane, on swerving to avoid a fleeing pony, glanced upwards towards the cliffs.

Santes, finished with his torch, hurled it into the darkness. In doing so he neared the edge and for an instant was in view. Tyrane's eyes were not the only ones to catch sight of the swirling torch. As Santes darted back to safety, a cascade of arrows bounced off the wall around him or shot overhead. So high was his position and so acute an angle he merely stepped back a few paces to be safe and the stinging missiles merely pinged against the walls.

Sitting down, knowing himself to be completely safe and out of harms way, Santes took out the makings and rolled himself a cigarillo.

"Do you think they hit him?" asked Ojo.

"Maybe, but I doubt it."

With no direct route to follow, the careering ponies split into different groups and raced in circles. The fire at centre of camp shone like a beacon, cooking fires overturned, sparks exploding into the darkness.

Avoiding any further contact with the Apaches, Tyrane pulled the string of ponies nearer to him.

Something, a figure, flapping in the wind raced towards them. It dropped to the ground. Ojo raised his pistol to look along the barrel. With the blanket discarded, the fair-haired figure became clearly visible.

"Don't shoot, Ojo, it's the girl I told you about."

Clementine clad now in buckskins, raced alongside the riders. She saw the tall stranger was leading a string of horses.

"How many of you are there, but no matter. Thank heaven you've come."

Before she could prattle further, Ojo shut her up.

"Where do they keep the gold?"

She gave him a blank look of disbelief.

"The gold from the Army, speak, you stupid -"

"You remember Clem, the night you cut me loose, those boxes they brought into camp with me. Where do they keep them?"

"What do you want to know that for, didn't you come to rescue me?"

"Don't be stupid. Do you think we'd risk our scalps over your account, now where's the gold?"

"Shut up Ojo," .

"Listen Clementine, tell us where they keep the gold, then we can get away from here."

Faced with long years in captivity before her, the reason why these men were here did not matter.

What did matter was that they were here and hence, rescue was a possibility.

Using her knowledge of the camp she led them. Avoiding where she knew open terrain to be.

Santes puffed on his cigarillo, the red end almost burning his lips. With a long drawn out breath he exhaled smoke. Picking up a stick of dynamite he put the red end to the fuse. The sudden hissing lit up his eyes. Watching it burn down he lit his next cigarillo. Then tossed the explosive over the edge. He miscalculated slightly, for it exploded in mid air.

The blast had a deafening affect on those below. Looking up, Tyrane closed one eye against the flash of light so as not to lose his night vision.

His chain of thought was interrupted by Ojo.

"Dynamite! Where did he get that?"

"Just a little something I gave him to play with,"

Tyrane caught Clementine frantically pointing towards a Brave, stood guard outside a wickiup.

"Right there, that's where they keep the gold, but it's guarded."

"Not for long its not,"

Ojo slid from his horse, passing the bridle to Tyrane. He strode quickly to the rear of the wickiup, slitting a hole in its side. Stepping inside he saw the boxes he sought. Ignoring them for the moment he gingerly moved back the flap to see the legs of the sentry.

The guard was watching the cliff top, with his back to the wickiup. Ojo followed the bronzed legs up to the buckskin around the waist, then took in the broad shoulders draped with long, matted black hair held together by a band around the head.

Throwing back the flap he arched his gun butt through the air. The movement did not go unnoticed and as the butt smashed into the skull Ojo saw the painted, contorted face of his victim before he fell to the ground. Standing still for a moment, Ojo smelt the putrid odour of sweat rising from his torso. Then acting quickly as Tyrane approached, he dragged the prostrate figure to within the confines of the wickiup.

"Help me with these cases,"

Ojo fought back his fear. He passed each box through the slit in the wall to Tyrane, the woman held back the flap.

Tyrane accepted each box in turn, fastening them to the backs of the ponies, checking each knot.

Santes from his position on the cliffs could not see where the dynamite he hurled was landing. He lit another fuse on the red end of his cigarillo and tossed it over the edge. Followed by another, then another. He threw them haphazardly in different directions and knew by the commotion coming up from below, he was causing havoc.

Down the sticks fell, one stick exploded in front of racing ponies, killing the first one and causing the next to mount a wickiup in its panic. The animal brought down its full weight on the dwelling, bucking and kicking, it became entangled in the structure. The other animals surged past in a flurry of hooves.

Another stick landed amid a group of Apache, exploding on contact it blasted bodies, some dead, some mortally injured, others dazed.

Santes hurled the sticks over the side, laughing at the top of his voice as he did so in his state of sheer ebullience.

"Listen to that fool up there,"

"He's happy at his work and he's taking the pressure off us,"

smiled Tyrane, not dwelling on the matter. As he swung astride a pony

"Let's go!"

He indicated Clementine onto the mount behind him. Pulling on the tow-rope he inched the ponies onward, he led them himself not relying on Ojo.

The Apache, having gotten over their initial surprise concentrated their fire on the cliff.

A Brave leapt over a prostrate body before him. Tyrane's bullet missed him by inches as he leapt at Ojo. The two men fell to the ground, Ojo's pony rearing off into the chaos.

The two bodies rolled over locked in combat. Ojo wheezed as the body smell reached his nostrils. Yet it could be no stronger than his own stench of fear. The two men's faces met, the smudged painted face of the Apache and the thin, moustached face of Ojo. Crashing his knee into the braves stomach Ojo leapt to his feet.

Tyrane moved on with the string of laden ponies. Ojo's gun leapt in his hand as it shot death into the ribcage of his advisory.

Realising he had been forsaken, Ojo raced alongside a bewildered pony clinging to its mane. As he pulled his weight onto the animal's back, the animal responded to his commands and both man and beast raced towards the moving Tyrane.

Tyrane hesitated, awaiting the right moment to pull clear of the cover of camp. The impetus was taken from him as the fast moving Ojo surged past.

Digging spur into his mount Tyrane chased after Ojo. The cavalcade behind him gained momentum, the bullion boxes bounced freely yet securely on the backs of the ponies. From the corner of his eye, Tyrane knew they were seen. He cut the lead pony badly with spur, enticing it to maximum speed.

Ahead of them as they raced, a rifle boomed. The Marshall emptied the weapon into the foremost braves. Taken unaware by this sudden fire, three Braves dropped to the ground. Two clutching their chests as blood spat through their fingers, another nursing his left side.

Discarding the now empty weapon Zeb rolled over to the opposite side of the rock behind which he hid. Picking up a second weapon he shot, the Apache were congregated at the encampment edge making his job so much easier. He concentrated his fire on those foolhardy enough to chance a quick arrow against a gun.

The perspiring figure of Ojo flashed past.

As Zeb fired, Ojo came to his side, gun already drawn.

Tyrane and Clem rode past in line with the free running Indian ponies.

Ojo felt his gun leap, a brave fell omitting blood from the mouth as he staggered forward.

The Apache were in a crossfire as the hysterical voice of Santes rang out. Working his way speedily down the cliff path, he emptied his pistol towards the village as it flashed into view at sporadic intervals. The Apache fell back for cover.

Before the ponies had stopped, Tyrane leapt to the ground, halting them alongside the saddled animals.

"Get onto another horse Clem. I don't have time to switch the lead rope to another horse."

Gathering up the reins he made ready for an immediate departure.

Appearing from the cover of the cliff path, Santes swept his eyes over the crates.

"Si si amigo. We have much gold, no!"

Even as he counted the boxes, Santes brain was systematically working out his share of the booty.

Ojo came at a dead run to join the trio. Thrusting the reigns into his hands, Tyrane ran back towards the Marshall who was collecting some of the rifles.

"Where's he going?" cried Clementine.

Ojo glanced in her direction, she was the only one mounted.

"To help the Marshall, he'll be back soon."

"He should leave the gringo bastard to the Apache, it would save me the trouble of killing him and give us time to escape."

Clementine looked from one to the other as the conversation took place.

"You mean you would leave that man back there to die?"

"Si Señorita, he is only a bastard not worth saving."

Ejecting the last cartridge from the chamber, Zeb reloaded. Scanning the village, he sighted a young boy wiping his eyes over the body of a Brave. The wickiup he had spent the afternoon repairing was a smouldering ruin.

Stopping short of the Marshall, Tyrane fired. Zeb turned and ran past Tyrane. Then Tyrane moved further back firing as he did so. The two men raced headlong towards the horses.

Both Santes and Ojo cut loose with rifles, firing over their heads. Their shots would score no hits, however would discourage the venom of the Apache for a moment longer.

The two fleeing men leapt into saddles. The Marshall soft-talked the piebald into action, as Tyrane mustered the pack animals. Zeb took the lead, Clementine rode alongside Tyrane as he struggled to get the gold-laden mounts running in equilibrium.

Ojo straddled his horse, sliding his rifle into its scabbard. The two men quickly gained on the gold-laden animals, firing sniping shots behind as they rode.

"That Mexican was going to leave you behind,"

protested Clementine.

"Forget it miss."

Said the Marshall.

"Santes and I have a mutual dislike for one another. Don't let it concern you, just ride."

"It concerns me."

Cut in Tyrane,

"You two had better forget your differences. It won't take the Apache long to muster their horses and be on our trail. We'd best have put a deal of distance between us and them before they do or we're done for."

Santes raced alongside, exchanging glances with the Marshall. Both men disliked the prospect of working alongside one another.

On they rode into the blackness of the night, glancing behind regularly for fear of pursuit.

The sky was aglow behind them. wickiups still burned.

"That's mainly your handy work Santes. You weren't exactly particular where you threw that dynamite, some of it landed real close to us,"

Ojo, began to get his wind back as the sweat grew cold on his torso.

"Si Amigo, but with you dead I would collect a bigger share of the gold."

"You idiot Santes, with us dead there wouldn't have been any gold brought out,"

"Thank goodness I missed then Amigo,"

The horses steadied to a gallop.

"They won't come after us until morning Tyrane. First they'll catch their ponies. Then mourn their dead. Finally they'll come after us. By which time we'd best be holed up somewhere for the day. We have to ride at night and rest by daylight."

Tyrane mused with the suggestion. His thoughts were preoccupied with the remark Santes made about there being more gold for him if some of them were not to survive.

"What you say makes sense Zeb. They sure as hell can't track us at night."

Chapter Nine

Race From Danger

For what was left of the night they rode.

The next day passed without sight nor sound of pursuit.

Keeping to a tight formation, each rider was alert for danger. Santes rode to the rear of the party.

Unable to determine if the Mexicans action was to watch for pursuit or to keep each member of the band in his sights, Tyrane did not pursue the matter. However he believed his latter suspicion to be correct.

Clementine could see Tyrane clearly now.

He was younger than she had imagined, by the authority he exerted over the others she expected him to be older.

She recalled the night she cut his bonds, remembering the rippling corrugated muscles of his torso.

Looking at his rugged appearance, she glanced down at her own tattered clothing.

Tyrane called for Santes to come forward.

"What is it you want gringo?"

"Have we disturbed your dreams Mex?"

Although Zeb spoke in a jovial tone he felt a relaxing of his muscles as Santes rode past.

Raising a hand Zeb rubbed his neck, sore from turning around in the saddle to keep an eye on the Mexican.

"Half expected a knife in my back at any time."

"One good thing about having you along Marshal, you are the one Santes will kill first." said Ojo.

Zeb continued to massage his neck.

The Indian pony drew alongside Tyrane.

Santes eyed the bullion boxes.

"What is it you want amigo?"

"You know this country Santes, is there somewhere we lay up for the day. A place you know of, a hideout you have used before?"

"I do not come here often amigo, but there is a place. It is not too far from here, there we can water the horses and rest."

Tyrane waved his hand in a gesture for Santes to take the lead.

Neither Ojo nor the Marshall could hear the conversation taking place between Tyrane and Santes.

Both men looked at one another, neither spoke yet each asked the same question with a quizzical glance ahead as Santes took point position and veered from a true course.

Liking this situation, the Mexican formulated a plan.

The place he knew of was on a plateau. He knew of only two ways to reach the summit, both of which were well concealed.

"Stupid gringo bastards."

He almost gloated too loudly.

"I shall take them up by one route, then I shall leave by the other with the gold.

The morning drew on, it was noon when Santes sighted that which he sought.

Increasing the pace he rode first in one direction before turning sharply in another. This tactic he repeated many times in hope that it would stop the Apache from picking up the trail if they should appear before nightfall. After which he no longer intended to be there.

They had been riding behind Santes for several hours.

At first it appeared to be a sheer wall of rock they approached. However upon reaching the outermost scatterings of rocks, Santes dismounted. The Mexican bade the others to follow as he ferreted his way through the mass of outlying boulders, which concealed a path, the way led upwards. Suddenly the animals were struggling for a hold.

Santes did not delay to assist, he proceeded alone. Despite its difficulty, the ascent did not take long, Tyrane joined Santes, who sat with his back against a rock, looking out across the desert, puffing on a cigarillo.

"They will know which direction we have taken Amigo. I hope they do not know of the existence of this place."

From this vantage point, Tyrane looked out across the arid, stretch of desert they had crossed the night before, squinting his eyes against the sun.

"We should see them coming a long ways off. How many ways can they get up here Santes?"

The Mexicans eyes shifted their focus from the desert to Tyrane.

"One Amigo, only one. That makes it easier to defend no?"

"Maybe, but that's if we're discovered, I'm hoping that doesn't happen. Where's the water?"

"I will show you Amigo."

Rising, Santes assured himself that Tyrane had believed him about there being only one path leading up onto the plateau. Clementine, Ojo and the Marshall arose as Tyrane and Santes rejoined them.

"How does it look, Tyrane?"

"It's good Marshall, we can rest up here for a while."

"I don't see why we have to stop, why not just keep on riding. The more distance I put between myself and those

Apaches the better I'll like it. That probably goes for the woman as well,"

said Ojo, jerking a thumb in Clementines direction.

"Well I -"

Clementine had no chance to comment before the Marshall took up the situation with Tyrane.

"What do you intend to do Tyrane?"

It was a high plateau, which dipped away from the edges to give the impression of being a crater. However it was not. There was plenty of growth, which belied the surrounding below. From what Santes had told him, Tyrane was fairly confident the Apache would view this as an escarpment and pass on by. Now he understood why Santes tried to cover their tracks below. . It was the kind of place only a man on the run would discover. A man such as Santes, but not the Apache for they reigned supreme in this hemisphere, afraid of no one, with no need to hide.

The sheer walls of the plateau, towering above the desert sands, made it appear impregnable from below. Certainly had he not been led, Tyrane was sure he would never have found this place.

"I figure we can rest up here for the day, and ride out tonight. Ojo, you take the first watch. You know the direction from which they'll be coming. They won't be here for a while, but stay alert."

Ojo, annoyed at not having any say in the matter slid his rifle from its scabbard. Cursing to himself he proceeded to take up position on lookout.

"It should be safe to build a low fire Marshall. You get some Chow going, I'm going to have a look around with Santes."

Clementine rummaged through the supplies for coffee as Tyrane and Santes moved towards the more vegetated area.

"Where-about is the water, Santes?"

The plateau was much bigger than Tyrane had first thought. There were many places where one could hide if the necessity came about. Gorse and Mesquite were plentiful. The sound of burbling water came to Tyrane's ears.

"It is this way Amigo."

A shallow basin, which made a natural water trap, was fed by a whirlpool. The pool was no more than a few feet wide, but the velocity by which it spun indicated to Tyrane it was fed by a strong current.

"I do not understand it Amigo. I have been to this place before and it was just the same, Santes has done good, eh?"

"Probably fed by some deep, underground river."

"It is a miracle that it should come to the surface here, where it would go unnoticed."

But for the concealment of the higher outer wall, Tyrane felt sure that the Apache would have discovered this place long ago. For a sharp-eyed warrior would surely have had his curiosity aroused by a patch of green in this no-man land.

"A garden in the wilderness."

"What is that you say Amigo?"

"Forget it."

Satisfied with the situation, Tyrane decided not to bother with further investigation.

Santes led the way back, eager to leave as much of the terrain unexplored as possible by the others.

"The coffee, it smells good Amigo."

"I will take the horses to the water when I am finished this, it is good." said Santes, between sips of the scalding black liquid.

Clementine fetched a mug for Ojo.

"Thanks, I thought I'd been forgotten about."

She stared out across the desert, then turned, returning to the fire.

Tyrane settled down and proceeded to strip his gun. Taking out a small pouch, he removed some papers and began to rub against the working parts. Zeb eyed Clementine.

"Where you from miss, and how come the Apache took you alive?"

Tyrane appeared disinterested in the question, yet Clementine was sure he listened.

"My folks they set out from Phoenix. We were one of many families going to new lands."

Clementine related how and where the wagon train was hit and why she was not killed with everyone else, leaving out only the personal details of the capture and rape. She told fully how the rest of the settlers including her folks were slain.

Tyrane watched, glancing up from cleaning his weapon as she gestured with her arms in the telling of the tale. His eyes lingered, taking in the figure beneath the tattered buckskins, revealed in every motion she made.

"We was going to Texas, pa bought a piece of land there."

"You must have passed through Tucson,"

"Yes, we did Zeb."

"That was the last town we passed through before – it was horrible."

"Then you were taken back to their village. It figures, they had no need to kill you, you represented no danger to them. That was where you ran into Tyrane here,"

Spinning the chamber, Tyrane was satisfied with his weapon.

"That's right, the Sheriff at Tubac warned me of an Apache raid on some wagons."

Santes re-appeared, catching the tail end of the conversation.

"So Señorita, you have been a guest of the Apache for many months no. You will have learned much?"

The lustful glare on Santes face left no doubt as to the implication of the remark.

"That's enough. We'd best get some rest. What did you do with the gold Santes?"

"It is with the horses amigo at the water."

"You take the next watch Marshall, let Ojo get some shut-eye."

The discussion ended as Zeb went to relieve Ojo.

Later with no sign of pursuit yet Zeb roused Tyrane to take his stint on guard.

"Where's Santes?"

"I don't know, he didn't come near me whilst I was on watch, and I wasn't looking at what was happening up here. I was concentrating all my attention out there,"

Zeb indicated towards the desert.

The Mexicans absence worried Tyrane.

"Where the hell can he be, and what's he doing?"

"I don't know and I don't care. For all I'm concerned he need never come back."

"Fat chance of that Marshall. Not whilst we have the gold."

The matter rested. Zeb spread out his bedroll whilst Tyrane took up position on lookout.

Snuggling his back against a rock, Tyrane laid his rifle over his knees. The sound of light footsteps came up behind him, his finger curled around the trigger, then Clementine appeared. Standing for a while, she did not speak. Tyrane eased the tension from his muscles and allowed his finger to come away from the trigger.

"Do you have any other family?"

Clementine was taken aback by the question.

"Someone you can go to, if and when we get out of here."

"You didn't mention a husband when you told us about the wagon train, is there someone waiting somewhere? You can't be much over twenty, most girls would be settled down with kids by your age."

The stark reality of her situation hit her. During those long months of capture she had given no thought as to where she would go or how she would live. Her one burning desire had been to escape.

"My folk, they bought a small holding in Texas. I suppose I shall go there."

"You ever see the land?"

"Why no!"

"Figured as much."

"What do you mean? Pa and a lot of others on the wagon train bought land they had never seen. Pa, he figured on raising horses. The land's no good to me, but I can sell it and return to Phoenix."

"Is that what you want to do?"

"I don't know."

She hesitated.

"Let me tell you something. I've heard of land sales before. Sometimes the land is there, sometimes it isn't. Even assuming it exists, is there any water on the place, what's the soil like, is it sand or rocks. Who sold your Pa the land?"

"The government, I think."

"Well that's something I suppose, but I wouldn't rely too much on being able to sell it."

"Why not?"

"Well if it was any good, like as not it would have been claimed long before your Pa ever heard tell of it. It's probably dry, barren land. So the chances of making a good sale are slim. What did your Pa do for a living in Phoenix?"

"He tended store."

"I don't want to worry you miss, but you've got problems."

As she wandered back towards the sleeping figure of the Marshall and the resting Ojo Clementine realised how casually she had spoken of her parents death. The long months of capture had hardened her, the innocent young girl, who had set out on a pilgrimage from Phoenix, was no more she realised. All that mattered now was survival.

Santes returned in time to relieve Tyrane on watch.

"Where you been?"

"I've been looking around Amigo. This place, it is exactly as I remember it."

"Don't wander off again, without telling me first."

"Si Amigo, as you say."

Daylight hours slipped slowly by.

Zeb checked on the horses. The gold was where Santes said it was, close to the picketed animals. Ojo took up watch again, followed by Zeb.

As he strained his eyes against the disappearing sun, Zeb saw them. "Here they come."

Tyrane, Santes, Ojo and Clementine arose as one, rushing to the lookout point.

"Look, there,"

Zeb, indicated a speck of dust in the distance which grew in size as they watched.

"That's them alright."

The Apache were not distinguishable as yet, however the dust they kicked up in their wake left little doubt as to their identity.

Fear gripped Clementine as she recalled her months of torment. Her absence would by now have been discovered and perhaps be connected with the attack on the village. The Apache she was sure, would show her no mercy.

"They'll know I'm with you, if they should capture me again!"

"No one's about to get caught. You Santes, keep that gun of yours in its leather,"

"Do not concern yourself Tyrane, I have no wish to shoot except perhaps at the bastard whom we allow to ride amongst us. Him I would kill for pleasure."

"I've had all I'm going to take from you Santes -"

"Cut it out, both of you."

"I should have killed you back there on the trail with your two murdering friends Santes."

Ojo's gun appeared in his hand.

"You two just simmer down."

"I should have killed him along with the other two murderers,,"

repeated Zeb.

"And I should have killed you along with the other Sheriff bastard in Sonora."

"You didn't, and your sure as hell not going to do it now. Not with that lot coming towards us."

Said Ojo emphatically as the dust thinned out and it was possible to pick out the faintest outline of the approaching riders.

"That was quick Amigo."

Whistled Santes, admiring the speed at which Ojo's gun had appeared in his hand. The impending danger from the Apache brought an end to all argument. They watched the riders' approach, however the sound of the the hooves proved a better guide as to their proximity as daylight ebbed away.

The riders stopped, congregating amid the outcropping of boulders.

"What are they doing Do they know we are here?"

"They followed our tracks this far, they'll stop and look around before making any move Marshall."

"Do not worry Amigos, I have spent the day making sure nothing is out of place. They cannot follow our tracks on rock, and I have made sure no stone was unturned."

"So that's where you were today Santes, covering our back-trail,"

"Si bastard, that is where I was."

Santes felt convinced they believed him. It was a plausible enough reason for his earlier absence. An absence he was sure would have been commented on.

"Can they find the way up here Santes?"

"Perhaps Ojo, however, the night is upon us and shortly it will be impossible to pick a route amongst the rocks."

Outriders returned to join those at the foot of the plateau. Sharp eyes scanned the topmost walls, searching for any sign of movement or any irregularity.

The quintet remained unmoved.

Darkness fell like a blanket across the desert.

"How many do you reckon?"

"About twenty or so Zeb."

"Nearer thirty of them I would say Ojo," Said Tyrane.

"In any event, they outnumber us."

A thunder of hooves reached their ears, below, the flashing paint of the ponies danced into the night.

"Are they leaving?"

"Can't tell, they followed our trail here, now it stops, so I doubt it."

Some distance from the plateau the noise died down to a bustle of movement.

"They're making camp, they must have seen something," cursed Ojo, eyeing Santes with distaste.

"So much for you making sure no stone was unturned."

Fires soon blistered the skyline, an occasional glimpse of movement was visible in the light thrown off.

"They're settling down for the night, we'd best do likewise. You stay on guard Marshall, me next, you Santes, then you can take the last watch before morning Ojo."

Moving back to the fire site, which had long been extinguished they bedded down for the night. The steady breathing of Santes indicated that the Mexican at least, had no difficulty in relaxing under such circumstances.

At midnight, Zeb roused Tyrane. He lay awake as the Marshall approached, still unable to get to sleep.

"They peer to be settled, best keep watch anyway"

"May as well, I can't sleep."

Ojo turned in his blanket, Zeb was convinced he was still awake. The woman certainly was as he saw the sparkle in her eyes whilst going past. The only sound was the steady breathing of Santes.

Zeb found difficulty in sleeping as his side began to ache, having put his pains and discomforts to one side during the period of danger. They now returned to torment him.

Yawning heavily, Tyrane roused the Mexican. All appeared to be asleep, as he pulled the bedroll over his tired body.

Santes remained vigilant on watch for some thirty minutes. His eyes moving regularly from scanning the Apache encampment, to checking on his four sleeping companions. His white teeth flashed in an evil grin as he contemplated the next phase of his plan.

The gold it will be all mine, he thought, while rising from his position on watch. No longer concerned about the danger from the Apache, Santes circled the sleeping quartet.

On nearing the water he calmed the animals before loading the gold filled boxes onto their backs. Testing the knots he satisfied himself that each box was held securely in place. The reason for this was two-fold, for besides the loss of gold should a box fall, there was the danger of arousing his sleeping companions. Speaking softly to the animals he secured a rope under their bellies to ensure the boxes did not move about whilst in transit.

Although believing himself to be at a safe distance, Santes took no chances. Moving each animal one at a time, he returned for another, then another. With each of the pack horses picketed at a safe distance, he quickly led his Indian pony to join them, glancing back frequently to ensure his movements had not been heard.

All roped together, forming a single file Santes led the animals. through the undergrowth, then across a stony flat.

Nursing his side, Zeb became alert to faint sounds.

Sliding out of the blanket he listened again. Once more the sounds reached his ears, fainter this time. Unconvinced it was not his imagination, he opted not to disturb the others who slept. Quietly he inched through the under growth towards the horses.

The splashing sound of water came to him, then he was amongst the horses. It was immediately obvious that the gold was gone, also a number of the horses.

Listening, there was still a faint clomping sound to be heard coming from the far side of the plateau.

Racing through the brush, Zeb went in its direction.

The undergrowth gave way to a stony flat area.

There was a glimpse of the last pack animals as they disappeared behind a huge rock.

The trail was narrow and difficult to see, however Santes relied upon the other ponies following his own mount blindly. The descent was a steep gradient, turning sharply with regularity. Still he egged the paint onward pulling the others closely behind, knowing that the way ahead was clear.

For the past day had not been spent in covering tracks, but in checking that this narrow trail had not been blocked by the passing of time and would be wide enough to take the cumbersome gold boxes.

As they moved, so too, did the stones underfoot. Undisturbed for so long, they rolled freely under the horses' hooves.

Reaching the huge rock, Zeb heard the low rumble of movement. He could not see the path but knew one must exist, for Santes could have gone no other way. He began to follow, then stopped, considering firing a shot to alert the others. He dismissed the thought from his mind for the Apache too would hear.

Turning, he raced across the stony flats into the undergrowth. The piebald became alert as he neared.

"Easy fellah"

Throwing the saddle onto its back, Zeb wanted desperately to arouse the others yet at the same time did not want to lose track of Santes. Picking its way through the brush the piebald soon reached the stony flat, then the huge rock.

Santes knew he neared the bottom of the trail as the walls fell away on either side, the way widened, and the pace was increased. There was a scattering of rocks to be woven through, as had been the case on the other ascent, Santes picked out his markers.

The piebald stomped, not wanting to proceed into the blackness of the narrow trail. Coaxing it onward, Zeb gave it its head, just egging it on every now had again. Pebbles rumbled underfoot, the horse whinnied, obviously afraid.

"Easy now, steady on fellah"

Knowing the correct course to take, Santes soon cleared all the outlying rocks in his path. The open prairie stretched before him, with the lead rope around the neck of his pony, Santes dug spur into the animal's side. There was a jolt before the other animals gained momentum, then they raced.

Unlike Santes, Zeb did not know the pitfalls to avoid. Several times the piebald went down on its knees, each time Zeb picking him up and coaxing him onward. It was a long, arduous descent, the walls fell away and he weaved through the out fallen obstacles.

Zeb realised all this delay was enabling Santes to steal a considerable lead on him.

As the first fingers of dawn stretched their light across the sky, Ojo awoke. A thunder of horses galloping reached his ears. Suddenly he remembered that he should have been awakened to take the last watch, and was not.

Ojo leapt to his feet, donning his gun-belt as he awoke Tyrane.

"What's wrong?"

"I don't know, the Marshall and Santes are both missing."

"What!"

"Check the horses whilst I see what's happening below,

Tyrane scrambled to his feet.

With long, bounding strides Tyrane soon reached the place the lookout should be. The reality of the situation hit him, for the Marshall, he was sure would not leave his post.

The Apache were gone from view. Surmising they must have ridden off on the blind side of the plateau, Tyrane turned, running to join Ojo.

Even before he reached the horses, Tyrane heard the cursing Ojo.

Clementine ran to him,

"What's happened?"

"I'll tell you what's happened," snarled Ojo, his face taking on a sickly, despairing look.

"That bastard Mexican and the Marshall have lit out with the gold. That's what's happened."

"What does it mean, Tyrane?"

"I don't know Clem Zeb would never tie in with Santes. There's something happened, or happening that we don't know about."

Clementine looked bewilderingly at the enraged Ojo as he searched fervently amongst the undergrowth for the gold.

"The horses have gone as well Ojo, so its pointless to think it could still be here."

"They're not going to get away with this,"

"The Apache have also gone Ojo,"

"Gone! What the hell's happening around here?"

Tyrane's mind raced trying to solve the mystery.

"The Apache can't know of this place up here. They followed us here last night, then left first thing this morning to try to pick up our trail." He mused.

"So what will they do, Tyrane?"

"They'll spread out and look for sign Clem"

"That doesn't get us our gold back, Santes I knew about and watched him, but that parasite of a law-man, when I find him -"

"We'll worry about that when we do find him Ojo. Meantime let's spread out, there must be another way down from here. They couldn't have left by the way we came up, not with the Apache camped out there all night."

As he searched through the brush, Tyrane would not have been surprised to have found Zeb dead by Santes hand.

For over an hour they searched. But for the piebald being missing it was easy to speculate as to what may have occurred the previous night. However, with three pack animals, Santes paint and the piebald gone, Tyrane began to have his doubts about the Marshall.

'Could he have taken both Santes and the gold back to the authorities?"

Ojo charged towards him interrupting his chain of thought.

"Git the horses saddled, I've found it."

Tyrane came running. The gap was narrow.

"They have a good start on us Ojo, and remember, the Apache are out there scouting for sign. Then there's the woman to think about."

"To hell with her, no one asked her along. I'm going after the gold with or without you and I aim to kill me a U.S. Marshall and the Mex."

Clementine reached them in time only to hear the utterance about killing.

"What's that, what does he mean Tyrane?"

"He means we're going after them."

"And the gold, don't forget the gold," cursed Ojo.

"Is the gold that important?"

"It is to me lady."

"And you Tyrane?"

"We'd best water the horses first," insisted Tyrane.

The canteens were filled. Ojo cursed Santes and the Marshall to hell and back as he tended to his horse's needs. Tyrane waited until the water stopped gurgling into his submerged canteen before turning his attention to Clementine.

"Sorry to drag you into this, it wasn't what I planned."

Whether there was anything heartfelt in the remark, Clementine didn't know. For, one moment, Tyrane appeared to be a strong lonesome figure, the type who could and would survive in this land. Next he seemed almost apologetic for his roughness, yet never leaving himself open to criticism.

"Anything is better than being back at that village."

Then hesitatingly she added, "You said we would travel at night Tyrane, it would be safer. I don't want to be captured again. If you knew what they did to me back -"

Tyrane stood up affixing the canteens around the saddle.

"I've seen what the Apache do to white women. It's time we moved."

An hour after first light Tyrane checked their approach to the plateau, the Apache were long gone.

Leading the horses, they crossed the stony flat. Ojo took the lead. The narrow path was comparatively easy to descend. now light was available, but the steep walls on either side kept the trio engulfed in shadow.

As the walls fell away there were numerous obstacles to negotiate. Still not yet clear of the outlying rocks, Tyrane turned in the saddle. He could not pick out the trail they had just travelled.

'This place really is concealed,' he confessed to himself.

Even in daylight the downward trip sapped both time and energy. Once on the open prairie the sign they sought was found.

"It looks as if the Marshall's with Santes after all,"

Tyrane had to agree as he gazed down at the tracks. The piebald hoof-print clearly distinguishable.

"That so-called Marshall's got some answering to do,"

"What does he mean?"

"It means miss, that where they go, we follow," answered Ojo turning his mount in the direction the prints led. Tyrane and Clementine fell in behind.

The trail was easy to follow, for the gold weighed heavy. Tyrane's face frowned, it seemed to have escaped Ojo's attention that if they could follow the tracks so easily then so too could the Apache.

Ex U.S. Marshall Zeb Pluckard gauged himself to be about an hour's ride behind Santes. He urged on the piebald inducing it to increase speed.

Santes had a crick in his neck from continually looking around for pursuit. Believing himself to be in the clear, he still refused to relax his awareness of possible danger, not least so from any meandering Apache.

The horses lathered, badly needing a rest. Santes had known for some time that he must stop to give them a breather. For the past two miles he had scanned the terrain around him for a place which offered concealment. The knowledge that should he be caught either by the Apache or by those he had betrayed would mean certain death spurred him into selectiveness. Many places where he would ordinarily have hidden were passed by. That the Marshall would be spearheading the hunt for him did not worry him as much as the thought of Tyrane hunting him down. He had said nothing, but he knew of the bounty hunters reputation, none had shaken off his pursuit, and almost as many had ceased to live.

The sun shone directly overhead, Santes shielded his eyes, wiping the sweat from his brow onto his sleeve. Cursing the dilemma he was in yet being unable to do nothing about it. Looking towards his back trail he picked out the sign he had cut. The pony stomped as it was forced down a steep embankment.

Santes stopped in the shallow between two dunes. The place offered cover, it was the best he had come across all morning.

Sliding from the pony the animal's back glistened with sweat. From each animal in turn he unburdened the strong boxes. After quenching his own thirst, Santes moved amongst the animals wetting their nostrils, giving each a drink.

A quick reconnaissance revealed he was in a shallow some thirty yards wide with steep embankments on either side. On climbing the far embankment, Santes eyed a cluster of rocks. Their number and height was not sufficient to hide the horses but he made a mental note of them as he did with all things pertaining to his safety. It was such a knowledge that had kept him at liberty all these years and was the same knowledge, which gave him an idea.

As the plan formed in his mind, Santes recalled a canyon he knew of. Deciding to follow the same plan as Tyrane, of hiding during the day and riding at night, the idea formulated.

If only capture can be evaded until the mouth of the canyon.

For long ago he had been trapped in the canyon, not knowing at the time whether it had been a dead end he had ridden there to evade capture. Faced with death at the hands of Mescalero, with whom he rode until they discovered his treachery, he had searched every crack in the canyon walls. Finding a trail which led to a precipice, there he forced his horse over the edge as capture became imminent, faking a scream he had hidden, watching, as those who sought to kill him looked down onto the bottomless abyss. Believing him to have fallen to his death, from then, with only a canteen of water he survived. Yet he was convinced that the canyon was not a dead end, but that there was a way through it.

A sneer crossed Santes face as he recalled on that occasion, as on this he was fleeing from those he had betrayed, and now like then, he would escape.

As the minutes slipped past, Santes moved from either side of the shallow keeping a vigilant watch.

=====================

With the tracks so easy to follow, Tyrane rode alongside Clementine allowing Ojo to retain the lead.

Ojo raged at the way in which Zeb had fooled them. Santes he had not trusted from the outset, but the Marshall he had reluctantly accepted. He intended to kill the Marshall when he caught up on to him.

Just out of earshot of Ojo, Clementine bombarded Tyrane with questions about the West. Tyrane chose carefully, selecting only the good points about the country. He had no need to tell her about the other side of its nature, for that she already knew from her short time here.

"It's the wide, open range I like. A man can feel free sleeping under the stars, moving from one place to another on impulse. The sheer beauty of this country is lost to the folks back east, they just can't begin to understand, not until they come here and see for themselves."

Clementine listened, enthralled, thinking of how it might have been if her Ma and Pa had not been killed. At the same time she listened as Tyrane's voice rang out names of places, some of which she had never heard tell of.

"There's the Staked Plains, the Sacramento Mountains, the Pinos Altos."

As she listened to his flowing voice, Clementine realised there was more to this rough man she rode beside than she had at first realised.

"Do you have another name Tyrane, and is it always so desolate here?"

"Barrington, Barrington Tyrane. And yes it is desolate here in the Madre."

===================

Santes tightened his grip around the rifle as he sighted movement in the distance, along his back trail.

Zeb Pluckard rode on unaware that he was being watched. He rode in Santes tracks, following them to the place where the land fell away to a shallow. Santes lay in wait.

As Zeb crested the summit he almost rode over the top of Santes. The Mexican let off a shot. Zeb turned instinctively, the bullet caught him in the side of his ribcage. The piebald reared in fear its nostrils bellowing, terrified by the suddenness and nearness of it all. Lashing out with its hooves it struck Santes a blow to the head. The Mexican fell down the embankment as Zeb rolled out of the saddle.

Quickly on his feet, clutching his side, Zeb scurried down towards the prostrate body of his attacker. The piebald had reached the bottom at a run. The other animals took fright and raced disappearing over the crest of the opposite ridge.

Approaching Santes tentatively, Zeb kept his gun trained on the Mexicans chest as he turned over the body. The trickle of blood from the side of his head told him that Santes would be unconscious for some time.

The immediate danger over, Zeb sighted the strong boxes. His mind awoke to the realisation that the animals had bolted. Racing up the incline, he peered after the ponies who kicked and bucked into the distance The piebald stood nearby, its head bowed the bridle trailing.

Resting, breathing heavily, the wound in Zeb's side began to ache. He felt a dizziness, grimacing he pulled himself together.

Knowing the horses to be gone, he had one of two choices. Either remain here and await the arrival of Tyrane, or to ride out and meet him. He reckoned on the shot Santes fired carrying far and with no knowledge as to when Tyrane and the others would have set out from the plateau, he decided on the later course of action, for it was likely the shot was heard by the Apache.

First, searching out a low spot in the shallow, Zeb dragged the strong boxes to it. Clawing with his hands he uncovered enough sand to inter them.

Satisfied all was well, and that Santes was still unconscious he beckoned the piebald to him. Exhausted he lay across the saddle, steering the animal with one hand while the other clutched his blood soaked side.

Zeb rode from the shallow taking a round about route. His head spun and his hold on the reins slackened as the effort from dragging the heavy boxes took its toll. Santes he reckoned could conceal himself amongst the group of rocks until he returned. Then everything went black.

=====================

The three riders reigned abruptly as the single shot reached their ears. Clementine turned to Tyrane, who simultaneously moved forward to join Ojo.

"Sounds a ways off Tyrane."

"Hard to judge out here, best take it easy from here on in,"

=====================

Santes stirred, his eyelids fluttered open to look for danger. There was none, he staggered to his feet. He stood alone in the shallow, no horses, no gold, no Marshall. The movement of standing brought a throbbing to his skull. As his hand came up it met with the sticky wetness of blood.

Santes eyes widened as he gaped at the redness in his hand, feeling cautiously he asserted the damage.

"Bastard gringo bastard."

As he staggered around screaming he came upon the freshly disturbed sand, much darker than that which lay all around it.

Falling to his knees, Santes clawed the ground. As the blood from his wound dripped amongst his fingers they struck the hard, wooden boxes.

Pulling the sand aside, Santes soon uncovered, the boxes. Then realising he could do little with them without horses, he cursed,

"Bastard Marshall, bastard, bastard, bastard."

Rising to his feet he moved to the top of the embankment. The sight, which met his eyes, he could not believe.

The piebald stood motionless some way off, with the Marshall on the ground. Santes eyes shifted to the appearance of riders in the distance. He felt for his gun, which for the first time he realised was missing from its holster.

Wagons came into view, kicking up dust as their tracks bit deep into the sand. Santes cleared his eyes, not understanding the sight in front of him.

The outriders neared the piebald cautiously. Then, sure that the man at its feet offered no danger, beckoned the wagons forward. There were three wagons, two open-backed and one canvassed. The Marshall's body was bundled into the canvassed wagon after some argument. The Sombrero clad riders rode on, searching the trail left by the law-man However, the piebald had criss-crossed its own trail so often after the Marshall slipped from its back it was impossible to tell from which direction it had come.

Santes watched, seeming to recognise the pose of one of the riders. He could not recall where he had seen that figure before, but the matter preyed on his mind.

Chapter Ten

Capture By Gun-runners

The wagons moved on and with them the riders, taking the Marshall with them. Santes arose, brushing the dust from his chaps.

He considered what to do next, as ideas flashed through his mind he discarded them as quickly. The one missing essential in each idea was a horse, of which he had none. Then a thought struck him.

He worked quickly, dragging the heavy boxes up the embankment to the cluster of rocks, pacing out an exact distance and re-checking his stride.

"Yes, that will suffice."

He pulled away the sand, with the hole deep enough to contain all three boxes. Santes replaced the sand over them. Taking handfuls of dry sand he sprinkled it over the darker area.

He wheezed heavily at the exertion of lifting the heavy boxes, the shirt he wore clung to his back. Convinced he could do no more to conceal the cache he returned to the shallow and climbed the opposite embankment.

He settled down to wait, knowing it would not be long before Tyrane and the others came upon him. Why they were not with the Marshall, he now began to wonder. Then feeling the blood hardening on his face he began to pick at it.

As he picked, he realised he had not eroded all tracks around the gold cache.

Working painstakingly he wiped out his footprints, working his way back towards the cluster of rocks as he did so.

Then he sighted the three riders, they had not seen him yet.

Standing on a boulder, Santes waved enthusiastically at them. Ojo was first to see him.

"What the hell's going on?"

"He peer's to be alone, best take it slowly just the same."

Santes flashed his teeth as they rode towards him.

Ojo rode past, looking for the Marshall, and the gold.

All attention was focused on the protesting Mexican.

"Si amigos, you have come at last. I have been waiting for you."

Ojo brought up his gun from its holster.

"Do not Amigo, for if you do, you will be killing the wrong man. Besides -"

He paused.

"I am the only one who knows the whereabouts of the gold."

Ojo flexed his finger around the trigger wanting to shoot.

"Talk Santes, and make it good," ordered Tyrane.

"That gringo bastard he crept up on me when I was on guard. The horses they were loaded, ready to move and he tied me to my pony. Then he say he is taking me to jail and giving the gold back to the soldiers."

"How did you get here by yourself, and what was that shot we heard?"

Tyrane did the questions as Ojo and Clementine looked on. Santes voice was shaky as he gestured to give emphasis to his words.

"Look at my head Amigo, could I lie about such a thing. The blood it is there for you to see. The Marshall bastard he was not well. I saw my chance to overpower him. The gun it went off as we struggled, he was hit, how bad I do not know. That horse of his, it is as big a bastard as its owner."

"Stick to the story Santes."

"It attacked me, it kicked me on the side of the head, Amigos look!"

Santes, indicated once more the dried blood near his temple.

"It looks bad," said Clementine.

"Shut up," cursed Ojo.

"No one asked you, get on with it Santes."

"I was struck unconscious amigos When I awoke I saw the Marshall bastard being taken prisoner by riders. They were not Apache."

"Who then?" asked Ojo.

"Mexican I think, they had wagons."

"What happened to the gold, Santes?"

"These men Senores, they rode off with it. It is very strange, why would anyone bring wagons to this place?"

"I don't believe a word of it,"

"I agree with Ojo why didn't you tell us about the other trail leading down from the plateau. On top of that, why did the Marshall leave you behind?"

"My horse it bolted amigo, he could not take me and the gold."

"You're a liar!"

"Hold it Ojo," interrupted Tyrane.

"He may just be telling the truth. Why didn't you tell us about the other route from the plateau?"

"I did not know of it Amigo. The Marshall bastard he must have found it."

"These Mexicans you saw, you recognise any of them?"

"No Amigo, they were too far away. Why do you ask?"

"Yea Tyrane, why do you ask? What do you know about them? You've been tight-lipped long enough," demanded Ojo.

"Never mind, we'd best get out of here. If we heard the shot, it's likely others did too."

"When I catch up with that Marshall I aim to kill him," vowed Ojo.

"Only after I have finished with him Amigo, then you may have him."

Clementine doubled with Tyrane, rather than ride the pack horse. Santes took her mount and rode to the fore. Ojo was convinced of Zeb's guilt, though to what degree Santes was involved he did not know.

Tyrane knew that the Mexicans with the wagons had to be Salvador Gonsalves and his gang of cut-throats. He reasoned, why if Gonsalves had the gold, was he still delivering the guns to the Apache. Not for one instant did he believe that the Mexican bandit would honour an agreement, besides the guns could be sold elsewhere. This was a gaping hole in the Santes story.

Tyrane knew Ojo could not determine this inconsistency for he had until now no knowledge of the gunrunners.

Tyrane toyed with the idea of putting a gun to Santes head to force him to talk, however the danger was that if Santes was harmed and it transpired that he was the only one who knew the whereabouts of the gold then it could be lost forever.

Following the trail left by the wagons was easy, Ojo too, now deduced how vulnerable was their position. Tyrane knew that all he could do was to wait until Santes made a move, in the meantime he kept the Mexican riding ahead of him.

=================

"Why do we not kill the gringo. What good is he to us Salgo?"

"He is a gringo Amine For what reason would a gringo come to this place, and who shot him?"

"We looked but the stupid horse it had roamed in circles before our arrival."

"The man who shot our prisoner was not an Apache Amine, it is this fact alone which concerns me. If there is one gringo, there may be others."

"Ah, I did not realise this amigo, but why do you say it was not an Apache who shot him."

"It is a pistol wound Amine, if an Apache was so close, he would not leave his victim alive."

"Unless he was dead himself Amigo."

"Perhaps, but for now it is necessary to allow the gringo to live."

The Marshall bounced off the hard floor of the wagon. The movement forced him into consciousness, hands moving instinctively towards his wound. Gomez shoved the hand away, delighting in the obvious pain he caused the prisoner by the unexpected movement. Zeb began to collect his senses as the incessant rumbling and jarring of the wagon continued.

Through blurred eyes he saw the frail little Mexican who watched over him. The pistol he held was not aimed, however he could bring it into play should the need arise.

Tentatively Zeb moved his hand once again to examine his ribcage. This time Gomez did not interfere. Zeb felt better on the realisation that the wound had been tended to.

"The bullet, is it out?"

Only a nod of the head gave any hint of a reply. Having no idea how far he had travelled or whom his captors were, Zeb surveyed the contents of the wagon. He himself took up a lot of its length. There were pots and pans and a coffee-pot Sides of beef and sacks containing various foodstuffs.

Out of the back of the wagon, with the tailboard dropped, he saw no other wagon. However he knew there were others ahead by the cries about him and the tracks left in the sand.

"You part of a wagon train?"

No reply came from the little Mexican.

"What are you people doing here, this is Apache country. How long have I been here?"

Zeb quietened as a sombrero figure galloped past the canvassed wagon. He watched, listening to the tailboard flap as the new arrival swung his horse around to face the wagon.

"So you are awake gringo, this is good!"

Zeb broke into a bout of coughing. As he did so his body turned, his eyes caught sight of a heap of dirty rags. Evidently used as a bandage for him, judging by the strips torn from them.

"So you do not talk eh, perhaps the Apache will loosen your tongue."

Amine turned his horse, galloping forward to rejoin Salgo.

"Si he is awake, but he does not wish to say anything Salgo."

"Since when have you let a little thing like that stop you Amine?"

"Let us kill him."

"What harm can he do us?"

Then Salvador saw a way in which he could belittle his second in command. Raising his voice for all to hear,

"That is why I am in command Amine, because I do not act rashly. You are too impatient my friend, the gringo will tell us what we want to know. I Salvador Gonsalves shall see to it."

Salvador flashed his gleaming teeth at Amine in a wide grin.

Zeb's side burned as he doubled up in bouts of coughing, Gomez looked on disinterestedly.

Salgo liked to put Amine in his place regularly, yet he also knew he would need the services of his second in command in the near future. In a low voice, so as not to be heard by the others he spoke to the sulking Amine

"You may kill the gringo when we have finished with him Amine"

A smile creased Amines face, he sat upright in the saddle.

The two men rode to the fore, directly behind were the two wagons laden with rifles and ammunition. The twenty odd sombrero Mescalero were strung out in groups of three and four, with the canvassed wagon at the rear.

It was the sixth day since leaving Janos, Salgo reckoned on reaching the Apache village sometime the day after next.

Darkness engulfed them and camp was made.

"Peers your unconcerned about being harassed by the Apache."

Offered Zeb, hoping for a snippet of information about his captors from the frail figure in the corner of the wagon.

He was bundled out of the wagon towards the fire. For the first time he saw the other two wagons and on counting the heads around the fire he came to terms with the fact that he was not going to escape from his present predicament without assistance.

"Mescalero," he spat, and was hurled to the ground.

The other two wagons he quickly learned were loaded with rifles and gunpowder. This knowledge he acquired from Amine, as the great bearded figure tormented him during the course of the evening.

"If you do not talk gringo, we shall give you to the Apache. They, I am sure, will loosen your tongue."

Amine longed to throttle the silent stranger, however, he held back for fear of a further rebuff from Salgo. He could be patient, for sooner or later Salgo would give the nod and the gringo would be his, and he too, like the Apache, had his own methods of persuasion.

"What are you doing here gringo?" continued Amine

Not knowing the situation between Salvador and Amine, Zeb decided to give an account of his presence here in the Sierra Madre. Up until now, the only reason feasible would be that he was on assignment. So that was the reason he gave.

"I was trailing a bandit."

"So, you chase men for money, perhaps one day you would chase me. Who was it you were after?" queried Amine

The reply spat like a bullet from Zeb's lips.

"Santes, Emanuel Santes."

A broad smile came across Amines face. The men within earshot began to discuss the name. Even Salvador turned his head slightly to listen.

"So, you know this miscreant Santes. I too, have known him, but no more. I rode with him, as did Gomez and others but he betrayed me. When we meet again I shall kill him."

Zeb was amused. For all their differences, both he and Amine had one thing in common, a hatred of Santes.

"It will do you no good gringo, that I have a dislike for Santes. For when we deliver the guns, and collect the gold, we will have no use for you, so we may as well leave you with the Apache, there will be sport no?"

Zeb realised these Mescalero were trading weapons and ammunition with the Apache, in return for payment of gold. He reasoned that his captors could not possibly know that the gold had been stolen from the Apache. Hence when they reached the place of the intended trade there would be trouble.

For with or without payment, Zeb was sure that the Apache would not allow so many guns to slip from their grasp.

Furthermore, he reasoned that somewhere on the back trail, Tyrane would be following. Not for one instant did Zeb believe that Tyrane was following out of loyalty. Tyrane wanted the gold.

What lies had been told by Santes when they finally caught up onto him, Zeb could not imagine.

Zeb thought it ironical, that the Mescalero should be taking him back to the Apache village. For all they wanted was the gold. All to do now, was to wait and remain silent.

The fires burned down before flickering away to embers with the coming of morning, but they had been seen by ever watching eyes and the Apache now waited near the trio of wagons, only they had no fires, and they unlike the gunrunners, were silent.

In the hazy light of early dawn, the outermost guards sighted the Apache. The signal was quickly passed back to the Mexican leader. The gunrunners formed a half circle around the wagons, the Apache stood their ground.

"Why have they come here Salgo?" questioned Amine

"Why do they stop now?" worried Gomez.

"They await the arrival of their chief,"

replied Salvador to the bothersome questions, bothersome because he did not know the answers.

Victorio, dressed in black, rode through the ranks of warriors.

Salvador greeted him with quizzical looks. At Victorios side rode a warrior with a broken nose. Salgo recognised the ageing sub chief, remembering him from the first meeting at the Apache encampment.

Amine advanced a few steps behind Salvador, eager that he too should be known as a leader, yet not so keen as to be up front.

"What are you doing here Victorio, we agreed to make the exchange at your village?"

The chief dwelt on the question for several moments, his eyes taking in the wagons, judging their load by the imprint of the wheels left in the sand.

"You have done well Salvador Gonsalves, you have brought many guns."

Zeb was forgotten about for the moment. He pulled himself aboard the canvassed wagon, eager to be out of the way. He could not understand what was being said, however he knew what must come.

Victorio was impressed as Salvador tossed him one of the rifles, at the same time, he gestured for his men to let the Apache chief know they were armed and ready to fight.

The motion was not unnoticed. The two chieftains conferred. Salvador waited. Amine moved more directly behind his leader, his fingers curling around his pistol. There was silence.

"There will be a delay."

It was the first time Geronobbi had spoken other than to Victorio.

"The ammunition is distributed amongst the wagons, one shot and it will go up. You will have no guns," said Salvador.

Broken nose's face hardened. He forced the words through his teeth.

"The yellow metal you seek, has been stolen."

Salvador took a pace backward. Victorio hastily added,

"The thieves are nearby. They cannot escape, we have sealed off the area."

From behind Salvador, Amine voiced his question.

"Who stole the gold?"

"White eyes, and one like yourselves. They have a woman with them now, they will be easy to find."

The two warriors paced their pony's back a few strides. Amine stepped closer to Salvador.

"The prisoner Salgo, do you think he knows anything of this?"

"Quiet, you fool."

Zeb did not hear every word spoken, but captured the gist of the exchange.

It would be simple for him to call out which may start both sides fighting, but he knew that he would be killed.

Some dozen or so paces away from Salvador and Amine, Victorio and Geronobbi turned their mounts to rejoin the hunting party.

"The next time you come, bring payment there are others with whom we can trade the guns," taunted Amine

Victorio's face twisted with anger as he turned astride his pony. He did not speak, merely glanced with impassive eyes towards Salvador who knew that words were unnecessary.

"That was a stupid thing to say Amine They will never allow us to leave with the guns."

"Perhaps not, however now they know that the next time we meet, it will be to exchange either gold, or lives."

Zeb wheezed heavily, recovering from the blow of a rifle butt, delivered to him by the weasel faced Gomez. The barrel of the rifle rested precariously near to his temple, Gomez itched for a movement, which would give him an excuse for hitting him again.

Salvador appeared at the rear of the wagon.

"What is happening here?"

"The gringo," said Gomez. "He had thoughts on leaving us."

With the rifle barrel pressed between his shoulder blades, Zeb was pushed from the wagon.

Salvador stood before him, hands on hips, gesturing elaborately with his hands as he asked his questions.

"So gringo it would seem you know more than you have cared to mention, about our presence here."

Zeb, held firmly between two bearded, barrel-chested men did not reply.

Salvador returned his hands to his hips, nodding to Amine Amine stepped between Salvador and the prisoner, arched his arm back, and smashed his fist into the side of Zeb's head. Already weakened Zeb reeled under the blow, his senses began to leave him. The next blow smashed into his chin, a tooth fell out and the body went limp, supported only by the two men who held him.

Amine braced to swing another punch, but Salvador intervened.

"Enough Amine He will tell us nothing if you kill him. Later he will tell us what we want to know."

Amine flexed his fingers, eager to continue with the beating.

Salvador organised the lookouts, stationing his men away from the wagons yet within sight of one another so as to give the earliest possible warning should the Apache return.

"We do not want the Apache to interfere with the games, eh Amine We will have sport with the gringo before he tells us where his accomplices are hiding with the gold."

Amines heart leapt at the inference of the remarks. His face contorted into an evil grin as he considered what method of interrogation to use.

The morning drew on, with the sun rising to its summit. Zeb awoke to find himself spread-eagled, with the sun baking his torso. His feet he could move a few inches on the cord, which bound them to two stakes. Flexing his arm muscles however, he found he was securely tied down with the only movement being the bending of his fingers.

Zeb eyed the intricate way in which his hands were bound around each stake, is such a manner as to afford no movement to the wrists.

A shadow darkened his torso as Amine looked down from above him.

"Now gringo, do you wish to tell us the whereabouts of the gold or must I extract the information from you?"

"I would tell him that which he wants to know if I was in your place gringo. For I know his methods to be very persuasive and they will cause you much pain," said Salvador, in an ever so casual manner.

Zeb looked at the faces of the men stood around him. Once they had the gold, the one and only reason for keeping him alive would be gone. Plus he doubted even Salvador of being able to restrain Amine.

Zeb wondered where Tyrane was right now. He could not be far off, but he feared they might not ride during the daytime for fear of discovery. Swallowing heavily he cleared his throat, his chest rose at the effort.

"I don't know what gold you speak of, I've told you why I'm in the Sierra Madre. If you don't choose to believe me there's nothing I can do about it. I don't know anything about any gold."

His pleading was aimed at Salvador, for Zeb knew no amount of reasoning would deter Amine.

Salvador stooped to pick up a tortilla, munching nonchalantly on it he nodded to Amine

Amine produced splints of wood, sharpened to a fine point.

"So gringo you do not know of what gold we speak of, eh?"

He gloated, as the watching men moved nearer their curiosity aroused.

"Perhaps I can help to refresh your memory."

Kneeling beside Zeb's head, Amine picked up a flat stone and placed one of the splints on his victim's thumb. With a sudden blow he smashed the splinter with the rock, forcing it between flesh and thumbnail.

Zeb's body writhed in agony, yet he let out little in the way of cries.

"One down and nine to go gringo. Do you still know nothing about the gold?"

'Thud.'

Another splint was forced into flesh. The sand beneath Zeb's body grew dark with sweat. Each finger on the right hand had a length of wood between flesh and nail.

Amine gleamed as he pushed his way amid the onlookers. He moved towards the fire, returning with a glowing ember. Touching the flame to the ends of each splinter, there were gasps from the spectators.

Slowly the flames flickered alight, each piece of wood grew hot as it burned down towards the pulpy mash, which was once fingers.

Zeb screamed as the burning ends reached his blood soaked hand. The stab of pain as the burning wood touched raw flesh was more than he could bear.

The screams brought Salvador hurrying over, where once a hand was tied to a stake, now was only a mass of burned, blood stained blistered flesh. Still conscious, Zeb's body was in a state of convulsion, unable to remain still, yet he was not able to move his hand in any way. His left hand held the stake so tightly his flesh turned colour, revealing veins.

Amine crashed his boot down on the charred hand, breaking bones and reducing it to a useless mess. Zeb's back arched as he received the blow, lights exploded in his brain, and darkness came.

Zeb awoke to find himself looking directly into the sun, his entire body exempting his head was submerged in sand.

"Can you still not tell me of the gold, or does your memory still suffer?"

The calm voice of Salvador Gonsalves pierced the wanderings of Zeb's mind. Straining his eyes against the sun he saw the taut Mexican moving towards him. His eyes searched upwards over the fancy boots, the embroidered chaps, the waistband, then the multi-embroidered shirt, still the clean shaven face with drooping moustache, topped by a huge sombrero.

The figure before him gave respite from the sun. There was no feeling in his right arm from the elbow down. Furthermore it was impossible to tell what damage was done for the only movement he was able to make was a slight turning of the head.

Zeb said nothing, his mouth was dry, the skin on his nose peeled.

Salvador turned on his heels and moved away.

=====================

Santes rode at the front, his head pivoting from side to side taking in the surroundings.

Ojo grew more restless with each passing hour. He had not liked having to stop for the night yet had to concede it was impossible to follow tracks in the dark.

Santes stopped his mount, putting his full weight into the stirrups he craned his neck forward.

Tyrane dismounted, leaving Clementine alone in the saddle. He indicated for Ojo to remain with the horses.

Edging his mount backwards, Santes passed the reins to Ojo. Then both he and Tyrane proceeded on foot. Keeping his voice to a minimum, Santes pointed,

"There you two Apache braves amigo. They are just over the ridge. I could see them from my horse."

"This isn't another trick is it?"

"I saw them Amigo. They are busy watching something else."

Tyrane belly crawled forward to the summit of the ridge. Removing his hat he peered over the top. The two braves were preoccupied with other goings on below. He eased his body back down the incline towards Santes.

"We have to take them, there's no way around. No gunfire Santes, we take one apiece, quietly."

"Let us hope they remain fascinated by whatever it is they are watching long enough for us to get near them Amigo."

"I'm curious myself to know what's so interesting,".

Santes slipped the knife from his boot. Tyrane on seeing the weapon once again returned to his horse for his own cutter.

"What's happening?"

"Couple of Apaches, Santes and I can take care of them."

His curiosity satisfied, Ojo calmly sat on his horse, content to wait whilst the others dealt with the braves.

Tyrane reached Santes.

"Listen Amigo, the first brave to turn I will kill, the other one, he is yours, Si?"

"Si."

The two men crept back up the incline.

The lookouts below, moved in more closely not wanting to miss any of the sport, merely because they were on guard.

The two Apaches also watched the tiny head on the prairie as it was left on its own after the departure of Salvador.

Santes was almost upon the brave, when Tyrane stumbled. Both warriors acted instinctively in diving to either side. Tyrane's knife hit the rock, the sudden jolt of the blade sent a numbing sensation up his arm. Santes released his blade, there was a dull thud as it forced its way through the sinewy muscles in the braves stomach. A slight groan as he retrieved his knife, turning the blade as he did so, indicated that the red man was dead.

Tyrane had no time to act, for the second brave was upon him. The warrior's blade drew blood from Tyrane's neck. He struggled with the wrist, which held the knife. Then the body went limp upon him.

Pushing the carcass to one side, clutching his blood soaked neck, Tyrane saw Santes retrieve his knife from the back of his second victim and wipe it on his chaps, just as he had done when telling the Marshall of how he killed the Sheriff in Sonora.

"Thanks Santes."

"It is all right Amigo, where the knife is concerned there is none can better Emanuel Santes."

He slid the weapon back inside the boot.

They observed below a line of horsemen galloping towards a small object. The object moved slightly and both men realised what was happening.

"That's the Marshall down there."

"Si Amigo," gleamed Santes.

Ojo came forward, leaving Clementine to watch the horses.

"What's happening?"

"They have buried him up to his bastard neck, now they will make sport with him I think."

"Where's Clementine?"

"Relax, she's tending the horses. Surely she can do that without assistance."

Tyrane, not content to leave the horses alone with Clementine slid down the incline. Then on scaling the opposite bank he beckoned her on, the riderless animals half slid half sat down the slope into the gulley.

"We should be here for a while, I advise getting some rest."

Tyrane, picketed the horses. Taking her by the elbow, Tyrane aided her up the slope to rejoin Santes and Ojo.

"My God, what's happening down there?"

"What's the set up Ojo?"

"They ride straight at him, then at! Look, they're charging again."

Nine Mexicans rode their horses towards the bobbing head of the Marshall The sand churned up all around, at the last possible moment they veered off a true course to either side leaving Zeb to choke.

After each charge, Amine sidled his horse alongside to taunt his victim.

The Marshall, trying to keep his eyes and mouth closed as the riders drew near, found it impossible to stop from swallowing dust.

"Have you anything to tell me gringo?"

Zeb could only cough a reply, his head began to spin and he could feel consciousness leaving him.

Amine rode to join the charge once more.

"How will it end, can't we help him?"

"It will end señorita, when the bastard is dead."

"How will they kill him Santes?"

"There are many ways Ojo. It is possible they will tie a length of rope around his neck. Then when they ride away, and the end of the rope is reached."

Santes paused.

"Snap!"

"Oh no," cried Clementine.

"His head it will come off his bastard body."

"Shut up Santes."

"On the other hand Amigo they may merely leave him to fry. I personally would favour this method with such a bastard."

"I suppose you've taken part in such goings on, eh Santes?"

"Si Amigo. From time to time I have had such dealings."

Clementine drew away from the Mexican.

"How can you sit there and calmly discuss such things. Aren't we going to help him?"

"Help him? he is a bastard."

"A bastard who knows the whereabouts of the gold, or had you forgotten that Santes?"

"There's nothing we can do. One shot and they'd probably kill him."

Salvador raised his hand for the riders to cease their charge. On one knee, he examined the Marshall, slapping the head about. Returning to the wagon he fetched a canteen of water. The sudden relief brought Zeb out of his delirium into a semi-conscious state. Licking his lips he attempted to wet his tongue before the water dried on his parched skin.

"Dig him up."

"But Salgo?"

"No buts, he will talk soon Amine, that is if there is anything to tell, which at this moment is in doubt."

"They're taking him out."

"Perhaps he's told them what they wanted to know,"

"I doubt it, Zeb's wise enough to know that as soon as he does that he's a dead man."

"What could he tell them?" demanded Ojo.

Tyrane answered Ojo's question, but looked directly at Santes as he did so.

"They usually kill their victims when they are finished, isn't that right Santes?

The only reason I can imagine for them keeping him alive is because he has something to tell them, isn't that right Santes?

Yet what can he tell them if they already have the gold, eh Santes?

Or do they?"

Tyrane snatched at the Mexicans throat, holding him hard against the rock. Santes eyes swung from side to side in their sockets as his mind raced to come up with an answer. Even as he spoke, he had no idea what his next word would be.

"Perhaps --- Senores --- He has --- But no --- That must be it Amigo. Don't you see, they can't have the gold yet. It must be buried back there, near to the place where you found me."

Santes thoughts hit on an explanation and he spat out the words as quickly as possible. Tyrane allowed his hold to slacken.

"Why would he leave it back there?"

"I do not know Amigo. Perhaps in the confusion the horses they stampeded. Now I think of it, I do not remember seeing the pack animals with the Marshall bastard when he was taken prisoner. Things happened so quickly, I had no time to think, my head it was aching." Santes, fingering the scar left by the piebalds hoof.

"They're lifting him out," beckoned Clementine.

The limp, unconscious figure was carried between the wagons.

"Well, he's alive, or they wouldn't have bothered digging him up. Though I'm still not satisfied with your story Santes."

"Seems plausible enough," said Ojo.

"Maybe, but the strong boxes would have been the first things Santes would have noticed, or missed."

Tyrane allowed the matter to drop for the time being. Not one bit did he like the company he kept, of Santes he had no doubts. Ojo, he was not sure where Ojo would stand should it come to a choice between them all getting out of this alive and Ojo getting the gold for himself. That left only the girl whom he could trust, should the necessity arise.

From the encampment came a shrill scream.

Amine, with a knife in the Marshall's left inner leg, forced the razor sharp blade to cut across the thigh.

"Stop, stop, I'll tell you. I know where the gold is. Just stop." pleaded Zeb.

His cries were heard yet not understood by those on the ridge. Amines teeth flashed as a gloating smile came across his evil face.

"So gringo, you have decided to talk."

"Take the knife out Amine," ordered Salvador.

Amine hesitated, then pulled the blade roughly from Zeb's leg. Zeb blacked out.

"Tend him, he must not die before he tells us where the gold is."

Gomez came scurrying towards the prostrate body to follow his leaders orders.

Ojo longed to know what Tyrane had in mind yet did not wish to appear to be awaiting a say so before acting. So he remained silent.

Santes watched on dispassionately.

The afternoon dragged on uneventful. Each man acted independently as he assessed the location they were in. From this present position on a rise surmounted by a huge rock, the encampment was below and to the front of them. Behind, the ground fell away and appeared to go on for some distance. The horses were in the gulley, amid an odd growth of Sagebrush. Apart from scattered rocks, this was the only ridge on the landscape. It did not appear to be a high rise when arrived at, but fell away sharply facing the Mexican camp.

Towards sunset there was a bustle of activity below. Tyrane watched intently as the Mexicans went about their chores. The horses were being saddled, not all however. The wagons were not being hitched.

Ex U.S. Marshall Zeb Pluckard was hoisted into the saddle, his arm in a sling, his left leg dragging heavily.

Chapter Eleven

Seek Gold

"Appears they're moving out,"

"Not all of them Ojo, but they're taking the Marshall,"

"Maybe they're going prospecting, what do you think Santes?"

Santes saw through the significance of the remark, yet he could not determine as to how much Tyrane suspected.

"It is as you say Amigos, the majority of them, they go somewhere. The rest, they remain behind with the wagons. I wonder why, eh?"

With his bad leg tied into the stirrup, Zeb clung to the piebalds mane. His right arm was completely useless.

Moving away from the wagons, Salvador and Amine rode on either side of their prisoner. Leaving ten men to guard the wagons they took the others with them on the hunt for the gold.

"They're coming in this direction,"

Santes ran down the incline towards the horses. Ojo followed Santes, who led the animals further along the gulley. Tyrane, snatching Clementine by the arm came at a run.

Santes soothed the horses as Tyrane drew his rifle from its scabbard and brought it to bear on the riders.

No one dared to breathe as the Mexicans rode first down, then up the other side of the gulley. Tyrane for an instant sighted the Marshall

"Whew, that was close,"

Ojo, wiped beads of sweat from his brow.

Santes knocked back his sombrero with the barrel of his pistol and breathed a sigh of relief. The Marshall's had not been the only face he recognised, he had also seen that of Amine

"Where are they going?" asked Clementine.

"I should have thought that was obvious, they're going after the gold. We'd best get moving."

"Hold it Ojo."

Tyrane watched Santes, who did not seem unduly worried that the Marshall was leading the gunrunners to the gold. Tyrane knew his hunch had been correct, in as much as it was Santes and not Zeb, who knew the whereabouts of the strong boxes.

The Mexican he knew would be eager to press on if there was the chance of losing the gold, yet he was unconcernedly watching for danger from the remaining gunrunners.

"What do you mean wait! We'd best get after them," said Ojo.

"It should take them a day to ride back to where the gold's hidden. That means two days before they get back, assuming of course that the gold's hidden somewhere near to where we found Santes,"

"They won't come back, once they have the gold they'll keep on riding."

Putting the final touches to his saddle, Ojo swung his body onto it ready to ride out.

"They won't leave without the guns Ojo, even with the gold, they can still sell the rifles to someone else for a good price. They'll return, what do you think Santes?"

Santes continued to watch the encampment.

"Si, they will return."

Leaving Clementine to watch the horses, Tyrane joined Santes. Ojo sat on his mount, unable to decide what to do.

Clementine saw the indecision on his face.

Ojo cursed at the dilemma he had put himself in. Knowing he stood little chance against the dozen or so Mexicans who rode with the Marshall, yet he believed them to be riding after the gold.

Using all his willpower, he climbed down from the saddle and passed the reins to Clementine.

By the time Ojo joined them, Santes and Tyrane had determined the positions of and strength of the guards on the wagons.

"Listen in you two, this is what I have in mind,"

Tyrane reasoned how under cover of darkness it was possible to overpower the guards and take control of the wagons.

"What the hell do we want with the wagons?"

"We don't want them Ojo. We're going to prepare a reception for them when they return."

"Si Amigo, I like that idea,"

"Well I don't,"

Neither Tyrane nor Santes paid Ojo any heed. Tyrane was pleased with the fact that Santes offered no objections. This further strengthened his suspicions concerning the Mexican. Yet he dared not force the matter, for fear of Santes acting hastily and betraying their position Tyrane told Clementine all she needed to know of the plan.

"You stay with the horses, at the first sign of trouble, you get the hell out of here."

Ojo too, pinpointed the sentries whilst the last daylight lingered.

With the animals securely tethered Clementine watched from her vantage-point as the three of them moved away into the darkness, to reappear minutes later moving in the direction of the wagons.

Tyrane lingered back with Ojo, allowing Santes to take the lead.

"Don't let Santes out of your sight tonight, if you can help it."

"Why?"

Santes turned at the noise, Tyrane waved him on.

"Quiet, just make sure that one of us has him in our sights at all times,"

Tyrane, quickened his pace to join Santes.

Ojo cursed inwardly at not being more involved in running things. He cursed the Marshall in his belief he had taken the gold, he cursed Tyrane for the way he kept putting him down, and he cursed Santes. For he did not know whether to believe the Mexicans story or not. He did not trust any of them.

The threesome huddled together watching the bright fire amid the trio of wagons.

"They are making a lot of noise for so few men Amigo."

"Probably been told to do so by Salvador before he left, just in the event they were being watched, which they were, if those two braves we came across are anything to go by."

"You mean there may be more of Apache watching,"

"More than likely Ojo, Victorio won't want to lose those guns."

Huge shadows cast by the movement of those in the vicinity of the fire were cast across the canvas wagon.

"They're sure as hell making enough noise,"

"Which is what we won't do Ojo. Use your knife or whatever comes to hand, but be quiet."

Tyrane, sure now that his eyes had become accustomed to the dark readied for the task ahead.

Santes removed the knife from his boot. Ojo caught the gleam of the blade. Santes stopped suddenly as the silhouette of a sombrero appeared from behind a rock. He moved quickly, before Tyrane could stop him. He positioned himself behind the rock, and waited.

The sombrero came into view again, its owner stepping from behind the rock before turning to retrace his steps.

As he disappeared, both Ojo and Tyrane heard a muffled cry.

Santes released his hold on his victim's mouth as he let the body slip from his grasp. Tyrane joined him in time to see him retrieve his knife.

As Ojo joined them, Santes wiped the blade against his chaps.

"That is how it is done Amigos, quiet no?"

Tyrane nodded, realising that he could not have a better man for the job in hand than Santes. .

With this guard disposed of, they had a much better view of the camp.

Some four men were moving around the fire, three more could be seen sleeping near the farthermost wagon to their left.

"I count seven of them, not including the guards," whispered Tyrane.

"I will take care of the guards Amigo."

Without awaiting confirmation of his intentions, Santes moved off into the night.

Tyrane was loathe to let the Mexican out of his sight, yet he had done just that.

"You wait here Ojo."

Leaving Ojo, Tyrane strode hurriedly back to where Clementine was tending the horses.

"Clem, Clem, it's me Tyrane."

"Over here,"

Clementines voice was shaky, she levelled the rifle with her waist.

"What's happening?"

"Take the horses one at a time and move them back along the gulley."

"How far, and why?"

"Never mind why," he snapped. "Just do it and make sure you secure them well."

He disappeared before she could ask another question.

Moving swiftly, yet with dexterity Tyrane rejoined Ojo.

"Where have you been?" Sweat now evident on his forehead.

"Just making sure Santes doesn't leave us during the night. Anything changed?"

"No,"

Ojo could not grasp why Santes should want to leave after being so much in favour of the present plan.

As some men moved away from the fires, others took their place. Somewhere out there in the night was Santes, doing the work he liked best mused Tyrane, killing. He did not relish being one of the guards.

Ojo, watching where Tyrane placed his body as he pulled himself towards the wagons tried to use the same ground as he inched himself forward.

Tyrane tested and cleared the ground before him, before allowing the weight of his body to come down Tyrane knew, as he eased himself nearer, that he must gain control of the encampment and this could only be achieved by the element of surprise.

The Mexican dialect became more coherent now they were much nearer.

"Can't make it all out, but it appears we got the gist of it right,"

"My Mexicans better Than yours. Zeb is taking them to fetch the gold, so what the hell are we doing here Tyrane?"

"You leave Ifn you've a mind to Ojo. I'm staying here, consider for a moment, Santes was out there with Zeb when the gold went missing. Yet he doesn't appear to want to go after them. I reckon he knows where the gold is and it must be safe or he would sure as hell have been the first to protest when we decided on this course of action."

Ojo was stunned.

"You saying that Santes knows the whereabouts of the gold and that the Marshall doesn't?"

"That's right, you catch on real quick, Ojo,"

"Then where has the Marshall taken the Mex.'s?"

"Damned if I know, only Santes has the answers to all the questions and he ain't saying. That's why I'm so sure they'll come back, and when they do, I aim to be ready for them. Meanwhile we can keep Santes under our noses and If he makes a slip we'll be ready for him."

Tyrane checked on the location of those around the wagons once more. Ojo was confused, things were happening too fast for him to keep tabs on the situation. He didn't like it one little bit.

"Thought you said no gun-play"

"Don't intend to use it, not unless I'm forced. Now come on, we don't have all of eternity,"

Santes slithered up behind the sentry and in one quick movement he arched his knife through the air, ripped open the man's throat, and caught the sagging body.

Lowering it to the ground, glancing towards the trio of wagons he could see no change as yet within the encampment. As he wiped the blade on his chaps he cursed under his breath, for he wanted to be sure that Tyrane had reached the wagons before making any move.

Santes re-traced his steps, keeping one eye on the wagons and the other on the ground in front of him. Quickly he scurried back to where he had left Tyrane and Ojo. Satisfied he could not be seen, Santes moved off in the direction of the ridge, and the horses.

Rounding the rock he felt the ground fall away and he slipped down the incline, then ran to the turn in the gulley where the woman would be tending the animals.

"Bastards!"

he cried, on discovering he was alone in the gulley.

Not delaying in trying to figure out where the horses were, he scrambled back up the embankment. Santes paused momentarily atop the ridge to view the wagons. All seemed the same, he stole off into the darkness.

One gunrunner lounged between the wagons puffing a cigarillo.

Tyrane moved along the side of the wagon. As the Mexican finished his smoke and turned to rejoin those at the fire, Tyrane moved swiftly.

Leaping up, he split the man's skull with the barrel of his pistol and caught the body as it fell.

Both Tyrane and Ojo stood expectantly behind the wagons watching. Most of the gunrunners had turned in for the night leaving only two at the fire and a third lounging against the canvassed wagon, which was more in the firelight than those they hid behind.

Tyrane nodded, indicating that the next to go should be the standing man and for Ojo to move towards the canvassed wagon. Tyrane, remaining with the two uncovered wagons stepped into view.

"howdy Amigo."

The Mexican dropped his cup. He stood motionless, in that instant he heard a voice from behind,

"Stand real still compadre."

Tyrane fanned his gun to cover those at the fire. They had seen Ojo first, and now froze as Tyrane's cool voice cut through the night air.

Santes strolled up to the guard,

"Si amigo, it is a quiet night."

Santes approached from the direction of the wagons.

"Si Amigo it is - !"

The guard stopped in mid sentence, sucking in long breaths as Santes shoved the barrel of his gun into the ribcage,

"Turn around, and make no stupid moves."

The guard laid his rifle on the ground and passed his pistol to his captor who stuffed it into his waistband.

The three men at the fire lay face down in the sand. Tyrane covered them whilst Ojo roused the others.

All were soon accounted for, and Ojo made a quick check on the wagons.

"I wonder how Santes is doing?"

As if in answer to his question, Santes appeared in the firelight preceded by his prisoner with arms stretched skyward.

"Where are the others?"

"Do not concern yourself about them Amigo, they will bother us no more. This one I kept alive for questioning."

Tyrane was taken by surprise by Santes entrance and allowed his attention to shift from the men on the ground.

One of the gunrunners leapt to his feet, kicking the exploding gun from Tyrane's hand, the others sprang into action.

Santes gun barked as he used the man before him as a shield. He let off six shots and three bodies fell to the ground. Ojo felled a further two as they lunged towards him.

Santes, whipping the spare pistol from his waistband, shot its owner in the back and kicked the groping body out of his way.

Tyrane struggled against his attacker, shoving the man from him onto the fire. The Mexican screamed as the hot coals scalded his back. He rolled over as the flames took hold on his shirt.

Ojo fanned the encampment with his pistol as the commotion died down as quickly as it had begun.

As all three caught their breath Santes thumbed fresh shells into the chambers of his empty gun.

Unexpectedly, before he could be stopped he emptied the replenished load into the bodies of the gunrunners who moved or even looked alive.

"They will trouble us no more."

The threesome stood alone amid the wagons. The flames licked into the darkness from the fire, revealing the glazed expression on a dead man's face. Prostrate bodies lay all around, a trickle of blood ran from one man's eye, another's shirt burned as it flapped in the wind. Tyrane rolled the body over, dousing the flames, before turning on Santes.

The Mexican faced up to him defiantly with his pistol replenished yet again, in his hand.

"Hold it both of you, perhaps it's better this way, they may have caused trouble, this way we can at least relax for the night,"

"That is correct Ojo, You begin to learn,, there is hope for you yet."

Tyrane, realising that nothing he said could alter the situation ignored Santes. However he noted that for the first time Ojo had agreed with the Mexican. He wondered what was going on in Ojo's mind.

"One of you go and fetch the woman and the horses. You go Ojo, you'll find her a ways back along the gulley, careful how you approach, she's moved position and she has a rifle."

In Ojo's absence Tyrane and Santes moved the bodies away from the fire, leaning them against a wagon.

As Tyrane propped up one of the Mexicans he felt a stickiness of blood in the back of one of those Santes dealt with earlier. Santes was nothing if not efficient, he pondered.

Clementine appeared leading the horses. The animals tethered, she picked up the pot replacing it on the fire. The smell of coffee soon engulfed that of gunpowder.

Each huddled around the fire avoiding the temptation of looking into the flames, yet at the same time evading one another's stares.

Clementine felt the tension building up between them, leaning against Tyrane's arm she asked,

"What happens now, do we wait here for the Mexicans to return?"

She hoped her question would give Tyrane the impetus he needed. There was a moment of silence.

When Tyrane spoke it was to tell the others what to do. There was no inference of suggestion in the tone of his voice as he laid out the following mornings procedure.

"Those shots will have been heard by every Apache for miles."

"They may put it down to the Mex.'s celebrating,"

"Perhaps Ojo" retorted Tyrane, with no conviction to his voice.

"In any event we must get some sleep, Clementine you take the watch for the rest of the night. You can lay up tomorrow, us three can get some shut eye that way."

Clementine acknowledged, by picking up a rifle and moving away from the light of the fire.

"Hey Lady,"

Clementine turned.

"Don't hesitate to shoot anything that moves out there."

Turning to Santes, Tyrane added,

"And if anyone moves about within the camp before morning, you shoot them as well."

She disappeared into the darkness.

"You reckon there's more Apache watching this site than those two we came across today?"

"Like as not Ojo even so, they can't do anything alone. They have to await the main party."

"In that event Amigo I would advise some sleep."

The night passed without incident.

Dawn broke, Tyrane awoke, donning his hat he moved towards the embers of the fire. It was safe to have a fire, he thought. In fact, it was safe to make as much noise as they liked, for if anyone was watching they would expect it.

Tyrane checked the two munitions wagons, calculating how much powder was available.

Ojo and Santes were up and about.

As he looked through the supplies wagon, Tyrane feasted his eyes on the strongbox.

Throwing it open he looked on mystified at the sand it contained. Running his fingers through the grains he was interrupted by Santes.

"Our supplies are low, we should replenish our needs from this wagon."

Santes too, saw the U.S. army box.

"What does it mean amigo?"

"Probably that there has been some double dealing going on here amongst the gunrunners."

Tyrane was knocked off balance as Santes clambered aboard for a look inside the box.

"Sand! This I do not understand."

"Victorio gave Gonsalves enough gold to buy rifles, what went on it the meantime we shall never know Santes,"

Santes, picking up the box hurled it from the wagon, the actions aroused Ojo's curiosity.

It was an hour after dawn when Tyrane called Clementine in from watch. Passing her a cup of scalding hot coffee, he clasped his hands around a cup himself whilst eyeing Santes and Ojo. Weighing up what must be running through both men's minds, wondering just how much they would tow the line.

Clementine trembled as the heat warmed her and the coffee burned her lips.

Santes figured on a way to get out of here with enough horses to carry the gold.

Ojo toyed with a stick in the sand. Contemplating on what Tyrane had said the night before about Santes and the gold, trying to fit all the pieces together.

"You see that ridge up there,"

Tyrane, broke the silence by indicating towards where the two Apache had been,

"You Santes, go up there and tell me if you can pick out targets accurately."

"What targets?"

"I'll indicate them to you when you get there. Just small mounds mind, but you must be able to see them from the ridge."

Santes, unsheathed his rifle and strolled away from the fire.

"Santes, when you come back, be ready to tell us where the gold is. You think about it whilst you're up there. When you come down be ready to talk, or don't come back."

Ojo stopped toying with his stick. Clementine looked towards Tyrane.

Santes, still with his back towards the wagons, listened, was about to protest, then changed his mind, remained silent and continued walking.

"You reckon he'll talk?"

"Don't worry Ojo, he'll talk, or die. Two onto one aren't the sort of odds Santes bucks."

The summit of the ridge was the only thing Santes saw, leaning forward, he took shorter steps up the steep incline.

'Was Tyrane bluffing or guessing,' he wondered.

The story about the Marshall and the gold was plausible enough, though not enough to risk Tyrane and Ojo pairing off against him.

Santes reached the summit. Tyrane moved from the enclosure of wagons indicating places for the Mexican to get a line on.

As Santes looked down the barrel of his rifle eyeing in each location he swung the barrel level with Tyrane's chest and rested his finger on the trigger.

'You are much hombre Senores, Santes may have need of you, now is not the time to kill you.'

More relaxed now, Santes levelled the rifle at each location, resigning himself to the fact that he may need to reveal the whereabouts of the gold.

Tyrane, satisfied the targets could be seen waved Santes down, swallowing nervously the Mexican began the descent.

Tyrane proceeded to explain how he wanted a charge of gunpowder buried at each place Santes had sighted, together with a bag of rounds.

"It is good Amigo, however we must be sparing with the gunpowder for it is not plentiful."

"How does any of this help the Marshall?"

"If he's still alive Clem then he'd best make the most of his chances during the confusion when this lot goes up, however the chances are slim,"

Santes felt each pair of eyes burning into him, yet remained unperturbed.

"Continue with the plan Amigo, it is good."

"We set the charges, wait for Salvador to return, then set them off from the ridge and get the hell out of here."

"Why do we wait for the gunrunners to return, if Santes here knows where the gold is?"

"Because Ojo, for one thing I say so, for another we don't know when we will run into them on the trail. Here, we can pick the time and place."

"It is too much to hope for amigo, but the Apache may return to their lodges when there are no guns for them,"

"Where's the gold, Santes?" demanded Tyrane.

He replied with a casual shrug of the shoulders.

"It is hidden near to where you found me the other day. Do not worry amigo, it will still be there when we return."

At each stash of powder and bullets a marker was left, a twig, a rock, not even that where it was deemed unnecessary.

With enough saddled horses to go around, and the sturdiest of the bunch picked to carry the gold later the remainder were tethered away from the wagons, visible to anyone approaching to give an appearance of normality.

Santes, returning to where each of the dead sentries lay, propped up the bodies and placed their rifles as if in use and made sure each man wore a hat.

In the encampment the bodies were leaned against wagon wheels. Two bodies laid as if sleeping with a sombrero over their faces, then the fire was built high.

Circling out of the encampment, riding wide Tyrane led the way towards the gully, which lay behind the high ridge.

From their vantage-point atop the ridge, all seemed right with the wagons.

"There may have been more than two Apache Tyrane."

"Maybe, but that's a risk we take. Which reminds me we must conceal the bodies."

Leaving Santes to keep watch, Tyrane slid down the embankment to rejoin Ojo who had the animals picketed.

"Help me move these two dead Apache Ojo."

No fire was lit.

Reckoning on it taking Gonsalves and his men a day to reach the place where Santes was found, Tyrane foresaw the Mexicans returning around sun up the following day.

For once the gold was not located, Salvador would drive his men hard, back to the munitions consignment.

The heat was intense.

Clementine rested up, donned a huge sombrero.

"It was of more use to me than its owner,"

Tyrane burst into laughter on seeing her beneath the big hat. Santes joined in, Clementine found herself unable to keep a straight face.

"Well, if I'm out of place in this hat, then you are equally silly in that coat, Tyrane I didn't think bullfighters and embroidery were your strong point."

Santes joined in the teasing.

"Si Amigo, I have been wondering about your coat. The stitching is very good, but not your style."

For a few short moments the danger of their situation was forgotten as each tried to contain their laughter.

"Riders coming."

The two sharp words from Ojo.

All was silent.

The three leapt to their feet, running up the incline to join Ojo pointing fervently towards movement in the distance.

"That is not Salvador Gonsalves, there are too many riders."

"Then who?"

"Apaches," spat both Tyrane and Ojo in unison.

Tyrane cursed at the turn of events.

"Now the trouble begins."

Salvador and his followers he had expected, not the mass of braves who were riding nearer.

"You two keep watch,"

Grabbing Clementine by the arm Tyrane pulled her down the slope. On reaching the bottom, racing towards the horses.

"Hurry, get everything together," Bellowed Tyrane, whilst throwing a saddle onto the nearest animal.

Quickly and effectively Tyrane continued saddling.

Clementine collected all the provisions nearer to the horses. Tyrane tightened and checked the girths and knots to ensure nothing would slip.

Roping all the animals together, with the four saddle horses on one cord, and the pack animal with the three bare-backed mounts and the animal carrying the ammunition on another.

"Stay here with the horses, don't let go of this rope whatever you do. They're picketed, but keep a tight hold just the same."

He picked up the three boxes of shells for the rifles, thrust the rope into her hand, and hurried up the embankment.

"What's happening?"

He gasped, whilst falling beside Ojo. Passing him two boxes of bullets, one to give to Santes.

"They're just sitting out there."

"Si Amigo, they have not advanced, they perhaps await a signal to say it is safe."

Apache were assembled a hundred yards or so from the wagons, they watched and waited debating the issue amongst themselves. The gunrunners camp some two hundred yards from the ridge, put approximately three hundred yards between themselves and the meandering braves.

With Ojo to his right and Santes now a similar distance to his left, Tyrane removed his bandanna Emptying the ammunition onto it he Set out the rounds in groups of six.

He was ready now. "Don't shoot until the wagons go up, then don't miss."

"Wait until the last moment Amigo, you will kill more that way."

"Remember, hit the stashes we buried on the far side of the wagons first, then when the Apache turn towards us, we can let loose,"

"That explains why you wanted so many explosives on this side of the wagons amigo!"

Ojo, leaned back and talked over Tyrane to the Mexican.

"You keep your head down Santes. We don't want you getting yourself killed, not before you take us to the gold least-ways"

'Bastards,' muttered Santes, placing the rifle butt into his shoulder.

Ojo, keeping a low profile changed positions. Scrambling below the crest of the ridge he moved nearer to Tyrane, where he could observe the Mexican as well.

Clementine clung to the rope tightly, more to steady herself she realised, than to hold the horses, which were well picketed. It was quiet, she could no longer hear any sound.

Tyrane raised his rifle, bringing it in line with the barrel of powder on the centre most wagon. Easing his finger around the trigger, he waited as the Apache still argued amongst themselves more cautious now with no sight of the braves left on watch.

Three of their number rode towards the wagons, veering to either side as they neared. Looking towards their leader they received the signal to move again.

This time they galloped through the encampment, whooping and letting out battle cries. Two of the three braves charged clear through camp. The third turned his pony to return, for as he brushed past one of the propped up bodies, it had fallen.

Tyrane felt the sweat in the palm of his hand as his finger curled around the trigger.

Ojo could feel the sweat running down his back.

Santes laughed as he saw the propped up body fall.

The brave leapt from his pony, which shied away from him. Moving cautiously, the brave approached another sombrero figure, the glazed eyes looked back at him as the body crumpled under his touch.

Racing around the wagons he pushed over more bodies. The other two braves circled the wagons, one leaping from horseback onto an open backed wagon.

Hurling a case onto the ground it smashed, revealing the dozen weapons it contained. The mounted brave swung low to pick up one of the rifles, holding it aloft he beckoned to the main war party.

The Apache rode forward, descending on the wagons, engulfing them. Warriors leapt from horseback onto each wagon, hurling the boxes to the ground in a frenzy.

The reins cut into Clementines hands, she held them so tight.

Santes viewed the spectacle before him dispassionately.

Ojo fidgeted, nervously shifting his weight from side to side. Keeping one eye on Santes.

Tyrane sucked in air, held it and slowly exhaled.

This he did several times as he awaited a clear view of the powder barrel on the wagon. Then it appeared, the target clearly in his sight.

He drew breath, eased it out again, and fired.

Chapter Twelve

Attack On Gun-runners

The cluster of rocks came into view before Zeb realised he had reached the place of the buried gold. The hairs on the back of his neck itched as he steered the piebald.

From the corner of his eye, Zeb saw Salvador slightly to his left and rear. Amine rode on his right hand side, every so often a prod from Amines gun indicating for a brisk pace to the kept up.

Zeb drew rein, Salvador and Amine came alongside.

"Where is the gold gringo, it had better be here,"

"I can't dismount with my hands the way they are, and with my feet tied,"

Forcing his blade between the horse's belly and the rope, Amine cut the leg loose.

The release from his bonds eased the pain in Zeb's leg momentarily before Amine sent him crashing to the ground.

Grasping the air for a hold, Zeb turned quickly to avoid landing on his mangled hand. His bad leg hit the ground heavily and he cracked his head, letting out a low gasp.

The weasel-faced little Gomez came running to check whether he was still conscious.

Zeb felt the last reserves of resistance leave his body as he was forced back to his feet. He knew also the dilemma he was in.

Once Amine could run his fingers through the coins, there would be no need to keep him alive. Death would come swiftly. Yet he had only made this journey to get respite from torment. Hoping somewhere along the trail, a chance of freedom would offer itself. None had come.

Raising his head in a last stand of defiance Zeb knew his delaying tactics had been to no avail. He stared Amine in the eye, teeth clenched, determined not to break.

As if he had expected such an action, Amine brought his mighty fist crashing down onto Zeb's temple. The force of the blow broke him.

"Where is the gold gringo?"

Salvador watched dispassionately whilst his second in command continued beating the prisoner.

Falling to his knees, Zeb pointed at the place he buried the gold. Weasel face Gomez released his hold, allowing the limp body to drop.

From his prostrate position, Zeb watched as sand was thrown in all directions from the place he had indicated.

Gonsalves eyed Zeb with suspicion as the men dug deeper, finding nothing.

"You are a foolish man gringo, to lie to Salvador Gonsalves,"

Gonsalves had been feeling quite smug with himself as his ridicule of Amine had gone so successfully. However, as the gold was not found, his logic in keeping the prisoner alive all this time was in doubt.

Zeb's mind raced as Gonsalves paced towards him. Santes he knew, must have the gold. Somehow he must convince Gonalves of this.

What story Santes must have told Tyrane and the others he did not know. However he must have been convincing, for them to have believed him.

Suddenly that faint hope of rescue was gone.

Zeb's chain of thought was interrupted as Salvador slapped him about the face, bringing him to consciousness.

"Tell me, where is the gold gringo, or you will die."

Salvador whipped out his pistol, shoving the barrel against Zeb's head. The cold touch of steel brought him around.

"I don't know. I must have come to the wrong place, or shown you the wrong place to dig. I've been ill, of course, that's it. You can't expect me to remember one sand dune from another, not in my condition."

"I expect you to tell me the whereabouts of the gold, gringo, or you will die right now!"

Amine ordered the men to spread out in search.

"Every rock must be inspected, no stone left unturned," he commanded, cursing at the men as they found nothing.

"You bastard, gringo!" snapped Salvador.

At that moment Zeb remembered Santes and how he always referred to him as a bastard whenever he spoke.

Zeb hunched his body, completely exhausted, devoid of resistance any longer, all hope of survival gone.

Once again Salvador placed his pistol to Zeb's head, once again Zeb felt the coldness of steel.

"We have wasted enough time with you gringo. We shall waste no more."

The pistol cocked, Zeb believed it would be the last sound he ever hear.

"No Salgo, do not kill him. This you promised I could do. I have a much better idea,"

"Then do it quickly Amine for we must return to the wagons, pronto."

Gomez would be glad when this prisoner died, he had meant nothing but extra work since he arrived.

Zeb began twitching and writhing. His body ached immensely. The shirt ripped from his body, Zeb was staked out in the sand under the hot sun.

Salvador rode to the fore of his men galloping at full stretch back to the wagons.

Amine remained, unable to tear himself away from the spectacle of Zeb before him.

The blood rushed to Zeb's head, he became delirious.

Amine towered over the staked out body of the Marshall.

"Tell me gringo, where is the gold."

There was no reply, only an innate murmuring.

Amine mounted up and rode fast to rejoin Salvador.

Somewhere in his subconscious, Zeb heard Amines question. Had he known the whereabouts of the gold he knew he would have told, for then perhaps he would receive a bullet, anything was preferable to this.

Amine dug spur into his mount, racing past the stragglers of the party.

Salvador rode ashen faced. He must get back to the wagons as quickly as possible - :

Chapter Thirteen

Explosive

The crack of the rifle was consumed by the explosion, which followed. The wagon splattered into fragments, hurling debris in all directions. Bodies were blasted, thrown by the terrified ponies.

Shifting the position of his rifle, Tyrane brought his aim to bear .

The weapon leapt in his hands once again.

The Apache were engulfed in a spray of bullets as a second charge exploded.

Clementine soothed the horses as they pulled on their lines.

Pandemonium reigned in the encampment. Ponies galloped bucking and kicking, sending their riders earthward.

Santes squeezed on the trigger, a gunpowder cache exploded amid those who had held back. The ponies reared, racing off into the desert.

Searching eyes scanned all around for the source of the shots.

They were seen as Santes could no longer contain his urge to participate. His small head bobbed above the crest of the ridge to set off another explosion.

The Apache moved back to re-group.

A line of charges drove them towards the last wagon as Tyrane, Ojo and Santes let rip at their targets.

The powder and cartridges exploded to create a wall of flaying bullets and smoke, leaving the Apache with only one way to go as they moved through the charred wagons and the twisted, deformed rifles laying everywhere.

Tyrane aimed once again. The canvassed wagon exploded, not as forcefully as the others, but lethal amid such a concentrated target.

The threesome on the summit, reloaded, waiting for the right moment.

Waiting for as long as he dared, Ojo fired. The explosion that followed stopped the running braves in their tracks. Santes fired.

A pony was cast clear of the ground, crushing the rider as it landed. Another pony thrashed wildly, its hooves flaying out, half its side burned and smouldering. It fell to the ground, kicked, then lay still.

Firing was rapid, explosion followed explosion. The area became littered with bodies, still the Apache broke through.

Tyrane's rifle cracked dropping the first brave to run through the barrage of pre-set charges. The victim fell to his knees, clutching at his stomach, blood oozing through his fingers.

A brave charged through on his pony. Santes rifle leapt once again throwing the warrior to the sand.

Ojo's rifle leapt in his hands, frantically he replenished the empty chambers. Sweat ran down his back.

A warrior charged up the embankment, Santes rifle scored, the brave was blasted skyward clutching his head.

Blasting shots into the frantically racing Apache, Tyrane signalled for Santes and Ojo to close in on him. Both men dodged below the rim sniping shots as they ran. Ojo stumbled twisting his knee, still he managed to fall alongside Tyrane.

The Apache gained ground during the movement whilst they had only one rifleman to contend with.

Arrows flashed, some going high overhead others bouncing off the rim where they lay. Some landing in the gully behind. Firing, reloading in sequence, the toll was proving too much for the Apache.

Tyrane fired, Santes fired, Ojo reloaded.

Ojo fired, Tyrane fired, Santes reloaded.

The Apache fell back, their dwindling numbers disappearing amid the dust and confusion.

Ojo, at Tyrane's instruction hobbled down the slope on his bad knee towards the horses. Clementine held the reins as he loosened each of the animals from their picket.

Santes shoved his rifle barrel over the rim, without taking aim he fired the six shots, pulling it back to replenish the load.

Clementine mounted, Ojo tied the pack animals lead to his saddle horn and slipped her the reins. Hurrying back along the gully he beckoned to Tyrane. Tyrane signalled for Santes to mount up, the Mexican ignored him, continuing to shoot. Tyrane raced down the embankment, the impetus of the steep run took him past the limping Ojo.

Santes let off another chamber load. Then he raced down into the gully for his mount, the animal was already running as he swung into the saddle.

Digging spur into his mount, Tyrane raced after him, followed by Clementine. The pack horses, most of them running free of any load ranged alongside. Tyrane accepted one of the lines from Clementine.

"Ride lady, ride for your life,"

Glancing back Tyrane saw the first Apache reach the summit of the ridge. Then they were out of sight as the bends in the gully lost them from view.

Santes was a clear leader as they raced at full speed, swerving one bend, then another. Clementine followed,

Tyrane and Ojo now brought up the rear with the pack animals.

Holding back to allow the woman to take the lead, Santes saw the black clouds rise over the disappearing ridge as the wagons burned.

At full stretch they raced, for an hour before easing back on the animals steadying them to a gait. There was no pursuit at the moment, nor would there be, Santes knew not until the Apache had regrouped.

Tyrane joined Santes.

"We must ride wide of the trail the gunrunners took, else we may meet up with them. Can you get us to the gold by another route?"

Only momentarily did Santes hesitate.

"Si Amigo, we must make a detour, that is all."

The Mexican eased his mount to the right, the others followed in close contention. The horses picked up speed as Santes increased the pace again. This he did periodically, a spell at a gallop, followed by an easy canter.

The Apache counted their dead. Many lives were lost. Others were mortally wounded. Geronobbi, sure that he had recognised one of the attackers as the man who had killed his sons felt a deep hatred for the tall stranger.

In the end he had his way and things were made in readiness for the hunt ahead.

=====================

Screening his eyes against the glare of the sun, Captain Houston viewed the vultures as they took flight.

This was not the raw officer who had left FT Thomas. Having panicked when first fired upon, he now had a cold expressionless face which betrayed none of his emotions.

The once so immaculate officer was no more. His epaulettes now tarnished, the dust-ridden uniform and lack of personal hygiene put him on a parallel with the wily O'Mallahan.

Scratching the growth on his face, he queried

"What do you make of it Sergeant?"

There were six of them, discounting O'Mallahan and Conrad, Houston could call upon only three troopers, Faheratty, Mornington and Cargen, all of whom were cast in the same mould as O'Mallahan.

The veteran sergeant scratched his whiskers as he too, pondered on the possibilities Someone or something was either dying or dead out there. Judging by the proximity of the birds it was probably the latter.

Houston edged his mount ahead. O'Mallahan indicated for the others to follow.

Those of the platoon not slain by the Apache had died from their wounds during flight, then latterly from lack of treatment for injuries. It was only recently O'Mallahan had found water, but it was too late to help those who had died. Their strength drained, they had fallen prey to the hardships imposed by the desert of Sierra Madre.

O'Mallahan noted the change in Houston.

Houston resolved his one burning ambition now was to find the gold at all costs. During their later skirmishes with the Apache, he had proven his first action under enemy fire to be all wrong.

"There's been a lot of activity here cap'n, and not so long ago neither," said O'Mallahan.

The area before them was ransacked, rocks were overturned, there were signs of digging.

The flapping of the vultures wings personified the silence all around.

"Over here cap'n," pointed Corporal Conrad, gaping down at the prostrate body before him.

O'Mallahan came bounding, slashing the bonds, which held the body in position.

"How long has he been dead, sergeant?"

O'Mallahan reckoned on it not having been too long, maybe a few hours to a day.

"Depends on how far gone he was before they tied him down. Judging by his hand I'd say he was in a bad way long before he died, but it's hard to say. Once the buzzards start on a man he don't last long."

"They were obviously looking for something, sir. What it was, or whether they found it we can't tell."

Two men took the watch whilst a shallow grave was dug. Whilst the men were digging, O'Mallahan nosed around.

"I found some tracks over yonder, cap'n," reported the sergeant.

"It weren't no Indians who did this to him, cap'n No sir, those horses were shod."

"Then we must follow the tracks sergeant, it's the first sign we've found other than Apaches. Maybe we're getting close."

"You mean the gold consignment. You think they was looking for it here, cap'n?"

"Perhaps sergeant, we'll find the answer at the end of those tracks."

Sergeant O'Mallahan swallowed heavily.

"How much longer do you propose to stay out here, sir?"

"Don't question my orders sergeant, we accomplish the mission, we owe that to those who died."

O'Mallahan stooped over the body, rummaging through the pockets for some identification, he found none, only a U.S. Marshall badge in the shirt pocket.

The body was lowered and covered.

O'Mallahan picked up the trail left by the shod horses. They would follow these tracks. Then he would have to consider the Captain's orders and propose returning to the Fort with the men.

=====================

Tyrane pulled to a halt to give the horses respite.

Ojo watched the back trail, ever impatient, not wishing to delay any longer than was necessary.

Santes wet the horses' nostrils, using the water sparingly.

After a short rest they moved on, Santes again taking the lead. Clementine rode alongside Tyrane who led one string of two pack animals. Ojo led the other two.

=====================

The night passed slowly for Geronobbi.

The first rays of daylight spread across the sky.

"Death to the White Eyes!" He shrieked .

Holding his Lance aloft with one hand whilst running his fingers along his broken nose with the other.

Caught up in the frenzy of the moment he charged his pony towards the high ridge the riflemen had occupied.

=====================

Amine sighted the camp. The suddenness with which he stopped his horse, caused those immediately behind to snatch up the reins.

The sun was not yet at its peak, though Amine was grateful for the shade offered by his sombrero. Salvador rode through those blocking his path.

"Look!" answered Amine

"The wagons are no more Salgo. They are gone,"

Pointing to the devastation below. birds took flight as the sounds of movement reached them.

Only black patches remained where the two munition wagons had stood.

"There are many places where explosions have taken place,"

The buzzards came to rest on rocks in the distance. They watched patiently as the riders advanced.

Moving amongst the carnage, the gunrunners came across the corpses of those they had left behind. Searching and rummaging through the wreckage strewn battlefield, remains of weapons were found, the barrels of the rifles were bent and mutilated out of shape by the blasts, which had carried them in every direction. The dead ponies were stripped of flesh by carrion. Only the framework of the remains of the wagons could be seen, a wheel here, a hub there.

The bodies of the dead, partly gored by the buzzards, who had first descended on the easier pickings of the ponies before the leaner offering of human sacrifice, were in evidence.

Salvador became insane with rage at the stupidity of the Apache in attacking the wagons.

"Stupedos, they were warned. I told them if they attacked, that the guns would be destroyed."

"Si Salgo, this you told them. But it does not help us now,"

Scouts rode around the perimeter of the camp, looking for what, they did not know. They had no desire to invoke Salgo's rage upon themselves. So when their leader told them to look, they looked.

Others searched amongst the debris of broken wagon frames, mangled rifles and arrows left by the Apache.

Salvador issued orders to his men not fully realising he did so. It came naturally, and served to suppress the innate hatred building up within himself.

A rifle boomed, all eyes turned to the direction of the shot. Gomez waved from where he surveyed them from his elevated position.

The tracks of the shod horses were distinguishable amongst those of the Indian ponies. Furthermore it seemed the battle had ended here on the ridge. For here amid the tracks in the gully were the last signs of battle, lances, arrows and hoof-prints.

"What does it mean, Salgo?"

Gomez was elated that he had found the tracks and that Salvador was paying so much attention to them.

"We will follow the tracks, they may lead us to the gold."

No sooner had he mentioned the word, gold! Than a buzz of excitement and dissatisfaction came over the men. It was Gomez, given courage by his find, who asked the question,

"The gold, the box of gold, where is it Salgo?"

Salvador stammered.

"We follow the tracks. Come Amigos, we ride,"

Cried Amine, leading the way along the gully.

Given his second wind, Salvador readily followed.

"Ride quickly, we must find the persons who have stolen our gold. If the Apache find them first, we must be close behind."

The lust for gold drove all other thoughts from their minds. Salvador breathed heavily as he rode at the rear, grateful for the impatience of Amine whom he realised must have foreseen the danger both of them were in concerning the whereabouts of the strong box.

That it was Amine who had acted so speedily, irked Salvador.

==================

The horses were rested, still no fire was lit. The respite from riding was welcome whilst it lasted, by all, that is except Ojo.

"Why do we stop here, when we could ride until nightfall?"

"It is wise to keep the animals fresh Amigo. Do not worry, we will have the gold, it is safe."

"All this trouble, we had it in the first place before you stole it."

"Si Amigo,"

Santes, moved nearer so only Ojo could hear him.

"However there were four of us then, I do not count the woman. Now the bastard Marshall is gone and there are only three. You understand me Amigo. Perhaps we can make it only two."

Santes waited while his words and their implication sank into Ojo's brain.

"Maybe, but not now. We may need his gun."

"Si Amigo I understand, later perhaps?"

====================

Sergeant O'Mallahan rode ahead of what was left of the platoon.

There was little difficulty in following the fresh tracks. Houston did not wish to have anything overlooked or disturbed. For this reason he wanted the Sgt. at point.

The sun had turned red, and in a short time would be disappearing from view, only the last lingering wisps of daylight remained.

O'Mallahan gave the signal to dismount. Houston came forward, the battleground lay before them.

"Appears the Apache have had themselves a war cap'n, and there were wagons here."

Faheratty, indicated a broken wagon wheel some distance from a large, burnt patch. Corporal Conrad joined them, then Mornington, leaving Cargen to tend the horses.

"Looks like we keep just missing out on something Captain,"

said O'Mallahan, as Houston surveyed the spectacle for himself. Houston waved Cargen forward with the horses whilst he and the others investigated.

Houston saw how the battle had been carried to the high ridge, and consequently moved the men in that direction. He crested the ridge, pistol at the ready, and looked into the gully on the other side.

"Search thoroughly here, it may give us the clue we need."

O'Mallahan ventured along the gully after the tracks. Faheratty and Corporal Conrad examined the area directly behind the ridge.

Houston looked from behind the rock on the crest of the ridge towards the scene of the battle below. Judging from the amount of empty shells, he was convinced the same scene had been viewed by others before him.

"Over here Captain,"

"Two dead Apaches cap'n, been dead for some time. Only reason they ain't picked clean to the bone is because of all this brush. They couldn't be got at. Been here days judging by the smell,"

O'Mallahan returned, emerging into view as Cargen sidled the horses down the embankment.

"I don't know what to make if it cap'n"

"Explain yourself sergeant."

"Well, it's like this. First we were following shod horses. Now these here tracks they're shod all right but the fact of the matter is there are unshod Indian pony tracks mixed in.

Houston considered.

"Can you distinguish the tracks sergeant?"

"Yes-sir no two are alike. the tracks we followed here are the last ones made and they go along this gully."

Houston hoped for some indication that the gold had been present. He contemplated making a more thorough search of the debris, however darkness had closed in on them and he was anxious to proceed. Things were happening and he did not want to waste any time by delaying here until morning.

"Can you follow the tracks at night sergeant?"

"I'll let you know when I can't, cap'n,".

===================

"We are nearly there Amigos,"

The night had come and gone and the sun was beginning to rise.

Ojo sped past Tyrane and Clementine, trailing the spare horses with him.

"That one has gold fever,"

Tyrane nodded in agreement.

The Mexican vanished from view momentarily due to the undulating terrain, and Tyrane did not trust Santes unless he could see him.

Tyrane urged his mount forward.

Ojo recognised this as being where Santes had been found some days earlier. He did not recognise anything in particular, it was the mass of hoof prints which alerted him. His suspicion was proven correct as the rock formation came into vision.

Santes dismounted, turning to speak. Ojo dug spur into his mount and left Santes to choke on the dust. Wheeling his horse around he sought for sign of where the gold might be.

"Bastard. You will not find it unless I show you,"

Tyrane felt a shiver run down his spine as he rode over the unmarked spot of the Marshall's grave.

Once amid the rocks they waited for Santes to reveal the resting place of the gold.

The Mexican found the boulder he sought and proceeded pacing, looking back continually to ensure his course was true. The boulders he had used as markers were just as he remembered them. Stopping, he checked his bearings then dismissed the markers from his mind.

Tyrane kept his concentration on the Mexican.

Santes clawed at the sand.

Ojo came at a run, not waiting for Santes to move out of the way he pulled at the sand.

"Bastard," shrieked the Mexican.

"You've got me all mixed up Santes. I'm not the bastard, it was the Marshall who was the bastard,"

Ojo, fervently moved sand. Sweat ran from his temple as each handful brought him nearer to the gold.

Santes dropped alongside clawing until his fingernails scratched a box.

Clementine kept the horses huddled together while Tyrane climbed a rock to check the back-trail His eyes scanned each horizon,

Before long the boxes took shape and were hauled from the ground.

Ojo, still discontent broke a box open running his fingers through the coins.

Managing without a fire a cold meal was eaten.

With the minimum of delay each box was secured to a horse and all was in readiness.

"Come over here Santes,"

Santes, picking up his rifle climbed the rock alongside Tyrane. Ojo checked the knots holding the bullion boxes. Clementine held the reins of the saddle horses.

"Think Santes, do you know of a way out of here that may be unknown to the Apache, because if you do then we can sure use it."

Santes was silent. The only sound omitting was as he scratched his diminutive head.

"Remember Santes the gunrunners will be coming too."

As if this last remark had given him an idea the Mexicans eyes lit up.

"Si Amigo, I know of a way,"

Replacing the sombrero to his head he indicated towards a range some half days ride away.

"There is a pass Amigo. It goes through the canyons. However, it has been a long time since I travelled this way and with the hazards and storms of late our way may be blocked."

Ojo ventured over in time to hear the tail end of the conversation. He was not pleased with the idea.

"I don't trust him. Remember what happened the last time he led us to safety. We had to go after him and the gold. We've only just got it back."

No one spoke, as each considered his own thoughts. Tyrane broke the silence.

"Lead the way Santes we're wasting time, but remember this. We shall be right behind you and watching for any sign of trickery. Make one wrong move and I may not be, nor may not want to be, fast enough to stop Ojo from killing you."

Santes flashed his teeth in an evil grin.

"All this talk of killing. It is silly. There was only one who had to die and surely the bastard is dead by now. Let us ride, we may be there by nightfall."

It had been over a day since the encounter with the Apache.

=====================

They had only been tracking for a couple of hours when O'Mallahan realised they were headed back to the place where the body had been found.

Houston took the opportunity to gain any ground possible, the adrenaline in him ran high. He pushed the animals hard.

The sun was ablaze.

Conrad trailed to the rear, still as yet UN-acclimatised to the heat he began to feel the strain and any relief from the sun rays was welcome. Even the dust churned up by those ahead of him.

==================

The scouts rode far afield hoping for a sighting of the enemy before the tracks led them to their prey.

Geronobbi led the main group. The fever of revenge burned deep within the old man. It was no longer a matter of the guns, he wanted vengeance against the tall stranger who had slain his sons.

An evil slit crossed his face realising the gold would further slow down his prey.

==================

Clementine swooned in the saddle, but for Tyrane's quick reaction to catch her she would have fallen.

"Hold up Santes, we'd best stop for a while. The horses could use the rest."

Ojo rode up from the rear in no mood to stop.

"If she can't keep up then she gets left behind. You didn't tell us about no woman when we started on this trip, so she's your problem not ours. Let her go back to her Apache friends."

Inching his gun out of its holster. Tyrane, lowering Clementine to the ground, stared coldly at Ojo as he finished speaking. A rage building up within him.

"Hold it Amigos,"

His pistol drawn Santes bore down on both of them.

"I agree with Ojo, if the woman cannot keep up then she should be left behind. However, on this occasion you are correct Amigo,"

Indicated the Mexican, swinging his pistol from Ojo to Tyrane.

"The horses they could use a rest. They are lathering badly. If we stop now it will be dark as we reach the mouth of the canyon."

A moment of indecision passed, then Santes flicked his gun back into its holster. The tension relaxed, and each dismounted.

Tyrane bathed Clementines forehead. Santes joined them after using his hat to wet the horses' mouths. Placing the wet sombrero on his head, its coldness gave a relieving feeling.

"Why didn't you make off with the gold Santes. You had the drop on us. It would have been easy for you to have killed us?"

Clementine switched her attention from Tyrane to Santes.

"I am not stupid Amigo. The Apache are gaining on us and I may have need of your gun. I cannot be sure the way ahead through the pass is clear, alone I would stand no chance if it was not."

"You could have gotten away if you had left the gold,"
Santes laughed.

"For me to leave the gold Señorita, would be like asking Tyrane to leave you. We are inseparable."

The sun dropped further as the quartet moved on again. After the break, each felt somewhat fresher and the horses moved easier.

=================

With barely an hour of daylight left the small compliment of Troopers rode into a dip overshadowed by a cluster of rocks. Sergeant O'Mallahan gave his horse its head as it crested the opposite embankment. The rest of the party did likewise and as they emerged they found that their assumption had been correct.

The rocks looked the same, the only difference being the number of prints all around the vicinity.

"There's a hole been dug over here sir,"

The size of the hole could have meant a lot of things, all Houston could think of were the boxes of bullion This hole fitted the bill.

"We've gained ground, cap'n,"

"The tracks lead off that-away"

"Explain yourself, sergeant,"

Houston, transfixed his gaze from the hole.

"Well there again appears to be Indian pony prints and shod prints."

Houston reckoning that if one party was following another then he had only to sight one of them.

==================

No sooner had the troopers departed than Amine arrived, riding at the head of the party. He gaped in astonishment on seeing the movement in the distance, too far away to be distinguishable.

He breathed heavily in relief that he had not ridden into view minutes earlier.

"They must have stopped for a considerable time for us to have caught up with them,"

Amine wiped sweat from his forehead and gingerly urged his mount. They emerged from the dip to find the cluster of rocks before them.

The realisation of where he was took Amine by surprise, for he was more concerned with the outgoing riders.

"Over here quickly, someone has been here,"

Gomez pointed profusely at the hole.

Salvador raced past Amine, in his haste to get to the hole first. He stood over the cavity, a rage building up inside him as he concluded the gold must have been buried here all the time.

Amine came alongside.

"What have you found?"

Two men, Miguel and Ramone scraped the ground for some sign and came up with a gold coin.

"It was here. Do you realise it was here all the time,"

The sand sifted through Miguels fingers as he tried in vain to find more coins from the strongbox Ojo had smashed open.

Salvador was only too well aware of the situation, as he profaned at the side of the hole. The men looked towards their leader for some sign or word of what they should do. Their leader issued orders quickly, as he paced in the direction the departing riders had taken.

The sun was almost gone, its shape shone red above.

"The horses, they are shod Salgo,"

"We must think compadres. Things are happening of which we know nothing. We will camp here until we are sure which course of action should be taken."

"Si, Salgo is correct," concluded Amine

A low fire was built in the dip. The wind howled bitterly as the night engulfed them.

Deciding it would be wise to await until daylight before going any farther, Salvador settled for the night. No sooner had he pulled the sombrero over his eyes than he was asleep.

Amine touched the handle of his pistol, Salvador was making many mistakes. Perhaps it was time for a new leader. The men were certainly dissatisfied enough to condone such an action on his part.

However, the fact that the gringo's body was no longer here worried him. Who would have taken the trouble to bury him, certainly none such as himself. This matter he had to consider, and thinking was not Amines strong point. The night cry of a coyote drifted in from afar.

==================

The moon shone its silvery light as Santes reached the first outcropping of rocks. He reined in his mount, turning to his followers as they caught up on to him.

"We can travel no farther tonight Amigos. It is a dangerous journey and it has been many years since I was last here. We should camp, and move out at first light."

No one was against the suggestion, for they had ridden hard to reach their goal and the dead weight of the gold was taxing the pack animals.

Tyrane quizzed Santes, as they rubbed the animals down.

"It will take us all day tomorrow, maybe longer to get through the canyon amigo. Then we must attempt the pass I know of. However, you can be sure it will be dangerous. It is a long time since I come here and there have been many storms of late. Any one of them could have caused a landslide, blocking our route. For this reason I am against going any farther in the dark."

"As if we don't have enough to worry about."

"Shut up Ojo, we're here and that's that. So it's tough luck if there's a blockage ahead. Moaning won't alter the situation."

"We should have a lookout Amigos,"

"Too bloody true, I remember what happened the last time you led us somewhere for the night,"

"You bastard, I will kill you."

"I'll do any killing around here. You take the first watch Ojo.

Santes you get some sleep."

Sliding the rifle from its scabbard, Ojo took his place amongst the outlying rocks.

Tyrane joined Ojo on watch.

"Let Santes sleep through the night. You do the first half, I'll do the remainder."

"Why,"

"Do you want to let Santes take a tour of guard, with us asleep?"

"I don't think he'll try anything with the Apache so close behind. On the other hand, like you, I'll sleep better knowing one of us is awake."

The Marshall entered Clementines thoughts.

"What do you suppose happened to him Tyrane? Do you think he's still alive?"

"I don't know lady. I don't all the answers. He's the only one who knows,"

Tyrane, jerked a thumb to indicate the snoozing Mexican.

"There are many ways a man can die in this country. He could die of thirst, or in a gunfight, or be bushwhacked, or his horse could throw him. A man afoot in this country is as good as dead. That's why the Apache put such a high value on their ponies.

Of course none of these things happened to the Marshall. I expect Salvador Gonsalves killed him when he couldn't show where the gold was."

Clementine liked Tyrane, but what did she really know about him. By his own admission he was a bounty hunter, a man who hunted others for money. By Phoenix standards she would not even have talked to him, but that did not seem to matter now. However, would he want in his life a woman who had lived with the Apache She nestled nearer to him. The comfort of his body was the only feeling of hope she had known since her parents were killed

A Coyote howled somewhere in the distance.

The silhouette of Ojo stood out in the moonlight with his arms crossed, clutching his rifle, gazing out across the desert.

==================

Geronobbi heard the cry of the Coyote. He brought his warriors to a halt as the lonesome sound reached his ears. It was safer to rest for now, he thought. For tomorrow he was sure to catch up with those who fled before him.

==================

"Best bed down for the night cap'n I'm afraid of losing the tracks.

Keep missing, then picking them up again,"

Houston was loathe to allow any more time than necessary to pass before having to stop. However he eventually agreed.

A Coyote howled somewhere far away, its lonely cry carrying on the night wind.

Chapter Fourteen

The Canyon

Daylight spread its first rays of light across the skies as the fingertips of dawn broke the morning.

Tyrane came in from watch to awaken the others. Santes looked quizzically at him, wanting to know why he had not been awakened for his stint on guard, yet not really caring, for he felt more rested than he had done for days.

The surroundings looked different in the light of morning. Their path led through an outcropping of rocks to a pass. The canyon appeared to go on for as far as the eye could see and its walls grew steadily in height as it deepened.

Santes assured them it was not a cul-de-sac, that he knew of a path at the canyon end which twisted through the rocky mesa's to bring them to safety.

"It will be a long journey, for there is much travelling to be done to take us clear of the cliffs. This is always assuming that we do not have to contend with rock falls, avalanches, or other such hazards, which may have blocked our path since last I was here in this accursed place."

"You sure know all the hell holes in this country Santes,"

According to Santes it was a day's ride through the canyon. Tyrane, glad to get a hot meal inside him, refrained from burdening the animals for as long as possible. He hoped to reach the canyon end by nightfall.

An hour after first light the bullion was loaded. The way ahead needed no direction, however Tyrane was pleased when Santes took the lead.

They led their mounts afoot over the treacherous terrain. The canyon entrance was some twenty feet in width, though Santes recalled from memory that in places it would widen to over a hundred feet, and in others narrow so as only one horse at a time could pass.

Ojo rested easier knowing that Santes was up front where he could see him. On the few occasions when the Mexican had ridden at the rear could feel those beady little eyes boring into his back.

Clementine was already mounted, Santes still led his horse afoot, Tyrane, collecting his own mount by the reins swung up into the saddle.

The movement of boarding the animal saved his life. As he landed in the saddle an arrow struck the horse in the neck where he had been standing. The roan dropped as dead weight under him as he kicked his foot free of the stirrup.

Ojo slid from his mount and lead the pack animals within the confines of the canyon. Another arrow hit rock above his head.

Santes, leaving his painted pony within the confines of the canyon, strode past Ojo who struggled to picket the horses.

"Clem, get back to tend the horses and tell Ojo to get out here."

Santes gave cover to Tyrane, who was struggling to retrieve his rifle from its scabbard.

"How many of them are there?"

"We were fortunate compadre,"

Santes pointed his rifle towards the approaching riders.

"These two, they were too impatient. If they had waited, the outcome it may have been different amigo."

To Tyrane the familiar figure of Broken Nose was singularly recognisable at the lead of the approaching riders.

The Apache slid from their ponies, knowing now where the White-Eyes were, they themselves became invisible blending into the background, using cover from the outlying rocks to inch forward.

Ojo having emptied his rifle scoring not a single hit, thumbed fresh rounds into the chamber.

Santes, more patient lined up his rifle on where he believed an Apache to be hiding. His finger rested firmly on the trigger, squeezed ever so gently as the brave leapt from one boulder to the next. The victim's body jerked as it disappeared from view.

"This blasted sun in my eyes doesn't help none," cursed Ojo.

A bullet struck rock near Ojo's head as he hurled his curse at the sun. The spraying fragments bit into his skin, the crack of the shot followed.

Tyrane and Santes turned to one another before continuing to lay down fire. Each in his own mind knew the significance of the Apache having rifles. The one shot discharged by the Apache worried Tyrane.

Ojo threw himself deeper behind cover clawing at his

Tyrane signalled to cease fire.

A moment of silence followed the instruction, superseded by two rifle cracks.

"Well it could be worse Senores Let us hope that they are the only two with rifles."

Ojo fired again, nursing his face. An arrow pinged off the rock next to him.

The Apache gained ground during the short lull in the shooting. Ojo merely shoved the barrel of his rifle from behind a rock fanning the immediate area, blindly pulling on the trigger in fear of being hit.

There was a spell, it lasted for only a few minutes, when it could have gone either way, as the Apache moved incessantly forward. The rifles were emptied, more shells pushed into the empty chambers at speed.

Geronobbi incensed his braves forward with screams of hysteria as he fired his rifle again, he used his shots sparingly as his ammunition waned.

Moving around as they did, dragging the injured or dead out of view whenever possible it was impossible to tell what toll had been taken.

Tyrane reckoned on having dropped two bodies, Ojo said three. However, Tyrane looked at him with cynical doubt. Santes gave his tally as four, this Tyrane believed.

"Keep them pinned down Santes."

Tyrane, crawled away into the canyon, pulling his body along the ground far enough back-a ways so as to be safe. Getting to his feet he ran towards the horses.

Clementine levelled her rifle as he approached.

Santes, showing complete disregard continued blasting away with his rifle. Keeping one eye on Ojo he waited his opportunity to reload. Between them they kept bullets going towards the Apache. Ojo however, was preoccupied by why Tyrane had left. He allowed his concentration to wane as he continually looked back into the canyon and towards the gold.

Tyrane breathed heavily, as he singled out the pack animal carrying the ammunition. Touching his hands on the last few sticks of dynamite, he hesitated only fleetingly before passing them over and sorting out the boxes of shells.

"Does it look bad Tyrane. They're not going to break through are they?"

Tyrane did not reply to her question but turned with the cartridges, running back towards the shooting.

Tyrane tossed a box of shells to the others, then his own rifle began to spit flame alongside theirs.

Santes aimed at a rock, the bullet bounced off and forward, a slight muffled sound told him to make his tally five.

The sun climbed, the shadows cast by the canyon helped.

"This is all your fault Santes,"

Ojo felt sweat running down his back again.

"If we hadn't stopped last night, we'd be well into the canyon by now. Not struggling at the entrance."

The rifle in Tyrane's hands leapt. A brave stood erect, clutching at his stomach. He staggered onward, his lance raised, Santes put another bullet into him, this time through the neck.

The velocity of the Apache onslaught diminished.

Ojo continued to curse the chain of events, which led up to the present predicament.

"The Apache must have stopped last night just as we did. They can't track in the dark and must have been real close at dawn to have come upon us so early. In any event stop whining Ojo, if you must think about something then think about getting out of here to spend your share of the gold."

Ojo seethed in anger at Tyrane To add further salt to his wounds he saw the wide grin from under the Mexicans sombrero. Thumbing more shells into the rifle he took out his venom on the Apache. Growing more and more irritated and more careless about concealment he cursedly thumbed more shells as the trigger clicked on an empty chamber. His mind was a jumble of hate, rage and desperation.

After all, was it not he who financed this undertaking. Why should he take orders and snide remarks.

=================

The incidents of the previous day appeared to be forgotten, thought Salvador, as he rode amongst his men.

Amine blazed the trail up front.

None mentioned how stupid it had been to miss finding the gold at the first search. This was not due to the fact they had forgotten, merely that no one wished to broach the subject for fear of invoking Salvador's anger. Knowing of their leader's hairline temper none wished to die.

They had moved out at first light.

Salvador not sure of what was happening, decided to depart quickly lest his men should question him on matters he did not comprehend.

There were many things he did not understand. First there had been the gringo who was now dead. Then the Apache had arrived unexpectedly. Next the wagons were blown up, but by whom? And who had fought the Apache on the high ridge overlooking the encampment and wagons?

Someone else, he deduced, must be here in Sierra Madre.

It was not inconceivable the Apache had asked others to bring them rifles, perhaps these other people had the gold? Furthermore, where was the body of the dead gringo? It was not at the cluster of rocks near where the gold should have been. The Apache would not bury him, nor would gunrunners such as himself.

All these things Salvador needed time to consider before catching up with those he trailed. He slowed his horse a little more, the others followed suit not realising they did so.

==================

Clementine fired alongside Tyrane and Santes. Ojo now lay with an arrow in his shoulder.

The wound was not serious, other than to deprive them of his firepower. The Apache moved forward, growing bolder, until the battle entered a crisis point.

Ojo, unable to shoot properly, attempted to reload. The arrow in his shoulder was broken off at the shaft. The fear he had experienced when the arrow struck him now gave way to a pungent odour of cold sweat. His hands shook, as he fumbled shells into the rifle.

Arrows whizzed past striking the cliff face. Tyrane caught a momentary glimpse of a chieftain's headband, then it was gone. He emptied his rifle around where he thought Broken Nose to be hiding, however could not be sure if he had hit the old chieftain.

=====================

They sat still astride their mounts as the echo of gunfire came to their ears. Houston strained to confirm that which he believed.

"Sounds like a stand up battle to me cap'n,"

The silence was punctuated only by the low murmur of rifle shots. Houston snatched on the reins.

"I agree corporal. Then let's go, move out at the double,"

Sergeant O'Mallahan saw the eager gleam of expectancy in the captain's face as his horse gained momentum.

"No gun-play Captain', not until we're sure what we're getting into."

Houston did not acknowledge O'Mallahan's advise as he urged his animal on faster whilst the others fell in behind. The shots became more distinctive.

Fear of detection passed into oblivion in the heat of the moment. They rounded a knoll, entered a basin, and crested a ridge as the adrenaline ran high in Houston's bloodstream.

The pace fell to a gait as the cliffs towered before them. Houston dismounting, signalled for the others to do likewise and lead their mounts afoot.

Peering through outcroppings of rocks the exchange of fire was evident. The Apache, hidden from those they fought, were plainly visible to the Troopers at their rear.

"Whoever it is they must have been holding them at bay for some time judging by the caution the Apache are showing,"

"Look sergeant!"

Houston pointed fervently towards the mouth of the canyon.

"That's a woman out there and at least two men, they're being forced back into the canyon."

"It is that, cap'n, it is a woman."

Faheratty and Cargen watched for any reaction from the sergeant as Houston told them his plan. Although the captain was officially in command they more willingly accepted matters when O'Mallahan gave his nod of approval.

==================

Ojo's fingers ached as he pressed shells into his empty pistol. The wound in his shoulder was temporarily forgotten in the excitement as they moved backwards into the canyon. With the motion, the dried blood on the wound cracked, open He felt the wetness about his shoulder as he staggered backwards and fell whilst attempting to find cover.

Tyrane, fired his pistol from the hip.

Santes could not believe his ears as the sound came to them.

Conrad's cheeks puffed as the notes rang forth.

"A bugle!"

Clementine was further into the canyon, Ojo joined her behind a boulder. Looking back, giving covering fire, he saw Tyrane and Santes backing their way into the canyon – out in the distance he saw a thin line of blue clad horsemen sweeping towards them, then he too, heard the notes of boots and saddles.

Houston rode at the head brandishing his sabre. The melodious sound echoed into the canyon.

Geronobbi too, heard the sound of the bugle. The Apache turning to face this new danger were caught without cover as the rocks which had proved so effective in providing protection from those at the mouth of the canyon were abandoned against this new foe.

Whilst fighting off the soldiers, the Apache revealed themselves to those at the canyon entrance. Again and again Tyrane's gun leapt in his hand as he ventured forward once more with Santes at his side.

The Troopers were amid the Apache. Houston took a mighty swipe with his sabre parting a fleeing brave with his life as the gleaming blade sank into flesh and bone.

Santes sniped at stray braves as they fled towards their ponies.

Tyrane took steady aim at the old chief he knew as Broken Nose. The bullet hit against rock, only inches from the old warrior's face as he ran. He turned to return the shot, but as his rifle clicked repeatedly on empty chambers he hurled the weapon to the ground as he fled.

Tyrane raced after him, firing repeatedly from the hip as Geronobbi ran towards a brave who led a spare pony. The bullets struck all around the old chieftain as he darted from rock to rock. Finally he clutched at the pony's mane as he raced alongside. One sweeping movement and he was laying across its back, urging it out across the desert.

The shooting ended as Santes emptied his pistol into a struggling brave.

Reloading his weapon, Santes proceeded to pump lead into the prostrate Apache bodies in the immediate vicinity.

"What does he think he's doing?" demanded Houston.

"I'll see to him cap'n,"

O'Mallahan stopping just short of the Mexican.

Santes bared his teeth, the barrel of his pistol was aimed at the sergeant's midriff.

"You would not be thinking of such foolishness as to try to stop me would you, gringo?"

O'Mallahan slowly and deliberately pulled his own weapon, pointing it at the head of an already dead Apache he pulled on the trigger. The gun leapt as the bullet spat.

"Well that's what the Captain had in mind, that I should stop you. However, on consideration I think I'll join you."

"You are a wise man Senores"

Tyrane approached the Captain.

"They have to do it, the Apache are treacherous. You must be new out here not to know that!"

Houston hesitated, the remarks rang true. Yet the many skirmishes between the platoon and the Apache between Fort Thomas and here would, he was sure, have made up for any lacking in experience on his part.

Before he could protest, a brave leapt to his feet lunging towards O'Mallahan with a knife. The sergeant half turned, taking the impact of the blade in his ribcage. The odour came to his nostrils as he gazed momentarily into hating eyes. The two men fell struggling, the Apache turning the blade as he rolled.

Santes took aim, his finger curled around the trigger as the weapon was steadied by his other hand. The struggling figure atop of O'Mallahan went limp as the gun leapt. Santes rolled the torso from the sergeant and the knife came out, held fast in the dead man's hand.

O'Mallahan blacked out.

Faheratty fanned the area whilst Santes checked on the sergeant's condition. Blood gushed from the pierced skull of the dead Apache lying alongside, mingling with long, matted hair it dripped onto the yellow sands.

Tyrane examined O'Mallahan's wound. He did not have to tell the old veteran the severity of the cut as their eyes met.

Geronobbi re-grouped his warriors at a safe distance. He knew he must kill the slayer of his sons, or die in the attempt.

The braves watched the skirmish as the blue coat was carried into the canyon. To attack now would be suicidal with their diminished numbers, especially as the White-Eyes had increased their numbers. Geronobbi relaxed his body, expecting to have a long wait.

Santes, with Faheratty kept watch from the mouth of the canyon. Clementine tended to the sergeant's wound, dressing it as best she could.

Tyrane was suddenly aware he had not seen Ojo since the cavalry's arrival.

Venturing deeper into the pass, Private Cargen stopped when he spied the horses. Examining the boxes he gauged their weight. The realisation of what he had discovered struck him, lighting up his face. Turning to report back to the Captain, he looked aghast into the barrel of Ojo's gun.

"Now just what do you think your going to do soldier boy?"

Cargens mouth opened, but no sound omitted.

Ojo squeezed on the trigger. The bullet smashed into Carmen's nose into his skull. The Trooper was dead before his body hit the ground. A horse kicked at the corpse as the echo rang throughout the canyon.

As one man, the party turned in the direction of the shot. Tyrane was first on the scene.

Ojo levelled his gun at the Captain as he approached.

Chapter Fifteen

Gold Found

Salvador Gonsalves reigned in his mount.

"We will make camp here."

The grumbles of the men were passed along.

Amine believed that now was not the right time to become the new leader of the men.

Too much was happening that he did not understand.

"Si, Salgo is correct. We should rest."

==================

"Captain."

Gasped Mornington.

"The gold, the gold is here."

His eyes then fell upon the body of Cargen.

Ojo firmed his finger around the trigger of his pistol.

Santes eyed the gold.

Houston gaped at the bloodied body on the ground.

Conrad shifted his feet.

Whether the movement by Conrad was an innocent gesture, or otherwise. Tyrane acted instinctively. In one motion his gun was in his hand, the loud click of the cocking mechanism being the only sound within the canyon walls.

"No sudden moves,"

"What is our the gold to do with you amigos?"

Sweat ran from Conrad's pores as Tyrane's gun pressed close to his chin.

"That's U.S. Army Gold," said Houston gaining his equilibrium.

"It's the payroll for the men at Fort Thomas. The convoy delivering the gold was ambushed, I was sent with a platoon of men to recover it."

Tyrane dwelt on the Captain's explanation for several seconds.

"What happened to the rest of your platoon?"

"Wiped out by the Apache,"

Contemplating on what to do to avoid further bloodshed Tyrane re-holstered his gun. Ojo eyed him quizzically, yet still retained his weapon at the ready. A feeling of release came over Conrad as the gun was removed from his chin.

Tyrane had no desire to fight the U.S. Army, especially as they had just saved his life. Equally he had no intention of surrendering the gold. Time was needed to think.

"I asked you already Captain, if you were new out here. You didn't answer."

"He must be amigo,"

"We fought for this gold soldier. We risked our lives many times. So do not expect us to give it up, however, now is not the time to discuss the matter of ownership."

"Si, Tyrane is correct."

Houston turned. Before him stood Mornington beside him stood the Mexican, the barrel of the Mexicans pistol pressed against the trooper's eardrum.

Tyrane looked quizzically at Santes.

"Do not worry Amigo. The woman, she watches for the Apache."

Houston appraised the situation. Mornington with a pistol pressed against his head, O'Mallahan critically injured, the corporal petrified, Cargen dead, himself and Mornington only a hair's breadth away from a bullet. O'Mallahan seemed to be the only one not covered. He recalled how quickly the apparent leader of this band hand brought his gun into play.

The seconds slipped slowly past, nobody moved. No sound, only silence.

"I agree – this is neither the time nor the place. For the moment we both have a common enemy,"

"How long have you been on the trail Captain?" Asked Tyrane.

Ojo eased his gun back into leather as Tyrane and the Captain moved towards the injured O'Mallahan.

Santes removed the muzzle of his pistol from the trooper's ear. Mornington gulped nervously, letting out a long sigh.

"For some weeks, we were getting nowhere, until a few days ago we found a body."

Tyrane looked apprehensively into Houston's face.

"Could you identify the body Captain?"

"Not especially, we saw the buzzards, so investigated. He wasn't a young man and he was in a bad way before he died. We took this from his body."

Tyrane accepted the U.S. Marshall badge the Captain had removed from Zeb's shirt pocket.

Santes eyes sank deep into his head as he watched Tyrane take the Silver Star.

"A big man, with black hair?" asked Tyrane.

"That's him, did you know him? We buried him as best we could. The sergeant said not to mark the grave."

Tyrane considered solemnly as the Captain continued his tale.

"We followed the tracks from where we found the body, to the scene of a battle."

Houston chose to omit various details of the pursuit.

"Finally we heard your shots and here we are."

Tyrane permitted no one to interrupt until he had all the details missing from the Captain's story.

"Like you said Captain, this is neither the time nor the place to decide on the ownership of the gold. The men who killed the Marshall were Mexican gunrunners, they're likely trailing us this very minute.

"We took the gold from the Apache, it is our gold now compadre"

Tyrane cast a cold glare towards Santes.

"We won't go into that now, in any event what happened was we exploded the ammunition wagons that's where you say you found the wagon debris. Hence we have both the Apache and the gunrunners to contend with."

"I see," considered Houston.

"Furthermore, I don't know how many Apache we have left to contend with but I killed the chief's two sons, so he won't let up until one of us is dead,"

"Now however, we must ride into the canyon for safety amigos."

Santes was eager to change the subject from that of the Marshall's death.

Ojo swayed, he crumpled earthward unconscious.

Santes took up watch, sending Clementine to tend the wounded. There was a lot of exchanges of information and filling in of detail whilst a fire was lit and water boiled.

Faheratty, still on guard with Santes, looked back towards the fire repeatedly.

"You say Cargen is dead?"

"Do not trouble yourself with them, problems have been resolved for the moment. Concentrate your attentions out there to our front ."

Houston wished to know what a woman was doing here. Tyrane explained everything as the knife in the fire turned red. He declined to inform the Captain of how he recruited his men.

Clementine made ready with hot water and strips of blanket as the blade in the fire turned white.

Conrad and Mornington held Ojo in a sitting position. Tyrane lifted the knife from the fire. Clementine looked away.

Holding the remaining shaft of the arrow, Tyrane inserted the blade alongside Ojo struggled to break free as the two troopers strived to hold him steady.

Inserting the blade into Ojo's flesh Tyrane twisted the arrowhead loose. The shaft with its pointed end emerged bringing no flesh with it. Ojo's back arched as the knife was turned, however the arrow was out. Clementine proceeded to bathe and bandage the wound. Santes returned.

"It is all right Amigos, the soldier, he watches for danger."

He answered to Tyrane's unasked question.

Mornington moved towards the canyon entrance to join Faheratty.

Tyrane looked upwards, the sun had shifted position.

"Captain, I'm in favour of moving as far into the canyon as possible."

Houston equally had no desire to remain in the present position.

Tyrane, removed his saddle from his dead horse.

Ojo was able to ride unaided.

The sergeant was in a bad way, he was tied into the saddle.

Houston gave last minute instruction to the two troopers on watch.

"Give us about a one hour start. Then get the hell out of here. It shouldn't take you long to catch us up, not with us laden down with the gold and the two wounded."

"Yes-sir,"

replied Faheratty and Mornington simultaneously.

The enlarged party moved deeper into the canyon.

Santes rode up front leading a pack animal. What ammunition was left he had transferred onto this mount.

Immediately behind him rode Clementine.

Next came Ojo and the sergeant.

Then Tyrane and Conrad leading the two horses carrying the gold.

Houston brought up the rear.

Tyrane did not share the Captain's concern, reckoning on there being little chance of the Apache getting past the entrance to the canyon whilst it was guarded The sporadic fire by the two troopers re-affirmed this.

Where the canyon widened outcroppings of Gorse struggled to grow. In other places it narrowed, the horses having to be taken through one at a time.

Faheratty and Mornington continued to fire shots, leaving a longer pause between each as the hours drifted slowly by.

Just before midnight, the hoof beats of the two racing trooper's horses could be heard echoing down the canyon. Houston became erect in the saddle, straining to look back for a sighting of the two men.

Minutes passed before Mornington raced alongside the Captain, Faheratty remained at the rear.

"What's it like back there?"

"Quiet, they didn't bother us none. We fired shots so as to let them know we was there Captain."

Slipping the lead ropes to Mornington, Tyrane and the Captain rode forward to join Santes.

Clementine strained her eyes to see where the canyon walls ended and the sky began, but was unable to distinguish.

A narrowing in the path was reached.

"We stop here for the night," said Tyrane.

"If we have trouble, the narrow Pass will be easier to defend."

Houston nodded his agreement.

Soon flames flickered against the walls, sparks rising high as the dry twigs crackled.

The moon, half obscured peeped into view.

"Isn't it quiet Tyrane. It's moments like this that make me realise why my folks wanted to come west. Just look at the moon, isn't it beautiful?"

Tyrane fixed his vision on the white ball overhead. He had never really considered the moon as a thing of beauty, merely as a guide to use to follow a trail.

"Yes it is, and when we get out of here things will be different. You may have your doubts now, but this can be a wonderful country."

The fire reflected its glow into Clementines eyes.

"In the meantime lady, you get some sleep. Who knows what's ahead of us tomorrow?"

Clementine curled into her blanket, a warm comforting feeling swept over her, the like of which she had not experienced since leaving Phoenix.

Tyrane and Mornington took the last watch. The back-trail was simplicity itself to observe, with little or no night noises, all rested easily.

The horses were readied at daybreak and the deeper descent into the canyon continued.

Houston rode with Santes.

Ojo's shoulder was on the mend.

The sun flashed its golden light overhead as the animals weaved their way from one side to the other of the canyon floor. Surmounting rock piles and avoiding formations, they skirted obstacles, always pushing forward.

One moment the sun beat down upon them, the next it would disappear and all would be cloaked in darkness as the walls cast their great shadows.

They discovered a natural rock formation, which was so shaded as to form a basin. The rains from some long ago storm or perhaps the condensation of the rocks as the bitter night wind blew after the scorching days, had gathered here. The water was clear and tranquil. Outcroppings of sparse grass grew in tufts nearby, the animals chewed on the meagre offering grateful for the nourishment it provided.

Sergeant O'Mallahan grew worse, his wound having opened under the incessant movement of travel. His injury unlike Ojo's was severe, the blood oozing from it was thick and constant.

Clementine cleansed and re-bandaged the wound during the short respite. Tyrane conversed with the Captain concerning O'Mallahan's condition.

"He's in a bad way. I don't believe he can last much longer, not if we keep moving as we're doing."

"I know Tyrane, but if we stop we shall be at the mercy of our pursuers,"

Houston paused.

"I don't have to tell you this, but this gold is important Tyrane. It's needed to pay wages, buy supplies, and fresh bloodstock, but most of all it's required to finance new outposts. The territory is getting too big and crowded for the few scattered Forts to handle. The danger is, we could have another badlands on our hands if things are left undone for too long. Then the territory would be thrown open to the Apache and all the riff raff lawlessness attracts, without this gold, law and order could cease to function in Arizona. Can you understand that Tyrane? So if I must balance one man's life, or even all our lives to ensure the gold gets through, then that's how it must be."

Ojo was listening in.

"That's as it might be to you soldier boys, but you don't have any say on how we run our lives. I don't belong to the army, so don't go giving me any orders. And I shouldn't worry none about the gold getting through, it'll get through all right, but not to build any Fort. I didn't risk my skin and scalp against the Apache just so you blue-bellies could come along to relieve me of my share."

The suddenness of the interruption caused Houston to pivot on his heel to face Ojo.

"You will answer to a charge of murder when we get back to the Fort!"

Santes listened from below the rim of his sombrero, his snatched siesta disturbed by the raised voices.

"You are all very stupid, the first problem is to get out of here. Then we can determine who shall receive the prize."

The moment passed, uneasiness in one another's company increased. More evidence of the split came as they rode out, in separate groups. The Troopers riding in pairs up ahead, Ojo continually whispering to Santes whilst bringing up the rear.

Taking a long bend veering to the right, Tyrane saw the troopers first then the obstacle blocking their path. Before them stood a rockslide. How long it had been there was impossible to tell. A week or a year, it made no difference. The fact remained, the way ahead was blocked.

Scrambling afoot to its peak, Tyrane surveyed the canyon beyond.

"Not much farther to go as far as I can see, looks like there's a trail ahead, does that sound right to you Santes?"

"Si Amigo, the canyon it ends soon. We must follow the trail and hope the storms and the passing of time have not destroyed our chance of escape."

"Peers like it already has," moaned Ojo.

Faheratty dug spur into his mount, charging at the blockage at full gallop. His mount started well, but soon lost its momentum as the stones moved under hoof causing a struggling ungainly backward descent. The impasse stood before them made up of rocks boulders and rubble, mainly rubble.

Tyrane dismounted to lead his horse forward, urging it onward as the rubble moved. The animal slid back two paces for every three forward.

With its forelegs hoofing for a hold Santes and Faheratty rushed to push the animal from the rear, falling over themselves in their haste to mount the blockage. The horse bellowed, scraping its belly on stone as it scrambled over the top disappearing from view, sliding down the other side it struggled for a hold from the cavalcade of movement under hoof.

Tyrane, tying his rope to the saddle horn, returned to the atop tossing the other end towards Mornington

"Get off, the horse will have enough trouble getting over without having to carry you as extra weight."

Mornington cast a look towards Houston, who nodded his consent.

The rope secured to his own saddle horn, Mornington led his mount up the stack. Tyrane walked his horse forward keeping the rope taut. Santes joined by Conrad and Faheratty pushed from behind. The animal disappeared over the crest amid a panic of bellows and snorts.

"Get the gold unloaded," cried Tyrane.

"Carry it over by hand."

The operation moved slowly as first another horse was sent over, then the two boxes of gold were hauled up. The troopers strained for a foothold, their hands preoccupied with the heavy boxes. Santes stood legs astride, on either side of the summit receiving the bullion, sliding the boxes down the other side to Ojo's eager hands. Hours passed as the horses and gold were safely transferred.

O'Mallahan was aided across, steadied by Faheratty.

The supplies came over last, Santes stood atop hauling them across with Conrad.

The Mexicans eyes widened.

"Apache,"

He screamed, leaping to safety, crashing down the embankment with the supplies as an arrow flew overhead.

The cries of the Apache echoed down the canyon as they fervently rushed forward.

A horse reared and took flight.

Mornington fell on his face attempting to stop the fleeing animal.

Scrambling back up the rubble.

Houston emptied his pistol as the Apache came forward.

A brave staggered backwards, taking his nearest companion with him crashing down the stack.

Santes, his sombrero pushed back, gained his feet and moved up to give support.

The Apache melted from sight,

Tyrane fell alongside, sniping off shots. The Braves retreated out of sight, protected by the turn in the canyon.

Bringing the horses under control, Faheratty quickly reloaded the bullion, assisted by Ojo.

Tyrane sidled down the stack indicting for Houston to join him.

O'Mallahan groaned heavily, the wheezing from his injury exaggerated by his chest's rise and fall.

"We could hold them here captain, it offers such a good defence."

"You surely don't suggest we should stay and fight them?"

Houston lapsed back to indecision.

"I don't know, I just don't know."

Sporadic arrows flew overhead.

Clementine tended to O'Mallahan's needs.

"If we make a run for it, we could be caught out in the open."

"I know Tyrane, the path ahead offers little cover."

O'Mallahan listened as the two men dwelt on their predicament.

Casting his eyes in the direction they must take he saw where the canyon ended and melted back into desert, the rocks around offered little protection.

"If we run, we shall be slowed by the gold and…."

Tyrane, nodded a glance towards the sergeant.

O'Mallahan pulled himself to his feet, ambling towards the impasse, loading his rifle as he moved. The weapon in one hand, he clutched his ribcage with the other as he scaled the heap to join Santes and Faheratty. Houston came at a run on seeing the sergeant fire then reload.

"Just had to see Ifn I could do it cap'n."

"Why? What do you mean?"

O'Mallahan glanced towards Tyrane, who looked earth-ward ignoring the sergeant's stare.

"I can keep them busy here whilst you and the others make a break for it cap'n"

"Nonsense, I won't hear of it."

"You must cap'n You've shaped up all right up until now, so don't spoil it. It makes sense. If we run I wouldn't make it, and those Apaches can wait out there forever if they've a mind to."

"Even so I!"

"Remember the gold cap'n, the gold is vital, you said so yourself."

Houston thought on the subject for several minutes.

Ojo, whilst listening to the conversation, made no one aware of the fact that he did so. Merely calculated in his mind that with one less Blue-coat the gold would be easier to keep later.

"I'm never going to make it cap'n, get going,"

O'Mallahan, clutched his side.

Houston had no idea of what he should say to his sub-ordinate.

"I shall make sure that Major Beresford learns of what you did, sergeant."

Santes emptied his pistol along the canyon and scrambled down not mincing his words as he did so.

"The man is going to die, he knows this. Should he stay then we have a chance, for the way ahead is treacherous and it would be impossible with Apache on our trail if we cannot ride swiftly."

The stark realisation of the situation hit Houston as he concluded he must act now.

"Best be moving captain, or we'll be stuck here for the night. If there was any other way, or I thought the sergeant here would pull through then I'd be against the idea."

"Reluctantly I must agree with you Tyrane."

Leaving O'Mallahan and Houston on the blockade Tyrane moved towards the horses, sifting through his supplies he located the last sticks of dynamite. Hesitantly, He left two sticks in his bedroll and took the others to the sergeant.

The others were mounted, all animals were at the ready.

"I heard what was said about the wounded giving cover whilst the others escape," Said Ojo.

"But if you think that maybe two wounded men would give twice as much covering fire then you can forget it Tyrane. Where the gold goes, I go."

Tyrane felt a hatred rising up inside of him. Pushing Ojo aside he powered past taking the explosives to the sergeant.

"I only agree to this -"

Houston ceased talking as Tyrane arrived.

"What are you going to do with them?"

Tyrane laid the dynamite beside the sergeant,

"Thought you could use them."

"Obliged,"

"Look I know I didn't always act like a commanding officer OMallahan."

"You was green cap'n You came through all right in the end."

"Maybe so, but I made life difficult for you, I'm sorry. We should have stopped at Fort Huachuca. The men would still be alive now if I had."

Tyrane grabbed Houston by the shoulder, pulling him towards the horses.

"Damn you, I wasn't finished."

"No but we may all be if you don't get a move on. If we're going to gain any advantage in the sergeant staying, then we must leave now. He knows how you feel, he's a soldier."

O'Mallahan checked everything was within easy reach, the rifle, a couple of boxes of shells, the dynamite, his pistol, and the makings.

Sniping off a shot he began to roll himself a cigarette.

Houston looked back once more as they moved out.

O'Mallahan exhaled the smoke, the relief to his aching chest was indescribable. Rolling several more smokes he laid them alongside the cartridges. He sniped another shot off again.

O'Mallahan kept track of the disappearing party as they moved farther and farther away from him, to become a blur. Placing the red end to the next smoke, he sniped another shot.

An arrow whistled back in return.

"Best make sure I don't put a stick of dynamite in my fool mouth and light it," He mused, cursing as he fumbled to reload the rifle.

Firing the rifle was easy, only a problem when it needed re-loading. It barked, its echo repeated time and time again until it became an indistinguishable din. The pain grew more intense, fervently he lit another smoke.

The Apache ventured forward, growing more daring as only the single rifle crack returned fire upon them.

Geronobbi galvanised his braves.

O'Mallahan fired repeatedly, stopping only to reload. He broke open another box of shells.

The pistol as yet lay unused, as did the dynamite.

A warrior leapt, the rifle cracked. The brave was sent backwards onto a sharp rock, which punctured his back. He screamed before ceasing to struggle.

O'Mallahan touched his wound, the dressing was wet, and as he removed his fingers they were red at the tips.

Cursing his braves onward, Geronobbi drove them at the landslide.

O'Mallahan emptied the rifle at them.

A brave fell clasping his kneecap, his endearing scream was echoed through the canyon as blood gushed through his fingers.

O'Mallahan twisted his body attempting to undo his braces. His face contorted in agony as he succeeded. Binding them around the sticks of dynamite he reached for the flint, but it was dislodged, lost somewhere amid the rubble.

The cigarette in his mouth grew shorter, he sniped another shot as the braves clambered up the stack. The stub burned his lips and he spat it out. The rifle clicked on an empty chamber, he hurled it after the smoking stub.

Snatching up his pistol, O'Mallahan knew he had only six shots left, there would be no time to reload.

A warrior towered above him, tomahawk raised. Two holes appeared in the braves chest as he fell forward. The third shot rebounded off the canyon causing a ricochet to land amongst the Indian ponies.

The fourth shot punctured a braves cheek, he fell as it exited behind his ear.

"Come and get it you heathen," shrieked O'Mallahan.

There was a moment of silence, a brief respite from battle when O'Mallahan put the muzzle of the pistol to the dynamite.

With no more shots coming their way the Apache charged in force, shrieking as they struggled up the incline to the prostrate figure atop.

Geronobbi raised his lance to drive it into the sergeant's heart.

Their eyes met, O'Mallahan saw the crooked bend to the warrior's nose. In unison Geronobbi released his lance, and O'Mallahan pulled back the trigger.

The blast, which consumed them, blew bodies and rubble apart, causing a further subsidence in the narrow pass. The small stones hurled for hundreds of feet clattering as they landed.

Others fell from the towering walls to take their place.

Gigantic boulders fell, crushing bodies underneath.

The Apache ponies tore loose from their moorings fleeing back along the canyon the way they had come.

Tyrane turned in the saddle as the explosion shook all around them. He watched the great cloud of dust arise over the pass as the blast echoed.

Houston looked back with Conrad.

"I wonder what happened back there,"

"I don't believe we shall be troubled by the Apache any more ."

Chapter Sixteen

The Adobe

The blast of the explosion echoed throughout the canyon. Salvador and his men drew rein as the noise vibrated in their ears.

"Aleeee" cried Gomez,

"the world it is ending, we must leave this place."

"Stupedos,"

cursed Amine, urging his mount forward.

"We must investigate, think of the gold compadres."

Amine dug spur into his mount, going forward opening up a lead which others followed. The remainder Salvador urged onward, relishing the rear of the column for himself.

Amine lashed at his horse. The big animal effortlessly negotiated the twists and turns.

A rock blocked its path, the roan merely hurdled the obstacle.

As the sun went down blackness engulfed them.

Reducing speed to a crawl, Amine pressed forever onward.

Then abruptly he came to a halt, signalling for those behind him to do likewise as the sounds of movement came to his ears.

Salvador rode forward to join his second in command, not wishing for Amine to be seen by his men to take any initiative.

The clip clopping noise of hooves were clearly distinguishable, also the splashing of water.

Dismounting, Amine waved two men forward to join him. Together with Salgo they crept forward.

The sheen on the white painted ponies was clearly visible, no other movement was seen.

"There does not appear to be anyone here Amine, it is strange."

"Si, it is as you say, we are alone."

The four Mexicans ventured amid the ponies who watered at the basin. They had fled from the blast and stopped here to chew at the brown, straw-like growth.

Salvador called for the others to come on in.

Salvador worried, so many things he did not comprehend.

"We shall camp here for the night, tomorrow we shall have the answers to all our questions."

Night passed without incident.

At first light Salvador had the men moving.

He rode to the fore setting a brisk pace.

Salvador pushed his sorrel around a long turning bend, the animal picked its way amid outlying rubble, then stopped.

"Amine come quickly,"

Amine rode from the centre of the pack, halting alongside Salvador. The men gathered, mulling behind as each rounded the twist in the canyon.

"The way, it is blocked. They must have done this. They have escaped. This must have been the explosion we heard yesterday."

"Si Amine, I am certain of it, they have blocked out path."

Amine started up the impasse, picking footholds, testing shingle as he climbed. His foot landed on a soft surface, he gaped down at the protruding arm of an Apache.

"They have fought here Salgo, that is why they have done this. The Apache are buried under the rocks."

"Can a way be cleared Amine?"

"Perhaps Salgo, however it will take many hours but we are many."

"Come you fools, do not sit. Clear these rocks we must get through!"

Reluctantly men dismounted.

The work was laborious.

The going was slow.

"Move faster you fools. If we want the gold then we must hurry,"

The significance of the dead Apache intrigued Amine.

Perhaps now was the time to become leader.

Unlike beforehand there was the Apache to contend with.

=================

"Whereabouts do you reckon we are Santes?"

"The Sierra Madre, the way ahead it should be easier."

The comfort of sleep was welcomed.

Tyrane shot his hand under his blanket, shifting his gaze he looked again from the corner of his eye. The figure moved, steadily making tracks towards him.

Clasping his hand around the gun handle he eased back the cocking mechanism and swung the holster into line with the target.

Tyrane saw the whiteness of Ojo's face in the glow from the fire and eased back on the firing mechanism.

"What do you want?"

"I've just come off watch. Santes is doing his stint now, with one of the soldier boys. I reckon we should take turns on one of us being awake, I don't trust these blue-bellies any more than you trust this Salvador Gonsalves fellah whose supposed to be trailing us. I don't want to wake up in the morning minus the gold."

Tyrane agreed, turning to roll in his blanket. Ojo, in no mood for sleep remained near the heat from the fire but continued talking.

"Who is this Salvador fellah? You seem to know a lot about him and what he's going to do. Have you met him before?"

"Uh hu."

"Where?"

"At the Apache camp."

"What! You didn't tell us that."

"You didn't ask."

Tyrane, deciding he was not going to get any sleep took out the makings.

"I've never met the man personally.
I was chasing a bounty on him.
The gold took precedence.
After all, he's only worth $5,000.
The gold's worth a lot more."
Ojo licked his lips at the thought.

"Of course the reward's only good in Arizona, where I'm not exactly of unblemished character myself,"

"This reward, dead or alive I presume?"

"That's right Ojo, you figure on collecting on it?"

Tyrane lay awake wondering as he finished his smoke.
Why was Ojo sneaking around? When all he had to do was casually walk over and say what bothered him.
The shifty way in which Ojo did things could bear some watching.

Santes now, he was a different pit of snakes.

The Mexican never having claimed to be anything other than a thief and killer, and in fact would resent being referred to as anything else.

The Captain, Tyrane just couldn't understand.

Was the man devoted to duty, or merely inexperienced in command and acclimatisation?

In any event he did not relish the forthcoming tussle, which must inevitably take place over the ownership of the gold.

Tyrane sucked in smoke, shoving the red ended butt into the dust.

Finally he managed to relax into a light sleep.

The sun rose high and it was noon when the river came into view.

"I thought we were never going to get out of the blasted desert,"

Nevertheless, Tyrane advised against stopping to rest the horses.

"They can rest up tonight. We'd best put as much distance between ourselves and the canyon as possible."

Ojo continued to find fault.

"I agree, we should press on," Agreed Houston.

This ended all discussion.

Crossing the river went smoothly, the waters reaching no higher than the horses underbelly as they crossed the border into Mexico.

At twilight they rested, then pushed on as darkness arrived.

Each rider leaned in the saddle, bracing, peering through squinted eyes. Spitting out dust as it stung their faces, their garments flapping in the wind.

Santes became erect in the saddle, bringing his mount to a halt alongside Tyrane's motionless animal.

"What is it Amigo?"

"Smell, Santes, smell."

"You are right Amigo, I can smell smoke."

"What's happening, why have we stopped?"

The words almost being swept away on the wind.

"We have company up ahead Captain. Perhaps friendly, perhaps not. Likely the latter. We'd best take precautions."

Santes pointed to a grey line of smoke filtering into the night sky, before being whisked away by the wind.

"It is an Adobe Amigos. I did not know of the existence of such a place here."

Clementine felt a pounding in her heart on hearing the news.

Only when she was in a house, with the door closed behind her, would she believe she was completely free from the Apache.

The rattle of shutters carried on the wind, then the braying of a donkey and hens squawking alerted their senses for danger. The building came into view. It was difficult to distinguish its size, however there appeared to be several smaller outbuildings. The light shone through the shuttered windows, its warmth beckoning.

"Oh let's go Tyrane, what are we waiting for?"

"We will. However first we ensure we are not riding in on a nest of rattlers,"

Dismounting, Tyrane, Santes, Corporal Conrad and Faheratty ventured nearer the Adobe.

Houston remained with the gold, not trusting it out of his sight.

Ojo was of similar mind.

Private Mornington and Clementine gripped the reins of the empty saddle horses.

Clementines knuckles turned white she gripped so hard. They watched on intently as the silhouettes moved nearer the house.

Tyrane's figure appeared near the flapping shutter, visible only momentarily before disappearing into the darkness. Then all was lost from view as the shadows blended into the night.

Tyrane took Corporal Conrad with him, whilst Santes and Faheratty circled the house. Entering the largest outbuilding first, Tyrane found it to be the stable as the smell of horse manure reached his nostrils and the donkey began to bray. A horse sniggered in the background and a goat rushed through the open door to freedom.

Poking around, Tyrane found only the various odds and sods he would expect to find in such a small building.

Much nearer and to the side of the adobe Santes disturbed the chickens as he opened a door to one of the small outbuildings.

The loud squawking alerted Tyrane as he emerged from the barn.

Crossing the yard he crouched behind the well, which stood some twenty feet from the house. Conrad knelt beside him, together they watched and waited. Conrad became aware of the alertness and readiness of his companion. His mind recalled the same awareness in Sergeant O'Mallahan. He wondered if he himself could ever adapt to this country, he doubted it very much.

His chain of thought was interrupted by the creak of the door opening.

The light from within cast its glow across the yard as a figure appeared in the doorway clutching a rifle. Its muzzle pointed into the darkness, held steady, as a frail voice croaked,

"Who is it? What do you want? Who are you?"

Tyrane, shielding his eyes from the sudden light saw the figure more clearly than the corporal who now blinked fervently to rid himself of temporary blindness.

The light from within, cast a long shadow of the frail bald-headed old Mexican. He bore a worried strain to his featured face, however the rifle remained steady in his hands.

Tyrane ventured to step from behind the well, then drew back as he heard Santes voice from within the house,

"Drop the rifle compadre, throw it out into the yard, or I will kill you."

The small figure trembled, almost reluctantly he tossed the weapon forward.

Santes was in the back room, which was the kitchen.

Ojo watched the murky events taking place around the buildings. He saw the figure appear in the doorway, then drop his weapon, and reach for the stars.

"All seems to be under control soldier boys."

Tyrane, sidling from the well, reached the house.

Scampering on all fours, he ducked the window and reached the doorway.

The sullen faced old man watched from the corner of his eye, not daring to flinch, for fear of a bullet.

Tyrane, poking his gun inside the entrance, saw Santes to the rear of the building.

"There's a horse in the stable Santes."

"Who is here with you old man, speak?"

A gringo," spluttered the ageing Mexican.

Whilst stretching his arms further skyward.

"Walk,"

Tyrane, indicating for the old man to move out towards the well.

As he drew level Conrad pulled him down beside him. Tyrane saw Faheratty appear in the back room with Santes.

"Gringo bastard. This is Emanuel Santes speaking. If you do not come out, then I will come in and kill you."

Tyrane couldn't help but smile as he listened to Santes utter his threat.

Santes, on seeing the smirk on Tyrane's face flashed his teeth in reply, these were the odds he liked, many onto a few, when he was one of the many.

Moments passed, the floor creaked.

The door off the front room opened and a large, portly man emerged with his arms outstretched above his head.

Santes waved him out with a motion of his gun, aware that Faheratty covered his rear.

Santes stepped into the room from whence the big man came.

He reappeared holstering his pistol.

A sign that all was well.

"It is as the old one says, just the two of them."

From the light of the doorway Tyrane waved the all clear for the others to come on in.

Mornington ushered the horses into what passed for a corral.

As soon as he entered the dwelling, Ojo Caliente, felt an emptiness in his stomach. The recognition did not go unnoticed by the big man either.

"You're the thief who stole my wallet,"

Cameron turned his attention towards the uniformed figure now entering the room.

"Officer! This man stole my wallet.

He's a thief.

My name is Earl Cameron.

I'm a Banker.

I demand you arrest this man."

The indignant accuser stood silently looking from face to face, searching for an inkling that someone was going to act on his behalf. All eyes focused on Ojo.

It was Tyrane who spoke as he recalled the name Ojo had given to Zen back in Sonora.

"Well now, it appears we have two Cameron's."

"You mean to say, he said his name was Cameron. Why, that's my name, he must have gotten it when he stole my wallet. Don't you see?"

The big man's eyes bulged in fear as he looked at the evil expression upon the face of the man he accused.

"What about it Ojo, what's this all about?"

Clementine, disinterested in what was being said, roamed into the back kitchen, touching the walls to ensure they were real.

The vital seconds whilst Cameron had been hurling his accusations were all Ojo needed.

"It's true Tyrane, he was on the stage. He got off before you got on. . After he had gone I found his wallet on the seat. There was nothing inside except some identification."

"He's a liar,"

"Let him finish amigo, it is an interesting story,"

Ojo switched from defence to attack.

"When you got off the stage in Nacozari fat man, you said you were going to visit your brother. If this wrinkled up, old coot's your brother, then maybe I am a Banker."

Cameron remained quiet.

"Just tell me Ojo, what is your real name, so as I don't get you two mixed up?"

"Caliente. Ojo Caliente."

"That is the name of a small village in Mexico Amigo,"

"That's right, it's where I grew up as a child."

The gold was brought inside.

Cameron's eyes bulged again.

Whilst stooping to place a box down Tyrane froze as the cocking sound of a pistol reached his ears.

Santes had his hands occupied with another box.

"Let it down real carefully Tyrane, then stand up, you too Santes."

From his stooped position Tyrane saw Mornington at the door, his rifle pointed into the house. Faheratty he could not see, however, logic dictated he would be covering the rear.

Ojo, having explained his way out of a difficult situation, had not acted swiftly enough. His gun lay on the floor beside him.

"What's this all about, Captain?"

Conrad motioned for Ojo to join the other two in a corner whilst Houston spoke.

"This is where I take control. Just in case you get any notions about helping yourselves to the gold, I had best take your guns."

Tyrane and Santes placed guns on the floor.

"Now kick those pistols over here.

I'm sorry it has to be like this Tyrane, but there's no way I can permit you to take the gold. Like I explained, it's needed to secure a vital military position out west."

Houston kicked the weapons over to Mornington along with the pistol Ojo left on the floor.

"Don't do anything silly, please!" pleaded Clementine.

"Not now we're so near to freedom."

Ojo Caliente slumped dejectedly into the corner of the room.

"Blue-coat bastards. It is as I have always believed, you are not to be trusted."

"Gringo bastards," seethed Santes.

"When you have all quite finished."

"Corporal."

"Yes-sir"

"Check the house."

"Yes-sir"

Houston detected a distinct clicking of heels from Conrad as he turned to leave the room.

Conrad returned after several minutes.

"There's this room sir, a bedroom to the side there and another room leading off from the back kitchen."

"Very well Corporal, I want all of them in the back room with a guard outside the door. The young lady here goes into the front bedroom put the gold in there with her. We can watch her door from in here and I want a guard on patrol outside."

Orders were swiftly carried out. Faheratty sat atop the kitchen table facing the bedroom door. Mornington braced himself against the wind whilst pacing outside, paying particular attention to the rear of the building where the prisoners were being held.

Houston and Conrad settled down in the front room, taking it in turns to check on any movement.

"The gold will be safe in there, Corporal,"

assured Houston, indicating the front bedroom door.

"She couldn't carry it out, even if she wanted to."

Clementine did not rest as easily as she imagined she would do with a roof over her head once again. Laying there, looking up at the ceiling, she wondered what Tyrane was thinking right now.

In the back room there were few that wanted to sleep.

Tyrane took out the makings.

Santes peered from between the gaps in the shutters to see Mornington pacing outside.

Ojo lay on the bed, contemplating what the next move should be.

whilst the old man who lay beside him, snored unreservedly. Pressing his ear against the wall, Earl Cameron listened for movement from the front bedroom, there was none.

Conrad went outside to relieve Mornington for a spell and did likewise with Faheratty. The night passed without further incident.

At first light, Clementine was up and aiding the old man in making breakfast.

Tortillas appeared to be the mainstay of the Mexican diet.

The troopers took it in turn to eat.

The others were allowed from the back room into the kitchen.

They clamoured around the filthy hardwood table.

Grateful for the first hot meal in days.

The aroma of coffee filled the room.

"I want to go outside," Said the banker.

"Let him go corporal, he can't do any harm on his own and unarmed. Besides, he and the old man aren't our concern. These others are,"

Ojo noted the remark, remembering the threat uttered by Houston back in the canyon, after he had killed the trooper.

Clementine moved around the kitchen refilling cups.

Cameron ventured out back, returning minutes later.

Corporal Conrad stirred to see to the horses needs. Standing at the front doorway he paused momentarily.

Was that a flash of light he saw?

Amine curled his finger around the trigger.

Omitting his breath he squeezed.

The rifle leapt in his hands.

Conrad crashed backwards, clutching his temple.

Falling in the doorway blood gushed from a hole under his left eye.

Chapter Seventeen

Fight For Life

The coffee-pot clattered to the floor and Clementine shrieked.

Tyrane, leaping to his feet, rattled the table, spilling the contents of his cup over Cameron.

The Banker howled as the scalding liquid scorched his thighs.

Faheratty and Mornington restrained any further movement from the table.

Houston, unbuttoning his holster raced into the front room. The pistol became limp in his hand as he gaped upon the body of the corporal.

Kicking the door shut, whilst pulling Conrad's body out of the way, Tyrane leapt for cover as a fusillade of shots erupted.

The door halted the bullets, as did the walls. However, the window spaces were a danger.

Houston, replied outside with three barks from his pistol.

Tyrane joined Houston.

Peering from the side of the UN-shuttered window space, he surveyed as the Mexicans shifted themselves around in the vicinity of the barn buildings, and the sparse cover of the corral. The only horses he saw in the corral were their own.

Faheratty assisted the old Mexican as he closed shutters across the windows, securing them in position with a cross length of timber. This left narrow slits in the wooden frames through which a rifle could be fired.

Mornington and Faheratty returned fire.

"Give us our guns captain," demanded Tyrane.

"They're moving around as they like out there.

You three can't hope to hold them alone.

Once they get positioned we're going to be in trouble."

Houston hesitated.

"If they get around behind us cap'n, and close in, we're goners,"

Houston resignedly agreed to the demands.

"You fool Amine,"

cursed Salvador at his second in command.

"Now because of you, we must fight for the gold, whereas we could have taken it from them by surprise, you idiot."

Amine, in no mood for talk, as a fire kindled in his eyes emptied his rifle at the house.

"What does it matter, we have them trapped, the gold it will soon be ours."

Ojo and Mornington occupied the front bedroom where the gold was kept. Faheratty kept watch from the kitchen, whilst in the back room the old Mexican leaned his rifle against the wall, watched, and waited.

Tyrane, Santes, the Captain and the Banker all blasted shots from the front room.

"Do you think two men at the rear of the building are enough?"

"Si Capitan. There is little cover to be had so the chances of them getting close from that direction are not good. All the buildings are to the front and side, with the exception of the hen house."

"Santes is correct Captain. The front is where we must concentrate our fire."

As he thought of fire, Tyrane thanked their good fortune the building was built of stone and mud bricks, else he was sure Salvador would try to burn them out, secure in the knowledge that the gold would still remain after the bodies had been incinerated.

Tyrane turned on hearing Clementine shriek.

On entering the front room, she clutched at her throat to hold back vomit as she gazed at the corporal's body.

Blood had run from the wound under the eye into the eye space itself to form a pool of crimson, which trickled down the soldier's face, ran around his ear and dripped onto the floor.

Houston scurried across to overturn the body, quickly rejoining Cameron at the window.

"How many of them are there?"

"Hard to tell exactly Tyrane. I'd say twenty or so at most."

The main concentration of shots came from the barn, with only single sniping shots from the corral area.

"There's one behind the water trough near the corral, two in the loft of the stable, doesn't appear to be anyone nearer than those. Certainly no one as close as the well,"

"You, Banker, get over here."

"Where are you going Tyrane?" demanded Houston.

"To tell your soldier boy in the kitchen to go easier on the ammo.

He's using it like there's no tomorrow."

"I don't like this, the odds aren't good,"

moaned Faheratty as Tyrane joined him.

"Just go careful with the ammunition."

A shrill scream sent Tyrane back into the front room.

Cameron slumped onto the floor gasping, clawing at his chest.

His hand pulled away quickly when he saw the blood.

Clementine, opening his shirt, attended the wound.

Tyrane took up position at the window.

The big man slobbered, gasping for help.

Dragging Cameron into the back room, Houston, with some assistance from Clementine managed to get makeshift bandages applied.

"Ask the old coot if he's got any ammo around here," cried Tyrane.

Houston, looking up from Cameron's prostrate body met the impassive glare of the old occupier of the house.

"Si, I keep bullets."

Leaving the window, he moved towards a cupboard, bringing out several boxes of shells.

It occurred to Houston that the old man had produced his rifle from nowhere. Had this second weapon been here in this room all night, whilst everyone was being held inside, he wondered.

Returning to the front room, Houston confirmed the first rifle the old man surrendered was here.

Cameron became delirious, raving incessantly.

"Money, money, my money, bring my money for me."

Clementine pressed her ear to his lips, trying to understand the words, whilst at the same time, continuing to bathe his forehead.

The old man looked on dispassionately, keeping one eye out the window.

The shooting abated.

Tyrane called for everyone to hold fire when it became apparent no one was shooting back.

Amines voice bellowed out over the area between the house and the outbuildings.

Only the chickens could be heard shrieking, the horses were out of earshot at the far end of the corral.

"You inside, I wish to speak with you.

Do not shoot, I am coming out. Do you understand?"

Amine swallowed hard whilst awaiting a reply, inwardly hoping none would come.

"I'm listening,"

Amine ventured out from the protection of the barn.

"What do you reckon they have to say?"

"We'll soon find out, Captain, and the only way, is to listen to what the man says. But I sure as hell ain't going out there."

Santes eyes widened as he recognised the figure of his old riding partner emerge into view,

"Santes, You listen in if he starts to talk Mexican."

No sound came from the other back room.

Tyrane opened the door slightly.

Clementine wanted desperately to know what was happening as the shooting died down, but did not leave Cameron's side.

The weasel-faced Gomez stood two paces behind Amine

Amine looked at the weapon in the window which was aimed at him and the blue uniform, which held it.

Glancing behind, he saw Gomez directly behind, so as not to stop the first bullet. He swallowed hard, his Adams apple bobbing.

"I have no gun, I only wish to talk."

"Then talk, compadre"

Amine recognised Santes sarcastic voice, and saw him appear at the window.

"Santes my old friend, why do we fight, we are friends no? There is much gold to share between us, there is no need for bloodshed."

A silence passed.

"I did not know we were still friends amigo. There was the matter of a small misunderstanding between us the last time we met."

261

"No matter, that is past. We must concern ourselves with the present, Santes my friend."

Amine broke into swift Mexican, smiling assuredly as he spoke.

"Join us Amigo and share the gold. You can help us from within, and later we can discuss old times no!"

"Speak English," broke in Tyrane.

"It is done," assured Santes.

"They want the gold. If we give it to them, they will allow us to live, if not"

He paused, hunching his shoulders.

"Then we shall die,"

Concluded Ojo, calling from the other room.

"And my Mexican isn't as bad as I led you to believe Santes.

I understood every word."

Santes face screwed up into a hatred.

Houston was in no mood to be parted from the gold at this stage.

Watching Amine back away towards the barn, Santes considered reducing the odds by one. Then he thought better of it, realising it would be wiser to wait and see which was the winning side.

Right now he would like to be over in the barn.

Ojo came through from the other room.

"Well, we needn't fight for the gold Tyrane. The soldier boys here decided last night that it was all theirs, so suppose we tell this Amine fellah we want to ride out."

Ojo waited as the implication of his words sank in.

He thought it would be just fine to leave the soldiers to fight the Mexicans for the gold.

Then he, Tyrane and Santes could return and take care of the survivors.

"You inside the house, have you decided what you must do yet compadres?" bellowed Amine

"You would be foolish to want to die in such a place as this."

Houston shoved his pistol out of the window and fired.

"You idiot,"

Ojo had his protestations engulfed in a volley of shots.

Tyrane fired alongside Houston.

"Feeling patriotic are you Tyrane?"

"No Captain, just a matter of necessity, nothing more."

Houston fired, his shot taking the sombrero from a darting man's head, its owner disappeared from view.

"I don't believe there's any way they're going to let us out of here."

Ojo disappeared back into the adjacent bedroom, his eyes swept the bullion crates as he rejoined Mornington there.

Houston was not certain where Tyrane's loyalties lay, and wondered if the Marshall's death had anything to do with his reluctance to surrender the gold.

Certainly when Ojo Caliente killed Cargen, it had been Tyrane who had been instrumental in stopping a bloodbath.

Tyrane had been first with his gun out, but it was also he who had called the shots

The morning drew on and midday approached.

The gunrunners fired at anything that moved within the Adobe building.

From within the confines of the building they sniped back warning shots at their attackers.

Santes being more free with his ammunition than most, dwelt on what Amine had inferred. However for the moment he could not foresee how he could switch his allegiance to the more favourably manned side. In any event he did not trust Amine to include him in any share out of the gold. Even so....

Hence he decided, he would remain where he was and take advantage of any situation if and when it occurred.

Ojo too, tried to figure a way out of his present predicament. Not for the first time since leaving Sonora had he tasted his own sweat. The odour was not pleasant, he unleashed a fury of shots towards the water trough.

Houston fired more vigorously as Tyrane moved away from the window. Possessed by an optimism that now he had procured the gold he was not going to lose it, he fired defiantly.

A bullet ricocheted into the room.

Houston knew they were pinned down.

Searching his memory he tried to recall some situation he had read about whilst at the academy, which was not dissimilar to the present predicament.

The thought seemed hopeless.

"He's been losing a lot of blood,"

advised Clementine as Tyrane entered the back room.

Removing the towel from Cameron's head she re-soaked it.

"Money, my money, it's all mine,"

Tyrane's eyes met Clementines.

"Go through to the front old man," indicated Tyrane.

"I'll tend here for a while."

Tyrane kicked the door shut as the old man departed, leaving only himself, Clementine and the wounded Cameron in the room.

Faheratty glanced over as the door slammed shut, then ignoring the incident he concentrated his attention outside.

"What's this he's saying about money Clementine?"

"I don't know. He's been raving for a while. It doesn't make sense, something about a Bank and money."

"Go into the kitchen and see if the old man keeps a bottle in there."

"What!"

"Tequila probably, just bring anything. Make a thorough search and keep down as you move."

Leaning over the body as Clementine left, Tyrane kept his voice low.

"Cameron, listen to me. What money do you mean?"

The seconds ticked slowly by as Cameron found enough strength to splutter a reply.

"Money, money from the Bank. Took money, blamed it on the robbery. Hiding here. Money, my money, get me my money."

"Where is it, Cameron?"

"Tell me where you keep it, so as I can bring it to you."

Several more seconds ticked past before Cameron again found the strength to speak.

"Front bedroom, top drawer, in black bag. My money."

"There's no Tequila, or anything else,"

informed Clementine upon re-entering in time to see Cameron release his hold on Tyrane. to lapse into unconsciousness.

"Watch him,"

Tyrane swiftly strode from the room.

Neither Ojo nor Mornington heard him enter the front room. Casting his eyes quickly over the gold, Tyrane moved towards the chest of drawers. The black bag was there all right, pulling it open, Tyrane now knew why the Banker had spent the previous night with his ear pressed to the wall.

Removing the bag from the drawer, he saw a bottle of pills. The bottle rolled as the bag was lifted, snatching it up Tyrane stuffed it into his pocket. Ojo turned on hearing the rattling sound.

"What the hell are you doing?"

His eyes fixing on the black bag, recalling the way in which the Banker had never let it leave his side during the stagecoach journey from the relay station to Nacozari.

Mornington glanced back only momentarily before continuing to watch outside.

"The Banker, I think he's dying. He asked me to fetch his bag."

Ojo scrambled over.

"Let me see that bag, the way he kept it with him at all times suggests there's something valuable inside."

"Maybe, but that's the Banker's business not ours."

Leaving Ojo, Tyrane returned to the back room.

Ojo, not convinced, searched through the drawers.

Santes, being the nearest to the adjoining room heard Ojo's moans.

"What is wrong Amigo, have you lost something?"

"Lost it even before I found it," muttered Ojo.

"You'd best go back to the kitchen soldier, I'll see to things in here."

Said Tyrane, for Fraternity's benefit.

Clementines eyes flickered from Cameron to the bag Tyrane was carrying.

"Give him some of these pills."

Placing the bag on Cameron's chest, Tyrane watched as the Banker curled his fingers around the handle. Clementine held up his head to administer the pills.

He's dead, pills are no good to him now."

Letting the head drop, Clementine allowed her own head to fall into her hands.

"Stop sobbing woman. Go up front and help with the reloading."

Her body became rigid, her eyes searched Tyrane's face for some sign of compassion. There was none.

In a blur of tears she left, slamming the door closed behind her.

With the noise of the slamming door still ringing in his ears, Tyrane released the catch on the bag. It fell open, the contents spilling out onto the banker.

Pulling the pillow from beneath Cameron's head, he slashed the top of the slip and began stuffing the banknotes inside.

'Must be over $30,000 here probably more,'

Patting the pillow flat once more, Tyrane replaced it below the Banker's head.

Rummaging around the room he found a pair of the old Mexicans long-johns and two vests. These he put inside the bag, satisfied that all looked normal, he opened the door.

Faheratty gave a quizzical look over his shoulder.

"He's dead,"

replied Tyrane to the trooper's unasked question.

"Keep a good lookout, I want to have a word with your Captain."

Clementine was positioned to the right of the main door, thumbing shells into a rifle.

"She said the Banker's dead."

"That's right Captain, like we'll all be if we don't get the hell out of here."

The old man ambled through to the back room.

Ignoring Cameron's body he took up his position on watch.

It was mid-afternoon,

Tyrane reckoned if they could hold out until dark then there was a chance of slipping away.

"I don't agree," argued Houston.

"The gold's too heavy for swift movement, besides, the old man wouldn't come with us."

"Then he can remain,"

Sizing up the situation outside, Tyrane saw that the gunrunners had improved their position during his absence.

Santes eyed him wonderingly.

"Have you some dynamite left Amigo?"

"Two sticks."

"Then let me have them."

Houston turned to receive the freshly loaded rifle from Clementine, as he took the weapon with his right hand, his left exposed itself at the window. The finger on either side burned as the index finger caught a bullet. For a moment he stood gaping at the space where the finger should be, then the pain began.

As his hand clasped around the last two sticks of dynamite, Tyrane heard the Captain's cry.

Securing the wrist tightly to stop the bleeding, he left Clementine to finish off.

"Here's the explosives Santes, what do you have in mind?"

"The Captain, he agrees with this?"

From his position, slumped against the wall, Houston in pain nodded his approval.

"You keep the dynamite Amigo, get yourself to the well if you can, then hurl it towards the barn. I will do the rest."

"Oh that's a real good idea Santes, why the hell am I going to go outside, why not you?"

"Because Amigo, I know I can hit the dynamite and I cannot be sure if you can."

Tyrane considered, before agreeing.

Houston was up and firing again, whilst Faheratty came through from the back kitchen to lend support.

"You get ready to fire Captain, and tell your men to do likewise. At my command I want you to throw everything you have at them."

Disappearing into the adjoining bedroom, Tyrane sidled up to Ojo and Mornington

"What do you want?"

Ojo, saw the dynamite.

"What are you going to do with those?"

"I'm going to get rid of their cover."

"You mean the stable mister?"

"That's right soldier, you stay here and concentrate your fire around the corral. You come with me Ojo, into the other room."

Ojo took up position alongside Santes.

"Christ, I hope you are as good a shot as you think you are Santes."

"Throw them real high Amigo,"

The Mexican experienced a surge of excitement pulsating through his body at the thought of the buildings going up with so many trapped inside.

Moving away from the window he replenished his rifle.

"Whenever you are ready Tyrane fire three shots."

Slipping out of the back door, Tyrane edged his way towards the corner of the building and dropped onto his haunches.

Gun in hand he crept, moving via the chickens.

The birds shrieked, however no more so he believed, than they had done since sun up.

The front-most coop was parallel with the front of the adobe.

Tyrane gambled that advancing towards the water well from this location would give him an edge, the distance was the same but they should be watching the house.

Taking three deep breaths, Tyrane aimed his gun towards the corral area, for from there he believed would he be most vulnerable.

One, two, three, Tyrane's shots rang out in quick succession, followed by a fusillade of rifle fire from within the house.

Thrusting his body from behind the coop wall, Tyrane raced then dived towards the well as shots pinged around his ears.

Breathing heavily he lay motionless, sucking in great lungs of air. The shooting from the house returned to normal.

"See Salgo, they try for water,"

Amine pointed hysterically towards the well.

"It appears you are correct Amigo, fire at the well compadres, do not let them get to the water."

Bullets crashed into and zipped past the well wall. From this position Tyrane saw the barrel of Santes rifle protruding from the window, signifying that all was in readiness. First he thumbed three fresh shells into his gun's empty chambers, then passed the weapon into his left hand.

"Any time you are ready Amigo,"

came the voice from within the house. Tyrane sucked in breath.

"Now,"

he screamed.

A fusillade of shots from within spat mercilessly into the barn.

Springing to his feet, Tyrane arched his arm back and then forward. The small stick flew high into the air. It was still rising when he hit the ground as bullets spat all around.

Every nerve in Santes body became alert to the situation as he awaited. Tyrane looked up to see the rifle barrel in the window move slightly, before leaping in its owner's hands. The dynamite fell short of its target by some ten feet or so, nevertheless when Santes rifle barked its crack was consumed in the blast, which followed.

The stable door fell from its hinges as the entire barn shook. Someone fell from the loft onto the already fallen door, the body remaining motionless where it lay.

"Ready Santes?"

"Si Amigo."

Again the gunfire from the adobe increased.

Once more Tyrane leapt to his feet, protected somewhat by the drifting smoke and rising dust.

He lingered momentarily longer to hurl the stick with all his might.

A bullet burned a hole in his sleeve as he fell.

Santes eased back on the trigger, the rifle spat once again.

Nothing happened.

Standing back from the window Santes scanned the dispersing dust. Levelling the rifle he let it bark, the explosion from within the confines of the stable hurled timber in all directions as bodies ran out choking.

Taking advantage of the confusion, Tyrane weaved back amid the hen houses.

Glancing back he let off two shots at a sombrero figure trying to mount one of the fear-frenzied corral horses.

Another staggered from the smoke filled building, stooping to retrieve his weapon. As he arose, Ojo snapped off a shot bringing him to his knees clutching his groin.

"Don't shoot old timer, it's me,"

Tyrane dived through upon reaching the rear room window.

No-one noticed as he sped into the front room to witnessed bedlam taking place outside.

The mechanical loading, firing, and reloading of weapons continued as the remaining gunrunners fled.

As shooting died down the old man came through to investigate the damage to his property.

Tyrane saw the look of resignation on the wrinkled face.

"Don't worry none old timer, I'm sure the U.S. army can afford to compensate you for any damage."

Houston turned to protest, however, changed his mind on seeing the desperate, imploring look.

"I suppose so,"

The veins on the bald Mexicans head seemed to recede on hearing this good bit of news.

"I would not thank him yet amigo, the trouble is not yet over,

"What do you mean?"

"The comancheros have merely moved back, they cannot know we had only two sticks of explosives. So they do the only sensible thing."

"Then they will be back?"

"Si, they will be back."

Tyrane knew Santes had read the situation correctly.

"We merely have a breathing space, so we'd best get organised."

There was little cover to be had outside now the barn and adjoining outbuildings had been demolished. Salvador regrouped his men upon reaching the horses. The two men left in charge of the animals let off shots as the bodies ran past, but the house was out of pistol range.

"They sure as hell can't sneak up on us now,"

"Perhaps not, however they can just wait out there Ojo.

We should get in some water before they close in again and

What happens when we run out of ammo?"

"I think it would be good if you went out for the water, Ojo."

"Not me."

The horses milled around in the corral, the hens shrieked and the old man waited for someone to take the initiative.

"Do you have any suggestions Captain?"

"I believe Tyrane that the best form of defence is offence, we should attack them."

"You can't be serious,"

"It would be the last thing they expected Ojo"

"Perhaps the Captain has a plan, allow him to speak amigos,"

"Very well, it has already known we can't make a run with the gold."

"Maybe you can't,"

Ignoring the interruption from Ojo Houston continued,

"Therefore why not attack, for if we wait here then they will surely attack us and under cover of darkness they may succeed."

"It would give us the element of surprise,"

Said Tyrane.

Ojo's eye twitched, he did not relish a confrontation.

Santes saw how nervous Ojo was, he knew many men like him Always shooting their mouths off and bragging. Then when it came to the test, they failed the test and felt the cold chill of sweat on their backs. But he knew Ojo would do his share of the fighting when the time came, for the man was more afraid of being dead than he was of the Mexican gunrunners.

Darkness fell over the small house.

The wind howled, banging loose boards against one another.

A goat bleated outside somewhere.

Sand lashed against the outside of the adobe.

In the back kitchen they ate.

Santes positioned the lamp in a corner so as to shield its rays.

Anyone lurking outside would get no assistance from those in the Adobe.

It was one hour after dark when Tyrane decided it was time to move.

"They're bound to have sentries out,"

"If we go out the back way Captain, quietly move back – a ways we may be able to circle around behind them. It'll take time, however they'd least expect an attack from that direction,"

Clementine was to remain in the house, as was the old Mexican. Each man looked towards the others, wondering who was going to go out first.

Santes disappeared into the blackness before anyone could comment.

It was a move, which surprised Ojo, yet not Tyrane.

For the first man out stood the least chance of being shot.

If there was anyone out back watching, they'd like as not miss the first man but be ready for a second to appear.

"Who's next?"

Ojo, geared somewhat by Santes success, stepped through the window. Next went Houston, followed by Tyrane, Faheratty and Mornington

Clementine watched from the rear of the building as the last departure vanished from sight. The old Mexican took up position at the front.

They moved away from the house, leaving it and the gunrunners farther behind.

The old Mexican moved from room to room checking outside through the shuttered windows.

Every now and sending out a shot.

Clementine listened to his movements as the old man wandered about, whilst she rested her body against the table with the rifle across her thighs.

A regular bullet fired from outside hit the front door.

Around the gunrunner fire, all that could be heard was the distant resound of shots being fired.

Salvador, having moved far enough away from the house so as not to be disturbed, parleyed with Amine

"They will be awake all night Amine, whilst we may sleep. In the morning before daylight we shall attack eh Amine"

Amine did not share his leader's enthusiasm for this present situation, nor did he relish the plan formulated by Salvador.

"Si, it is a good idea to have someone watch the well Salgo, however I do not think we should wait."

"You are too impetuous my friend."

"We should ride now and kill them tonight Salgo,"

"No Amine we have more guns than they, they are a mere handful and a woman."

"Si, Salgo, but how many were inside the house before we arrived."

Some of the men had turned in for the night, others sat in close proximity with the fire, their sombreros pulled over their eyes.

Others straddled amongst the sleeping bodies, readying themselves for next day by cleaning weapons, checking ammo, and rolling enough cigarillo's to see them through the day.

Out on the boundary of the firelight a red end glowed in the dark. It disappeared, then came into view again as the guard puffed on his cigarillo.

The sextet, three civilians and three military men lay watching through the campsite.

The adobe was not visible at this distance.

They were now in position to come upon their enemy from a vantage point they least expected.

Over to their left, the horses were picketed away from the campfire. It had taken an hour to reach their present position, and they made good use of this respite.

The sound of rifle fire could be heard from the adobe.

Tyrane clutched the knotted shirt in his hand,

"The dynamite would have been better for this, but no matter."

The knotted shirt held twenty rounds of ammo inside.

"Spread yourselves out, however don't shoot until I land this little present on the fire."

"I will take care of the guard first Amigo."

He was gone into the darkness before anyone could stop him.

Santes painstakingly moved forward, testing each foothold before putting any weight behind it, ghost stepping, he neared the sentry who watched over the horses.

Santes stealthily moved only inches at a time.

Then the the characteristic movement of the hand to the top of the boot, for the knife.

The two Troopers were circling around, leaving Tyrane, Houston and Ojo huddled together.

"You two had better get yourselves into position. Make sure you keep your heads down when this little lot goes up. Then come out shooting."

Chapter Eighteen

Departures

"Just hit anything that moves within the confines of the camp."

Were the last words heard by Houston and Ojo as they left Tyrane.

Santes moved alongside the guard, so close he could hear the chest wheeze as he exhaled smoke from the cigarillo.

Laying pressed against the ground he awaited until his quarry turned his back.

Flexing his muscles, Santes with one motion leapt to his feet, arched his arm back then forward.

The blade flashed in the twinkle of firelight before it sank deep into the lower spine of his victim.

Catching the body as it fell, Santes released his hold over the mouth.

Amine rose to his feet.

"What is wrong amigo?"

"I do not know Salgo, I believe I saw something out there.

"Si Amine it is Carlos, he is on guard."

"No Salgo he is not."

Tyrane reached Santes as he was helping himself to shells from the dead man's gun-belt.

Santes wiped the blade on his chaps, returning it to his boot.

Salvador arose from the fire to his feet, calling out,

"Carlos, where are you?"

Tyrane quickly tossed the bundle to Santes.

"Throw it onto the fire damn you,"

Tyrane brought his rifle to bear on Salvador's chest. He eased back on the trigger as Santes hurled the bundle into the air, the two landed together.

As the rifle leapt in Tyrane's hands, Salvador threw open his arms under the impact of the bullet. Standing motionless for an instant as he frothed garbled blood from his mouth, his eyes glazed as the sparks cascading from the fire drifted skyward and the echo of the shot rang loud. The heat took its effect and the knotted shirt exploded with the assistance of a bullet from Santes.

A vision of Zeb's face flashed before Tyrane in that moment.

The whole encampment came to life at once.

Salvador's body was carried by the blast, it landed, riddled with holes down one side blood seeping from the wounds.

Cries rang out as gunshot also targeted the gunrunners.

The bullets from the fire flew at random, striking into running men as they attempted to clear their minds of sleep.

One of the horses reared as a bullet scarred its rump, pulling the securing ropes from the ground it incited the other animals into flight as horses reared in confusion.

Santes, emptying the guard's pistol at those in the area of the fire, discarded the weapon once empty and pulled out his own piece.

Faheratty reloaded whilst Mornington fired.

Houston picked his targets carefully, unable to reload swiftly due to his injured hand.

"One for O'Mallahan, one for Conrad, another for O'Mallahan."

He swore as each bullet hit its intended target.

A shot zipped near Tyrane's head, turning he saw Santes alter his aim, he could not be sure if Santes had fired the shot.

Mornington buckled as a bullet tore into his thigh.

Faheratty fired Mornington reloaded.

A wild gleam flashed in Santes eyes as he sought out Amine.

Faheratty dropped his weapon to open up with a pistol snatched from a dead man's holster.

Mornington fired, supported on one knee.

Tyrane moved towards the fire, his gun blasting lead.

Houston shot, as the flash of light spat from the barrel a fleeing Mexican dropped, shuddered, then lay still.

Amine returned fire from sparse cover.

"Leave him to me Amigo,"

Came a voice from the dark above the all consuming din.

"We have old scores to settle, him and I."

Tyrane returned Amines fire, while Santes circled around behind.

At the house the shooting ceased, watching breathlessly the old man peered from the window, but could see little.

Clementine came through from the back kitchen to join him.

"Can you see what's happening?"

Tiny figures could be seen moving around in the firelight in the distance, the shots were not distinguishable, merely a noise which seemed to repeat itself over and over again.

Resistance petered around the fire, the gunrunners not dead other fled into the night.

Houston snapped off shots after them.

"Another for Conrad."

Tyrane had Amine pinned down.

"Drop it compadre, or your old partner will kill you now rather than later."

Santes brought his pistol to bear on Amines head.

Amine froze with his face still pressed against rock, gun still in hand.

"I have him Tyrane. Leave him to me."

Tyrane moved to assist Faheratty in checking the bodies.

Even if he wished to, he was sure he could not reach Santes in time to stop him pulling the trigger.

"Santes compadre," pleaded Amine

"I have much gold."

As Santes finger tightened around the trigger he heard Amines plea, unable to keep from firing he pulled his weapon to one side. Amine took the bullet in the hip, the great brute of a man dropped his weapon, clutching at his side.

"You spoke of gold Amigo, speak quickly and true or I will kill you."

Amine caught his breath, leaning back against the rock.

"The Apache Santes, they gave us gold to purchase the guns. A box of gold Amigo."

"Where is this gold, do you have it here with you?"

"It is buried, hidden near Janos you know the place."

"Si, I know it."

Santes mind flashed back to the box of sand Tyrane found in the canvassed wagon.

"This gold you speak of, was it in a box or a bag?"

"Santes, we put sand in the box and buried the gold."

"Who else knows the whereabouts of the gold?"

"Only Salgo and myself, we buried it whilst the men slept. Now Salgo is dead and I am the only one who knows where it is."

Amines voice took on a conversational tone as he realised Santes was taking the tale to heart. Nevertheless, Santes kept his pistol trained while his mind raced.

All Amine said about the gold made sense, even the soldiers said some of it was missing. He reasoned that Amine must be telling the truth, and calculated the odds. There were two cases of gold back at the adobe. However, first the soldiers must be dealt with.

Then the gold must be divided between himself, Tyrane and Ojo.

It would be a lot of trouble for the same booty.

If Amine did have two gold, he could lead him to it. then Amine could be killed.

His mind made up, Santes smashed the barrel of his pistol down on Amines head.

"That should hold you for several hours my friend. I will return for you later."

Dropping the barrel of the pistol, he fired two shots into the ground and scrambling over Amines body, he moved towards the diminishing ring of light thrown by the fire.

"What took you so long?"

"We went back a long way together amigo, we had much to discuss, ."

"Is he dead?"

"Si Tyrane, he is dead. Have you checked all these bodies for bullet holes?"

"I don't get caught out on that one twice, yes they've been checked," said Houston.

Counting the guard Santes had disposed of and Amine, Tyrane totalled fourteen dead.

"Some of them got away,"

"That is correct Amigo, however they will bother us no more. We are many now and they are few. So their spirit will be broken."

"They're also afoot,"

Tyrane turned agreeing with Faheratty and moved in the direction of the house.

Ojo walked faster, catching up with Tyrane with each stride.

"What are we going to do about the gold? These soldier boys ain't about to hand it over to us without a fight."

"I'm not interested, Ojo or Cameron, or whatever you want to call yourself."

"It's that woman! She's turned your head. Come to your senses man, we can take them easily."

"Then you take them easily Ojo,"

Ojo stopped walking, hissing abuse at Tyrane.

Not realising he was now walking alone.

Tyrane increased his pace. The Banker's money he intended keeping, so saw no profit fighting the U.S. Cavalry.

Tyrane froze, his gun leapt into his hand. He thought he saw someone moving near to the corral. Believing it may be his eyes playing tricks on him, he called out to the house.

"Don't shoot, it's us."

The old man lowered his rifle, it had been aimed at Tyrane's heart.

As he entered the house, Tyrane squinted a last look towards the corral. He was sure he had seen someone there, however could see only the horses.

The three uniformed figures reached the house as lights were going on.

Helping Mornington into a chair, Faheratty ripped away his leggings to inspect the wound.

Ojo lingered behind to speak to Santes, who for some reason unbeknown to him wanted to bring up the rear.

"What about it Santes, we can share the gold between us if we work together. All right, so Tyrane doesn't want any part of it. That just means all the more for us."

Santes considered for a minute. He could not foresee Tyrane standing idly by whilst he and Ojo killed the soldiers.

"No my friend, I think I shall ride out in the morning, alone!"

Ojo was insane with rage.

"Has everyone gone mad around here,"

Santes, moving towards the well, let the bucket drop.

Ojo still cursed.

"The bastards, Santes is right they're all bastards. And he's the biggest bastard of them all."

Santes smirked as he heard Ojo's protestations and turning the winch the only sound to be heard was the brimful bucket spilling out into the well. As it reached the top, Santes picked up the dipper and wet his parched throat.

Even the chickens has stopped their shrieking.

The smell of hot coffee filled the bustling back kitchen as everyone moved inside. Although the atmosphere appeared relaxed, Houston did not relax his vigil. Faheratty was posted outside on watch.

"I'll take the second watch," offered Santes.

This unexpected offer did not go unnoticed by Tyrane who now decided he was going to have a sleepless night.

"I'll go fetch some more coffee,"

Moving from the kitchen, sure he could not be seen. Ojo opened the door to the back room. In the darkness, Cameron's body seemed large and bulky. Snapping open the bag, he cursed as the pills fell onto the floor. He plunged his hand into the bag. Tyrane heard the bottle drop and came to his feet.

"Vests, what!"

"Peers he only kept his long-johns in there Ojo, some pills as well,"

Tyrane, lounged against the now open door. Seeing that the pillow was undisturbed, he helped himself to some more coffee.

Clementine retired into the front bedroom.

Mornington leaned against the bedroom door in a sitting position with his rifle across his lap having been told by Houston to guard the gold.

Seeing that the floor space was being taken up, the old man snuggled up on a scant rug and pulled a blanket over himself. He shortly breathed evenly in slumber.

Ensuring the shutters were secure Tyrane opened the back bedroom door.

He bedded down for the night under the kitchen table, the most uncomfortable place he could find. It would ensure to keep him awake for the remainder of the night, and offered a good view of where the money was stashed.

He pulled his coat over him and puffed on a cigarette.

Ojo too settled in the kitchen, on a chair slumped across the table.

Santes found a corner in the front room, pulling his sombrero over his eyes.

The night sounds soon drifted into nothingness as the weary eyed succumbed to the call of sleep.

The steady pacing of Faheratty moving around outside to keep himself warm, was still heard by Tyrane as he lay awake.

An hour passed slowly, then part of another. A sudden gust of wind blew through the Adobe as Faheratty stepped inside.

The stifling closeness of the room after the howling wind sent dust into the air. Santes opened his eyes from under the sombrero as the figure in the dark hovered over him.

"Your watch," voiced

Pressing the sombrero tighter onto his head, Santes closed the door behind him as he stepped outside.

Faheratty settled down in the now vacant corner.

Tyrane listened as Santes moved around to the rear of the building, catching a glimpse as his huddled figure walked past, drowsiness though soon overcame him and his steady breathing could be heard by Ojo, who lay awake.

Content he had made enough noise and movement to ensure those inside knew of his presence outside, Santes strode towards the corral.

The horses sniggered in the background their sounds like whispers in the night.

Searching around, Santes found a length of rope, cutting the lengths he wanted, he discarded the remainder.

The corral gate creaked as he led two animals out.

Securing the gate, Santes led both horses behind the remains of the barn and circling around still on foot made haste towards the scene of the attack on the gunrunners.

As the house was left behind he mounted and allowed the horses a steady gait.

Amine was still unconscious as Santes poured a canteen over him.

"What happened, my head, it is killing me."

"No matter Amigo, help me to saddle the horses then we can be away."

"Si,"

Santes pulled a saddle out from under the head of its dead owner. The dead man's hand was on his half-drawn gun, the position he had died in.

Staggering to his feet, Amine with some difficulty saddled the spare animal. He doubled over in pain as the wound in his hip reopened and began to bleed.

"Where is my gun?"

"I will keep your gun Amine, until we reach the gold."

=================

Tyrane's coat slipped from his body.

Ojo held his breath expecting it to be retrieved, it was not.

Calculating it had been many hours since Santes went outside, he had heard no sound for sometime and dawn would be coming soon. With it daylight, which did not fit in with his plans.

The wind died down outside, yet it was still bitterly cold.

Rising gingerly, Ojo donned Tyrane's coat and moved towards the back door.

Tyrane's eyelids fluttered as the silhouette appeared in the doorway.

'I wonder where the hell's he going?'

Glancing into the bedroom to ensure all was well with the money. The bulging body of Cameron lay undisturbed, a shadow crossing its length as Ojo passed by outside at the rear of the adobe.

"Brr r it's cold,"

Halting at the corner of the building, Ojo surveyed the outlying area looking for Santes.

He was nowhere in sight.

The chickens squawked sending a shiver down his spine.

Biding his time he strode towards the corral.

Finding discarded rope Ojo rode one animal bareback, leading a another.

He noted that horses were missing.

The matter bothered him for several moments, then it passed.

Tyrane listened, nothing was to be heard.

Suddenly he was cold, and Ojo had taken his coat.

"The thieving bastard,"

Tyrane chuckled inwardly realising he had acquired some of Santes vocabulary.

Light spread across the sky.

Two gunrunners horses, which had taken flight the night before were mulling around the water trough.

Houston appeared behind Tyrane as Ojo, leading his spare animal disappeared from view.

"Where's he going Tyrane?"

"Who knows, he's bitter about losing the gold."

"And you Tyrane, what do you think about losing it?"

Tyrane collected his thoughts whilst lighting a smoke.

"Me, I've accepted the situation Captain. So in a way we all have one thing in common Ojo, Santes and myself, we all read the situation the same and decided to pull out."

Suddenly Houston, for the first time, realised Santes was missing.

"When did Santes leave?"

"While he was on watch, some time during the night.

Certainly before Ojo."

The smell of strong, hot coffee drifted out, catching the whiff Tyrane ventured back inside inside.

=================

Ojo drew rein alongside Salvador Gonsalves body and dismounted. Rolling the carcass over, he viewed the bullet holes down one side.

"Yes you'll do, they'll still be able to identify you,"

Steadying the animals Ojo pulled the carcass over, lifting it across the back of the spare horse. After much struggling the body stayed in position long enough to be tied secure. Breathing heavily after his exertions, he sat down.

"Damn you Gonsalves, you are as awkward dead as you were alive. But the $5,000 I get for your hide will compensate some for that."

Putting one of the many available saddles onto his mount, Ojo swung his body into place and dug spur into the horse's side.

The animal lunged pulling the spare mount in close contention.

================

Having fled from his position as sniper at the house, Gomez, his weasel face longer than usual trod wearily on.

Constantly looking over his shoulder for fear of pursuit, his eyes locked on movement far in the distance. Climbing a rock he strained his vision as the tiny speck on the horizon grew.

"The swine they leave me to die, with no horse, they betray me."

The dust speck drew nearer, becoming more distinguishable.

Thoughts of events of the previous night flowed through Gomez mind.

"First they send me to shoot at the house while they sleep, next they run away and leave me, I heard the horses galloping away. Then when I try to steal a horse from the corral I am almost discovered by the gringo,"

Ranted the insane little man to himself.

"I will have my revenge."

Perching his body across the rock, Gomez brought his rifle to bear.

================

Having finished eating, Houston counted out five gold coins onto the table in front of the old man.

Tyrane coming from the back room with the pillowslip under his arm hesitated only momentarily as he met Clementines wondering gaze. Hoisting his saddle onto his shoulder he strode towards the corral.

"Si si.,"

thanked the old man, as Houston upped and ran after Tyrane.

"What do you plan on doing Tyrane?"

Tyrane, tightening the girth, affixed the bundled slip to the bedroll. His eye caught Clementine watching from the doorway.

"I thought perhaps.....you and the young lady!"

"I don't see myself as a dirt farmer Captain, or as a storekeeper."

=================

The two riders came near enough for Gomez to recognise the outline of one rider, the other he could not make out.

An evil grin creased his face as his finger tightened around the trigger.

The rifle leapt, and Emanuel Santes was blasted from the saddle to lay spread-eagled on his back, a blank expression set in the deep, vacant eyes.

Amine leapt from the saddle, his head aching as the shot rang out.

The rifle swung around to bear down on his chest.

"Do not shoot. Do not shoot Amigo, it is I Amine"

His cries were lost as the rifle leapt once more in his killer's arms. Clasping at the air, Amine with his dying breaths attempted to scale the rock. Gomez crashed the rifle butt into the great shaggy mane of black hair, then leaping, landed into the saddle and dug spur into horse flesh.

================

Both Tyrane and Houston turned simultaneously as the far echo of the shots reached their ears.

"What!" protested Houston,

"was that?"

"Gunfire,"

Tyrane hoisted himself into the saddle.

The occupants of the house spilled out into the yard in curiosity. The bald old Mexican stood alongside Tyrane's horse, peering into the distance.

Tyrane pressed a $100 bill into the old man's hand, whilst whispering in his ear.

"Bury the Banker, bury him deep."

Giving his horse its head Tyrane allowed it to break into a steady gallop, then turned it easterly.

Clementine watched until he disappeared from sight.

"I expect you want to come back with us miss?"

Resignedly Clementine hunched her shoulders, thanking Houston.

"Bring the gold out Faheratty, it's a long ways back to Fort Thomas. The sooner we start the better."

================

It was six days later when a saddle weary Tyrane rode down main-street Casas Grandes.

He hadn't hurried, but would be grateful for a respite from the saddle. The town was a bustle with activity.

Depositing some $30,000. at the bank for transfer to Silver City, Tyrane sold the horse and saddle then cleaned up.

The following day whilst waiting on the platform for the stage to arrive Tyrane fixed his eyes on the elaborate stitching of the coat he so disliked, with the red blotches he recognised at once as his own.

His eyes swept to the badge pinned onto the chest, then to the face of the wearer who was not Ojo Caliente.

"Tell me Sheriff,"

inquired Tyrane, as the law-man drew level.

"Where did you get that coat?"

"Do you know who owns this coat Senores?"

"I did once."

"The man who wore this coat Senores, is dead."

Removing his badge, the Sheriff revealed two holes in the material.

An incessant banging was heard and the noise of wood sawing from the courtyard behind the Stagecoach Office.

"What happened?"

"The man who owned this coat was a bounty killer. He was bringing in the body of one Salvador Gonsalves."

The Sheriff waited for some reaction from Tyrane, there was none.

"His arrival caused much interest Senores, especially to one hombre by the name of Thorburn, Kid Thorburn."

On hearing the name, Tyrane's memory flashed back to the warning from the Sheriff at Tubac about the two brothers after he shot the first Thorburn. Then to the fracas in Sonora where he killed Duke Thorburn.

"Then there was none."

"What do you mean Senores?"

"Nothing Sheriff, go on with your story."

"This Thorburn, he murdered the bounty killer."

"Why?"

"It appears he made a mistake Senores, he mistook him for another hombre in his fancy coat."

At that moment, Tyrane was grateful Ojo Caliente and stolen his coat.

"What happened to Thorburn?"

The Sheriff hitched a thumb towards the noisy courtyard.

"They are building the gallows now Senores"

"First there were three Thorburns.

Then there were two.

Then there was one.

Now there are none,"

The

    Arizona

        Alliance.